Twelve Lessons Lived

KATE SPENCER

Published by
Katherine Spencer Publishing

Copyright Kate Spencer 2024

ISBN
Hardback: 978-1-7385775-1-4
Paperback: 978-1-7385775-0-7

Typesetting by Michelle Emerson
www.michelleemerson.co.uk

Cover design by Leanne Kelly
www.facebook.com/Jakenna.creative.design

A CPI Catalogue for this title is available from the British Library

CHAPTER 1

The fingers of fear tightened around my throat; breathing came fast and shallow. I slammed my laptop shut and closed my eyes tight. Tears of anger and shame burned my cheeks, and I silently swallowed back sobs. "No, no, no!" I shook my head. I tried steadying myself by laying my hands flat on the desk.

Breathe, just breathe.

But panic had taken hold and she wasn't about to back down. She'd only just started.

My heart rate was soaring.

My thoughts were racing.

Future scenarios flashed through my mind at lightning speed.

Damien's devastation, my marriage in tatters, my reputation publicly shredded.

But the worst thing would be Mia knowing that her mother was a cheater and a liar. I'd broken the trust which bound her parents together and thrown away the love of a lifetime for one shallow moment of drunken fumbling that meant nothing.

Nothing could cost everything right now.

How could I have done this to Damien and Mia? My two treasures, my reason, my world. I could recover from losing anything else. But not them.

I'd known how dangerous Jay could be, he'd broken me before. And in a single moment of weakness, he'd reeled me in again, but this time, the stakes were so much higher. Damien, with his endless love and patience, had brought me back from the brink the first time. The brink that I'd returned to now, but this time, I've brought him with me, as well as our daughter.

My breathing wasn't slowing down and tears were blurring

my vision. I needed air; I must be hyperventilating. Something about a paper bag came to mind, so I started to rummage through the desk drawers, grabbing at notebooks, envelopes, post-it notes and crying, crying from my soul for forgiveness I knew I didn't deserve. I pushed myself to my feet and walked the two steps to the open window, gulping in summer barbeque air and fanning my face as the scene around me started to drift.

Please don't let me pass out.

The room swirled and sound moved in and out of my awareness. Damien's voice, the splashing of water, and Mia's laughter. I could see her in the pink bathing suit with white spots that I'd helped her wriggle into just half an hour ago – when everything was still perfect.

I felt like I was flying and watching from above, strange, weightless and dream-like. I could smell cut- grass and sunscreen and feel powder-puff clouds brushing my bare arms. For a few moments, it was remarkably peaceful. Then Damien's voice, loud and urgent. He was shaking me and calling my name. Taking a deep breath, I opened my eyes and stared, confused, at the ceiling.

"Steph, what happened, love?" he looked at me intensely as I raised my hand to the back of my head and winced.

His hand followed mine.

"You've gone down like a sack of spuds. Don't try to get up yet just give yourself a minute." He reached over to the office chair for a cushion and slid it under my head.

"How long was I out for?" I asked as I raised my wrist to look at my watch. I remembered feeling hungry just after five; that's what had prompted me to finish work for the day and think about starting dinner. My watch said four minutes past.

"I don't know, but it can't have been long. I sent you a text to ask if you wanted me to light the barbeque, and when you didn't reply, I came up to ask." He was speaking softly and scanning my face for clues.

And there it was - the crossroads.

That moment in time which could change everything.

A pause. A gap.

The Universe taking a breath.

Tell him the truth.

Right now I could reach out to the man who loves me with a depth and breadth that I'd never thought possible. I could trust that he would hold this sacred space between us with the courage, strength and compassion I knew ran through him. I could lay my heart bare and pour out my shame and guilt at his feet. We could break together, cry it out and promise that although we needed to retreat into ourselves, we would find a way back to each other. Because our love was the rarest, purest and most precious thing we had, it could conquer anything and everything. This is a man who already knows my darkness and fear and loves me through them. He is my anchor, my safety net and my rock.

The truth will break him.

Rewind four years, to the morning I'd done the walk of shame up our garden path and confessed to spending the night with another man. Damien had crumbled in front of me, the light extinguished from his eyes and his expression changed to despair as he shook his head in disbelief. The only words he had uttered were to ask if I'd known the man. I'd almost said yes, and every part of me now wished I had. But the way he looked at me filled the void between us, made the truth catch in my throat. I couldn't hold his gaze, and I couldn't tell him what I should have.

His heart had broken in front of me that morning, and twisting the emotional knife would have felt like adding the ultimate insult to injury. Some faceless random guy with no history or context was hard enough to forgive, but my ex? So I said no, and Damien had left the room, leaving me alone with the weight of my lie that was had held me captive since.

He can't ever find out it was Jay.

Years ago, Damien had helped me to search for the pieces of my broken self and patiently put me back together. He'd sat with me in the shadows of my past as I healed and cried out my story, each word hurting him as much as it did me to share it – but he never asked me to stop. He shouldered the cost of listening to me with dignity, love and understanding. He was my safe space.

I can't believe I did this to him, to us.

One night, a lot of alcohol and now a lifetime of regret. I'd been in a strange place that night. Damien and I had been disconnected for months, and I felt rejected, unworthy, unattractive and not enough for him. I'd numbed myself with too much wine too quickly, and then a horrible woman called Rosie saw her opportunity and moved in fast. Rosie was a nasty piece of work who thrived on pulling other people's lives to pieces, and that night, it was my turn. She accused Damien of having an affair. I was aghast; the pain and humiliation were unbearable. Everyone looked at me, and she sneered, smirked and slurred her way through telling me I was a doormat and he was shagging some woman at work with big tits.

Like Alice in Wonderland tumbling down the rabbit hole, I couldn't find my way back once I'd fallen. People avoided eye contact everywhere I looked; some were moving food around their plates and others were pretending to be engrossed in something on their phones. It was a small restaurant and Rosie had a big voice, and she kept going strong. The waiter had come to our table and asked Rosie to leave, but by then, I was on my feet and heading for toilets. I'd left the restaurant through the emergency exit and into the back lane, grateful to be alone and escaping humiliation in the taxi that was waiting.

Little did I know that fate was about to step in. As I closed the door and heard the driver speak, my head and my heart betrayed one another. I had just made one of the worst decisions of my life. Jay's familiar voice wrapped around me and felt like the comfort I needed. And so it began – the night I risked everything for nothing. Falling right back into the arms of the man that Damien helped me to recover from. The man who had ruined me financially, emotionally and psychologically. The same man who was now blackmailing me with the pictures he'd taken that night.

"Steph, can you hear me, love?" Damien asked. "You zoned out. Maybe you've got a concussion."

I cleared my throat and took a breath. Closing my eyes for a second and gathering myself, I heard my voice out loud.

"I think I'm ok, but can I have a glass of water, please?"

Tell him the truth.

"Of course, don't move. I'll be right back." Damien made his way to the bathroom. I heard the tap running and his footsteps returning.

He helped me to sit up and take a sip.

"What do you think happened?" he asked with concern.

I shrugged and sipped again.

"Maybe we need to get you to the doctors?"

It was now or never. Tell him I told a lie, or live it for a lifetime. The choice was mine, and I had to decide. And then I heard the patter of feet. Mia appeared at the doorway.

"Mummy? What's wrong?"

The Universe exhaled and the moment evaporated.

"I'm fine, sweetheart. I just got a bit dizzy and hot, so I'm having a sit on the floor," I said, trying to sound upbeat.

"You're sure?" Damien asked.

"I'm sure." I smiled to reassure him as he helped me stand up, shifting the chair towards me with his foot so I could sit down.

"Ok, well, finish your water and I'll go and get you a biscuit and a cup of tea. No falling down while I'm away, mind. Mia, are you going to stay with Mummy for a minute? Tell her about the paddling pool and all of that puff we needed to blow it up."

Mia blew out her cheeks to demonstrate, and Damien left the room.

My beautiful daughter stood beside my desk, covered in happiness and polka dots. Oh, how she filled me up and lit up my life with her curls, freckles, and giggles. She was perfect in every way, and I couldn't imagine life without her. Behind her, I could see my laptop, which contained the photographs that now held my life hostage.

STEPHANIE'S JOURNAL - LESSON 25
THE COST OF LYING

The truth doesn't cost you anything, but a lie could cost you everything. ~ Unknown

People lie for many reasons: to avoid punishment or judgement, side-step loss of face, to gain approval, and make themselves look more successful. There are, however, so many costs associated with lying. The ongoing mental energy it takes to remember details, and build context around the lie is an ongoing emotional and psychological drain. The fear of being found out is ever present. You waste time and energy preparing for exposure and rehearsing your response, defence or more even lies to cover up your original untruth.

The stress of lying means you constantly live in fight or flight, affecting your well-being in all kinds of ways. Life, relationships, and work can all be contaminated with hypervigilance, anxiety and becoming easily triggered. Mental and physical health can decline, and your self-worth slowly erodes as you move further away from the connection with your authentic self.

Lies steal energy from your present and spoil times that should be happy and joyful. The more time that passes, the harder it is to tell the truth.

CHAPTER 2

When I'd slammed the laptop lid shut, I hadn't closed the message box. The images would be the first thing to confront anyone who used it next, and that needed to be me. Before bed, I steeled myself to open it again.

Even though I knew what was waiting for me, I was still horrified. I quickly deleted them and closed my eyes, but I could still see myself lying there wearing next to nothing, tied up in bondage ropes with a riding crop in my hand. There were a couple of tubes of lube and some flavoured condoms on the bedside table, along with scrunched-up tissue and a half-empty glass of wine. I'd never been so ashamed in my life. I was disgusting. Nowhere near worthy enough to wear the wedding ring visible on my left hand. When we had been together, Jay had called me boring in bed. Although I'd tried to spice things up, I'd always felt really self-conscious and body-shy. How the hell had I mustered up the confidence to do something like this?

I must have been blind drunk. I can't remember this at all.

I decided the best thing to do now was to ignore it. Hopefully, it would go away, and I'd stop seeing the pictures in my mind's eye and instead focus on being the best wife ever to Damien. I know I can create my own reality by aligning with what I want, and I choose peace, love and my family – cue deep breath in.

Who was I kidding?

I was never going to be able to feel that everything was ok because it definitely wasn't.

So what if I'd deleted the pictures? They were still in Jay's possession and, of course, in the cloud. A storm cloud that was gathering force. The moment to come clean had passed, and from now on, every day that passed would make telling the truth more difficult.

Would I ever have to?

Jay might have a moment of decency and leave me alone. Maybe I could silently slink away and disappear from his radar. If only it were that easy. Part of making my work a success was media. The more book signings, social media posts, appearances, and general buzz that we could create, the better the sales were. A publisher expects and encourages it, and this was only just beginning.

Jay had obviously been watching me, lurking and getting ready to make his move. I couldn't remember how much I'd said about my writing that night, and, in fact, I couldn't remember much at all - a blessing and a curse. However, my mental blank and, of course, the pictures were his ammunition. I prayed I'd seen every one, and there was nothing else, nothing worse. The thought made me feel even sicker.

I heard Damien making his way upstairs.

"You're still up?" he whispered.

"Yeah, I was just double-checking a date for a book signing. I'm done now," I answered. The lie came so easily.

Who was I becoming?

We made our way to bed, and after an hour or so, I blamed the hot summer night for making me restless. Damien blamed the bump on my head and asked me again if I thought I should go to the doctors tomorrow, just to make sure. I fluffed over it and before long, I could hear his soft snoring in the blackness of the bedroom and, outside, the distant hoot of an owl looking for its mate. I wondered if animals ever betrayed each other the way us humans did, and I guessed not. Owls, especially, were meant to be wise, and that was certainly something I couldn't claim to be right now.

Morning came eventually, and I felt like I had done a night shift, which, in essence, I had. Hours of worry, overthinking, second-guessing and holding back tears. I'd woken with a start as Damien placed a cup of coffee on the glass coaster on my nightstand. His hand touched my brow and he spoke softly, telling me he was heading to work.

"Mia's been fed and watered and she's downstairs watching something to do with a zoo. Are you still going out with Mel today?" he asked as he opened the curtains slightly, letting in a shaft of morning sun without dazzling me.

I'd forgotten we had to go and get Mia and George fitted for their first pair of proper school shoes. I sat up, rubbed my eyes and gulped some coffee. "Yes. I'd better get in the shower first if I've got to face the crowds at the shoe shop."

"Just take it easy. Keep your phone with you and call me straight away if you need anything.

Has Mel got my number?" Damien asked.

"Yes, I'm sure she has, but I'll double-check. Honestly, I feel fine, just a bit tired. I didn't sleep well because of the heat." I lifted the coffee cup and gulped some more. "This will sort me out."

He leaned in for a kiss and I could feel myself starting to tear up. Blinking them back, I turned my face away into a mock yawn.

"I've got to go, sleepy head. See you tonight. Love you."

"Love you too," I answered, thankful the sentiment was short and he wouldn't hear my voice break.

His footsteps echoed through the house, and I heard him telling Mia it was an exciting day and she'd be getting her big girl school shoes. As I heard the front door close, I couldn't hold back the tears any longer – what on earth was I going to do?

After a quick shower, I carefully dried my hair around the bump on my head, which was thankfully receding. Mel would be here any minute and I'd have to stop myself from going over and over the night with Jay. I'd put this to bed years ago, and tormenting myself was not going to help. I needed to be present at least this morning. It was another milestone in Mia's young life - her first school shoes. They would only be on her feet a few months before being wrapped in tissue paper and put in the memory box in the attic.

I wondered what life would look like then, in a few months. *Will this nightmare with Jay have gone away?*

Maybe his message was a one-off to scare me, threaten me – that definitely worked. If he was really desperate for money, he might be prepared to play the long game, though. Was he getting ready to turn up the heat right now?

The doorbell rang, and I jumped. The dregs in my coffee cup went flying, puddling near my phone as it lit up and pinged. It rang again and I could hear Mia shouting hello to George through the letterbox. I wanted to open the message; I needed to, but I had to keep it together. The bell rang a third time, accompanied by a knocking and Mel shouting, "Yooo hoooo!" Turning my phone face-down, I ushered Mia out of the way and swung open the door. George tumbled in as usual and Mel looked me up and down.

"Bloody hell, Steph. Rough night?" she laughed.

I turned and looked at myself in the hallway mirror as she closed the door behind her. Yes, she was right. I'd looked better. I had some weird cowlick-type affair going on with my hair, and I'd accidentally mopped up the coffee puddle with the cuff of my sweater. Add to that no make-up and zero sleep.

Rough as chuff – confirmed.

"I'll put the kettle on," I mumbled and made my way to the kitchen.

"Just half a cup. We need to get going!" Mel said.

I spooned coffee granules into two cups and asked Mel to take over while I nipped upstairs to tidy myself up a bit, which, of course, meant I was about to open the message that was making my palms sweat. I saw the thumbnail profile pic of a sweet-looking blonde-haired woman called Suzie Rainbow; obviously not her real name, but a good choice for Facebook. She asked me about one of the posts I'd shared the day before and if I really believed in karma.

Wasn't that just the question of the day?

I sighed and gathered myself. Even if I never heard from Jay again, was I going to jump out of my skin every time my phone pinged?

"Coffee's ready, Steph," shouted Mel up the stairs, bringing me back to the now.

"Two ticks, I'm coming." I quickly put on some blusher and mascara, changed my top, bobbled up my hair, and felt slightly more comfortable. I wished I could tell Mel what was going on, but she'd feel so compromised, and it wasn't fair.

Maybe there was nothing to tell anyway.

It could end up being a total one-off. By not responding, I was sending out a good old Fuck You, and he'd get the message. Although, deep down, I didn't believe it, I was still going to practice thinking it until I did.

Fuck You, Jay - I'm ignoring you and you've gone away.

One last look in the mirror confirmed I was ready to face the shoe shop, and I made my way downstairs for half a coffee more.

CHAPTER 3

I faffed with the radio to distract myself, as Mel indicated to pull out and the kids chatted in the back about big school.

"It's happening, Steph. They are growing up." Mel spoke over some kind of rapping that I quickly turned to an easy listening station – music for the middle-aged.

"Yes, and this is just the start. When people say that time flies, they should add that it flies even faster when you've got a kid."

Mel approached the roundabout in the right lane, and I wondered if her coffee had kicked in yet.

"You're in the wrong lane," I said. "You'll have to go all the way around now and come off left."

"No, it's ok, sorry, slight change of plan. My neighbour told me that the shoe shop on the high street has started to stock kids' shoes, and they are doing a back-to-school discount this week."

"But won't it be loads busier if they are doing that? Should we not stick to plan A and go to the shopping centre?" The high street shoe shop wasn't a place I'd been back to since the incident with the boot, and I'd rather not go back ever, especially not today when I'm feeling like a jangled bag of nerves and likely to get triggered as soon as we walk in.

"No," she said, "hardly anyone knows about it because the girl who does their social media dropped the ball and didn't get the message out in time. We should get straight in and sorted, and they have the same shoes as the one in the shopping centre. They will measure the kids' feet and give them a sticker and all that jazz, it's fine."

"I hate that shop," I mumbled, as if I wasn't anxious enough.

"What are you going on about?" Mel laughed. "Why on

earth would you hate a shoe shop?"

"It's a long story, and it was forever ago, but I was shamed for having chubby legs."

"No, you weren't." Mel was laughing even harder now. "I'm not saying you've got chubby legs, mind, so don't get all offended!"

"I have got chubby legs, Mel, because I am chubby! My legs are sturdy because they have to carry the rest of me around, and just in case no one noticed, I'm certainly not skinny, and I never have been – hence the historical incident."

"You've got to tell me about it now. Come on, it's better to share these things, then I can support you if you have a wobble." Mel was laughing full-on now and I couldn't help but join her.

The woman who served me must have been knocking on the retirement door back then, so she wasn't going to be around anyway, and the retail industry is notorious for having a high staff turnover, right? So I could probably chill out about it, really. Even if someone was there who had been working that particular day, I doubt they would recognise me now anyway. Recognise me! Who did I think I was? I was just some woman who once got a boot stuck on her foot in a shoe shop. It probably happens all the time, and it's a non-event in a shoe shop assistant's life.

"I got a boot stuck on my foot. That's it, really," I said.

"And how did they get it off?" asked Mel through snorts and giggles.

"Oh, it was a bit of a thing, and they had to get different people to try and what not, but it was ok in the end."

"Different people to try? Try to get it off? This is hilarious!" Mel was wiping tears of laughter from her face with her coat sleeve.

"Yeah, maybe it was funny after the event, but at the time, it was just awful! Who knew I had one fat leg?" I corrected myself. "One fat leg and one very fat leg."

"Stop! I'm going to pee myself!" pleaded Mel, fanning her face.

"Well, you asked," I said. "God, I was mortified and the woman helping me was trying to be nice and all politically correct and not say that I was overweight, but it was bloody obvious and there I was with my leg in the air, all hot and bothered with a stuck boot. She tried to save my feelings and talked about faulty zips and sometimes them being on the small side, but it was still excruciating. And when I say excruciating, I mean both contexts - excruciatingly embarrassing and excruciating for my calf, which quite honestly felt like it was in a torture device being squeezed to oblivion inside a luxury fleece lining."

"Wow, what an adventure for you! And look, we've arrived!" Mel parked up easily, as she'd predicted, and unbuckled her seatbelt. She turned to me and patted my knee, still giggling.

"You've got this, Steph. I believe in you."

"Come on, kids, let's go and get you measured up for your big school shoes," I said and we all got out. Although banners were strewn all over the window, we were the only people waiting for the shop to open.

"Told you it would be quiet, didn't I?" said Mel, checking the time. Only three minutes to wait. "If we were at the shopping centre, the queue would be right back to Buffet King by now."

I saw movement in the store, and another mum with a child in tow approached the shop, ready for opening. Mel shuffled forward slightly, making it obvious she was first in line. The key turned in the lock, the closed sign flipped to open and there she was – Brenda. She hadn't retired, and she'd hardly changed. I hoped I had changed, enough for me to have no idea who I was. I tried to avert her gaze and Mel and George shuffled past her, exchanging good mornings, but she was from the school of good manners, customer service and repeat business. She's been on courses about retention and upselling.

"Hello again!" she smiled widely.

I wanted to believe she couldn't possibly recognise me, but on reflection, how could she not? It had been a pantomime with me as the lead, and no matter what I told myself in the car, they had probably never had an incident like it before or since. Of course, she knew it was me – I bet she even called me 'boot woman'.

"Hello," I replied, and there was an awkward pause.

"It's lovely to have you back," said Brenda with a questioning expression I couldn't look at for more than a blink. I needn't have worried because, like a true professional, she took complete control of the situation. "We've got a fabulous new *comfort* range in-store today," she began walking, and I followed her towards a stand of footwear called Amblers, boasting that they offered style and comfort in generous sizes. The shoe equivalent of the elasticated waistband has arrived. The next chapter in your life will be spent in sensible slip-ons with sturdy soles for putting the bin out all year round.

I clocked a rotary stand nearby full of socks with a 'sympathetic cuff', whatever that meant. On closer inspection, I worked out that these were the sock of choice if you had thick cankles (where calf and ankle meld into one). Brenda was good; she knew her customers' needs and delivered them straight to the shoes and socks they needed for their sturdy legs and fat feet.

Now, this was even more awkward. There was Brenda, being all customer servicey and helpful, and here was I, trying to get school shoes for my kid, something I should have said straight away before it got this weird.

"Is there anything you'd like to try?" she asked and cast her eyes down to see what I was wearing today. I was sporting pumps, mummy pumps, that had been a panic buy from a supermarket. They had seen better days and, on closer inspection I realised they had copped for some of this morning's spilt coffee.

Luckily, Brenda wasn't one to let a customer down. No one was ever left behind on her watch. By the time Mel came around the corner, me and Brenda were staring down at the pair of navy sandals on my feet, complete with cushioned soles and thick Velcro fastenings that made me look ready for a nursing home. To be fair, the small wedge heel and arch support were actually comfortable, but wow, they were ugly and aged me by at least thirty years. Brenda explained they also came in 'sand', which was a good neutral choice for casual or smart days, with a slight inflection in her tone that gave a bit more emphasis to smart.

Mel peeped around the sock stand and mouthed, "*Smart days.*"

Just as I was about to crack, Mia started tugging my sleeve and showing me a black patent leather shoe with diamante sparkles.

"Mummy, I like these ones," she said quietly and thankfully stole the moment.

"I like them too, Mia. Shall we see if Brenda can help us find your size?" I looked at Brenda and stage whispered that we'd really come for school shoes and I'd gone a little off-piste, but I'd take the sandals in sand because, yes, they were comfortable and versatile. My mum's birthday was coming up, and ever since I was 16, we'd had the same size feet, so the pensioners' footwear would be going in her direction for the next coach trip – which, as I recall, might be Ilfracombe.

Brenda smiled widely and raised her hand in the air to attract the attention of one of her minions to measure Mia's feet. She had more important things to do, like trying to sell me the £9.99 shoe care package. Yes, the sandals are suede, but no thanks,

Brenda, I don't want a small, overpriced spray and brush set.

Scorned but still wearing her professional smile, she made her way to the till with the sandals and I joined Mia in the kiddie corner with a lovely girl kneeling in front of her and asking about big school.

The name badge told me the girl's name was Valerie, but when I got closer, she explained she was actually called Jo, but she was quite new and her name badge hadn't arrived yet. It was against company regulations to have no badge, so until then, she was Valerie, a shoe shop sales floor veteran who retired two months ago with her husband and was now living in France. Good for you, Valerie. I hope you went with some Amblers, so you've got both smart and casual days covered.

Once Jo had measured Mia's feet, she disappeared into the store room and brought out the shoes Mia loved. She slipped them onto her tiny feet and thumbed the end to see where Mia's toes were, then held them by the heel and gently tugged to check they wouldn't slip off or rub her heel.

"I think they are gorgeous on you, Mia," she said and then asked her to stand up and walk around the shop floor a couple of times.

"Do they feel ok?" I asked, and Mia nodded with a big smile.

"I like them, Mummy."

"They are perfect, thank you, we'll take them," I confirmed as Mia sat down on the small pink chair and Jo started unfastening them.

Mia slipped on the shoes she'd arrived in just as a whole load of kids tumbled into the small shop. The mums followed, each with the regulation mummy bag and one with a big bump that looked like she was due to add to her brood any day. A man lurked beside the door, holding the hand of a boy who looked shy and overwhelmed, just like his dad. Jo went to assist.

I made my way through the pack and approached the till. Mel was beckoning me and I could see that Brenda was a bit rattled by a kid using a school shoe like an aeroplane and running up and down the shop floor making a racket.

George was quite a sensitive child and didn't much like crowds or noise. He shuffled closer to Mel and attached himself to her leg like a vertical limpet. This was a habit he'd had forever, but he was built like his stocky dad, and Mel was only just over five feet tall.

"George, let go now. Everything is fine," Mel spoke calmly as she dragged her right foot and her hefty child towards the till. I was surprised she didn't put her back out or dislocate her hip. Her swing and shuffle technique was impressive but hampered her handbag action when she needed to pull out her purse and pay.

"George, do you want to play on my phone for a bit?" she asked and nodded to a couple of chairs behind the Chapters shoe display that was strategically placed for those wanting to try on the feeling of comfort and style before committing to navy or sand.

George wasn't allowed too much screen time, so this was a treat and it worked like magic.

"Go over there and I'll be five minutes." Mel passed him the phone and he unlocked it in a flash, the familiar sound of Minecraft blended into the noise of the kids, the chatter of the mums, the mumbling of the dad and the traffic outside.

"Can I play?" asked Mia. She loved the game just as much, and it looked like the till roll was being changed now, so we weren't going anywhere fast. I reached into my bag and gave her my phone, and she joined George just as Aeroplane Kid finally knocked over the sock stand. Brenda had to find out who had guardianship of this "spirited" little boy.

"Have you eaten yet?" asked Mel. "We could go for breakfast after this if you like. It's still early."

"Great idea, I'd like that," I said as the till ate the new paper roll and spat out little shreds of confetti.

"Bloody thing!" Joan muttered under her breath, and I wondered if she was, in fact, Joan or if she was waiting for her name badge too. She looked like she'd been here a while but obviously didn't have the knack with a new till roll. Brenda came to the rescue, a true retail veteran, calm and professional even in the face of adversity. She teased the edge of the paper over the tiny silver teeth of the cutting edge and clicked the plastic cover shut. Job done. She nodded at Joan as if to say *I hope you were watching and you learned from that.*

Joan flushed slightly but carried on regardless, asking Mel for £39.99 and, "Is it cash or card today?"

As Mel declined the shoe care kit and Joan apologetically and quietly explained that they had to offer them to everyone in case someone was the mystery shopper, I thought I heard my phone ping. It could have been the card machine as Mel tapped and the payment registered, but even so, I turned to look at Mia. Then it happened again, and Mia huffed at the game to confirm it had been interrupted.

Oh my god.

Mia was a few steps away from me, but it felt like a million miles.

"Mia, bring my phone here, please," I tried not to sound as scared as I felt.

"Just let them have two minutes. They're fine," said Mel.

"No, it's not fine. I want my phone, Mel," I said.

Another ping.

Oh my god.

"Mia, bring my phone here please now." My voice was louder this time and my tone was stern.

"But Mummy, I'm playing," she whined. "You said I could."

Joan launched into the shoe care kit pitch and I found myself snapping an abrupt response as I wondered how long this would take.

Another ping.

"Messages, Mummy," Mia said as I stormed towards her and snatched the phone from her little hands. She looked up at me with fear that mirrored my own as I quickly turned it off.

"I told you I wanted my phone, Mia. That's really naughty and you've ruined this for yourself now because you can't ever have it back," I shouted, towering over her and shaking with rage and panic.

The shop became quiet and people looked away. Mia started to sob and George ran to Mel. I grabbed Mia's arm and dragged her out of the seat with such force that it fell over and I marched her out of the shop, desperate to get away from the onlookers.

Standing in the street and crying, I bundled Mia up into my arms and rocked her like a baby while sobbing, "I'm sorry," over and over.

She cried too, and after a while, she pulled away a little and held my face in her little hands.

"It's ok, Mummy, we all have bad days."

I cried even more. "It's never ok to be shouty and mean to you, Mia. I lost my temper at something else, and it wasn't about you or the phone and I should never, ever have done that."

"What was it about, Mummy?" Mia asked in complete innocence, an innocence that would be shattered forever if she found out I'd betrayed her father.

"Just grown-up stuff," I said as Mel came out of the shop with two bags and asked me if I was ok.

"No, not really. I'm a complete psycho who shouts at her kid and terrorizes her in public. She'll need years of therapy now." I smiled weakly, but the tears were still falling. Mel put the bags down.

"Steph, that's so out of character for you. What's wrong?" she hugged me tight.

I couldn't look at her as she asked if it was about Damien's health or maybe money stuff.

"Can we go for breakfast, Mel?" I managed to mumble. "I don't know if I can eat much, but the kids can go in the soft play, my treat."

"Of course we can."

We started to walk towards the car and Mia asked about her shoes.

"I've got them right here, along with your mum's new sandals for smart or casual days."

I forced a smile that I couldn't feel and wondered what the hell I was going to do now.

The car journey was subdued, to say the least. I watched life pass by from the passenger window and wondered if mine would get back to normal. I apologised to George and Mia and said that I shouldn't have been so shouty and snappy in the shop and that it wasn't Mia's fault, it was mine.

"We all have bad days, even mummies," Mel chirped in support and patted my knee.

I teared up again and sniffed. This was the consequence of my lying and betraying Damien, I was getting what I deserved. Even though I hadn't opened the messages, and even though they may not be from Jay, the desired effect was playing out. I was exactly where he wanted me, terrified of losing everything.

"I'm so sorry, Mel," I said. Shame was swallowing me slowly and it was so painful. I wanted to hide away and cry my heart out. I wanted Damien to know and to somehow love me still and help me through it, and I desperately wanted to erase shouting at Mia. Would she remember this later on in her life? Might it be a moment that affects her confidence and relationships? If Mel could hear my thoughts, she would say I was overthinking, but I'd never, ever spoken to my child like that, and the regret of doing so in public was a heavy burden to bear. It's not who I was – but it seemed to be who I was becoming. The unravelling of who I used to be had begun, and I needed to stop it fast.

I felt a little hand on my shoulder and Mia whispered in my ear,

"It's ok, Mummy. Don't cry. I love you." I reached to hold her hand in mine.

"I'm so sorry I lost my temper. It wasn't your fault." I turned in the seat and saw her perfect face.

"It wasn't your fault either, Mummy. I think you were tired and that makes us grumpy," she said as she wiped my tears with her thumb and spread them over my cheeks.

It is SO my fault, Mia, and I hope you never need to know that.

I managed a smile and she smiled back.

"Can I have waffles for breakfast?" she asked, knowing full well they were a sugary treat she was rarely allowed.

"Of course you can. I think it's the least I can do. Breakfasts are on me today and we can all have whatever we like." I knew I wouldn't be able to eat much. My stomach felt like a washing machine on a spin cycle, but I'd show willing and order something anyway.

On arrival, we were ushered to a table near the window, overlooking the outdoor play area that the kids would be dying to use after we'd eaten. Two stacks of waffles, a full English and one eggs benedict later (which I could only manage half of) the kids were swinging on monkey bars and Mel was leaning in to find out what was going on.

"If I tell you, you've got to promise not to tell Damien." I stirred the coffee that I probably wasn't going to drink and the spoon clinked against the cup.

"Steph, of course, I won't tell him, unless it's something that puts you or Mia in danger and then I'd have to." Mel spoke with integrity. She was a straight shooter and I usually loved that about her; what you see is what you get. But if I was going to tell her the truth, I'd have to know that she could lock it up in the vault of our friendship and never allow it to be shared with anyone. Perhaps her innate sense of honesty would compromise that and, therefore, me. She was right, of course, but this wasn't the cast iron guarantee I needed right now.

"You'd say the same to me if it was something really bad, and you've got me worried now. I've never seen you like this and certainly never seen you fly off the handle with Mia like you just did. What the hell is going on?"

I took in a deep breath and then slowly exhaled. And then I started to share. I'd had time to think in the car and while Mia and George were eating their waffles about how this might play out. The best I could do was deliver a version of events that was close enough to the truth to explain how I had behaved, but not the whole truth. Yes, I was protecting myself, but I was also protecting Mel. At least that's what I had to believe right now before I lied by omission, and the two things I was about to omit were the one-night stand and the fact that it was Jay – the two key and relevant details, really.

"I'm being trolled online and it's really getting to me," I said, stirring again and looking at the cup.

"Trolled? What do you mean?" Mel asked wide-eyed.

"Someone has been sending me really pornographic images through messenger and threatening me, asking me for money and stuff."

"Oh my god, that's awful! Have you told the police? That's a cyber-crime, you know." She jumped to my defence straight away.

"I haven't because I am hoping it's just some loony tune who will leave me alone if I don't react. I'm deleting them as they come in and hopefully, they will get the message soon that they can do one and they're getting nothing from me."

"Yes, good for you. I think that's a really good idea," Mel nodded. "I can see now why you wanted your phone back in the shop. You'd never want Mia to open something like that."

I hated that the lies were coming so easily, and I felt guilty for getting some sort of relief from Mel buying into the story. This had to stop after today. I needed to find a way to get out of this as unscathed as possible and stop deceiving the people I loved.

"You should tell Damien. He'll support you, and you'll feel so much better if you do."

"I can't tell him, Mel."

"But why not? Surely it's better if he knows and then he can help you?"

"It's not that easy. This guy wants money and he knows where we live. I have no idea how serious he is about getting it and what will happen next, so I'm bricking it. I hope that he fucks off if I just keep ignoring him, but I've actually got no idea what could happen next."

"What do you mean he knows where you live?" Mel sounded worried.

"I'm not hard to find, Mel," I sighed. "Since things started happening with the book, I'm pretty visible on social media and you only have to look at Companies House to see where I am registered as a business, which, of course, is home."

"No wonder you are all over the place," she said and reached for my hand across the table. "You have to tell the police, though, Steph, and you need to tell Damien."

"Mel, you promised!" I could feel fear fuelling anger. Surely she wasn't going to betray me? After all, it might still go away, and we could go back to living happily ever after.

"I'm not going to say anything, honestly. But as your friend, I've got your back, and the right thing to do is to tell them. You can't carry this on your own; it will drive you mad. Just look at what happened earlier."

As if I needed reminding.

"Steph – you're being blackmailed. It's extortion and it's illegal."

"It's probably some fruitcake from the other side of the

world who would never in a million years get into the country, never mind my house, Mel." I forced a shrug.

"I agree with you, but it's enough to make you super anxious and stressed out, and if you share it with the police and Damien, you don't have to carry this on your own."

I knew she was right, but she didn't know the full story. The stakes were just too high. Of course I desperately wanted to tell Damien, my safe space and best friend. But my confession might mark the beginning of the end. I'd have to have no other option if I was going to risk it all, totally at the end of the road with no cards left to play. But in truth, I'd already risked it all - everything for nothing.

And here I was in the middle of a nightmare of my own pathetic and weak-willed creation.

"I'll think about it, Mel, I will." I tried to diffuse her insistence and offer a compromise that might help me to breathe. "But hopefully, it's going to come to nothing and I'll have been trolled and a bit spooked, but soon it will be old news and Damien might never have to know."

"I don't understand why you just don't tell him, though. He has always supported you and he would want to do that now too." She was a good friend and if the circumstances had been as I'd described them without the key omissions, she would of course be right.

"He's got loads on at work, and, anyway, there's nothing he can do about it. I don't want to pile more stress on him for no reason at all. It's not fair. This could end up being a storm in a teacup." I was getting frustrated and made a conscious effort to temper my tone. Time to shut this down and hope with everything I had that my lovely, well-meaning friend would back off and leave it there. "Look, I don't want to talk about it anymore if that's ok, I'm done in. If anything happens, I'll tell you, I promise. You are the only person who knows, so you are the only one I can tell anyway."

She wasn't satisfied but knew it was time for a change of conversation.

"Ok, I hear you," she said reluctantly. "To be honest, although this is awful, I'm actually relieved in a weird kind of way." She sighed.

"Oh?" I was the curious one now.

"Don't hate me!" she giggled a little to lighten the load. "When you were telling me that I had to keep this secret from Damien, I was certain you were going to tell me you'd had a one-night stand or an affair, or slept with your ex or something like that!"

I gave a little half laugh too. What a ridiculous notion.

"As if! I honestly don't know if I could! I'd feel so compromised, and I'd have to tell Damien, even though you are my friend, I'd just feel so torn."

Status confirmed – never tell Mel the truth, ever.

"Yeah, I get that, but please don't tell him this." I looked over to where the kids were playing instead of looking at Mel.

"I won't, I promise. But keep me posted, won't you? Like you say, hopefully it's nothing, but if things escalate…"

"I know. I'll have to go to the police and tell Damien," I said a bit too abruptly.

"You will, Steph, you will."

Just then, her phone rang out from the bottom of her bag and she started rummaging through everything a well-prepared mum takes out and about; baby wipes, a snack bar and an activity book were unpacked onto the table. She turned her phone to show me that it was Damien calling.

"What should I do?" Maybe I shouldn't have said anything to Mel at all and blamed the menopause for my meltdown instead. I'd passed on my anxiety to her and was already starting to regret it, along with everything else. I was digging a deeper and deeper hole, and the panic that I'd never get out was only ever a moment away.

"Answer it and act normal." I tried to portray the calm that I didn't feel and probably wouldn't ever feel again at this rate.

Mel swiped to answer and I could hear Damien's tinny voice asking if I was with her. She looked at me for guidance and I nodded and mouthed the word, "Yes."

"Yes, we've just been to get the kids' school shoes and we stopped off for breakfast. She's right here. I'll hand you over."

"Are you ok, love?" he asked, his voice full of concern.

"Yes, I'm fine. We're just finishing up here and I'll be heading back soon. Is something wrong?"

"No, I just couldn't reach you. I think your phone is switched off. It kept going to voicemail and I panicked. I'm sorry I didn't mean to scare you. It's just after you passing out yesterday and all that, I wanted to be sure you were ok." The love and consideration in his voice were almost too much listen to. He deserved someone so much better than me.

"I think my battery must have run out without me knowing. Sorry for panicking you."

"It's ok, as long as you and Mia are ok. Did you get sorted with her shoes?"

"Yes, she loves them, and she's got a sticker to show you when you get home."

"I'll hear all about it after work. Please charge your phone up when you get back, love, and text me this afternoon so I know you're alright."

"Will do, love you." And I really, really meant it. But I couldn't blame love for the lying, even though I was doing it to save us. Deep down, I knew my lies were destructive and already eating away at me.

"I love you too."

"You passed out?" she asked me.

"Yes, yesterday. It was just after I got that awful message with all the images and the demand for the money. I just got all hot and panicky, and before I knew it, I was on the office floor.

I've still got a bit of an egg on my head."

"No wonder you looked terrible this morning, Steph. Are you sure you can't tell Damien? This is really affecting you."

"I can't, not yet. Please just let's see what happens, give me a couple of weeks and if it continues I'll have to tell him. I'll have no option."

"Ok, a couple of weeks it is then."

STEPHANIE'S JOURNAL – LESSON 26
TRIGGERS

*Be grateful for your triggers, they point you to where you are
not yet free. ~ Uknown*

A trigger is something that happens in the present, which
reminds you of a traumatic event in the past and causes you to
experience associated feelings. This is a subconscious
connection, and in the moment, your brain fails to differentiate
between the past and the present.

A trigger can generate the same feelings you had during the
past traumatic event; therefore, the same behaviour and
physiology can appear. As old feelings ignite, it feels in many
ways like you are 'back there' in the past.

Because it's your subconscious, you may or may not realise
you have been triggered or the cause and connection. Triggers
can make you overreact and appear from nowhere. They
usually have a sudden onset and can be out of context. People
around you will probably not know you are being triggered and
you may not know yourself. You just know that you have a
bunch of uncomfortable feelings suddenly coming up that you
can't make sense of.

Common reactions to a trauma trigger can be panic attacks,
crying, shouting, being defensive, feeling nausea and
hypervigilance.

If you are triggered, do your best to try and pause. Take a
breath and make yourself really present, notice what is
happening around you and look for anchor yourself in the
present moment. Take some conscious breaths and remind
yourself that the past is not happening right now and you are
safe.

Once the moment has passed and if/when you feel up to it,
revisit the trigger moment to help you find out what might be

unhealed within your past, thus helping you to see what needs working on to reduce or eliminate the trigger. Triggers are connected to our unfinished emotional business. When this is no longer active in our emotions and vibration, triggers don't affect us anymore.

CHAPTER 4

After Mel dropped us off and Mia was settled, I reached for my phone. It had to happen sooner or later, so it may as well be sooner. Sending up a silent prayer, I switched it on. The message envelope was ready for me to click, and my finger hovered above the icon ready for the reveal. Whatever had been sent was already done. Waiting wouldn't change anything, but it felt like I was buying myself time, even though I knew it was an illusion. That would suggest I had some control, but in reality, I had none. I was cornered, and I'd done it to myself.

There were three messages: one was spam and two were about the book I was working on. Relief was welcome but laced with remorse as I reflected on how I'd shouted at Mia. I couldn't live like this - on a knife's edge, waiting for him to make another move, scared to look at my phone and overreacting. I either needed to reply to Jay or completely ignore him, and both felt terrifying.

I pep-talked myself up the stairs and into the office, sat at my desk and opened my laptop.

"Stop it," I told myself out loud. "You know those messages are not from him, so chill out."

You can do this.

I'd start by checking my emails, which were usually harmless and verged on boring, so they were the perfect neutral task to start with. There were the usual spammy messages from web design companies, something about shrinking four dress sizes and a special offer from a hotel chain for weekend breaks. I trashed them all and then noticed an email from my agent telling me the interview I'd done a couple of weeks ago was going to be printed in the *Sunday Times* supplement this weekend.

There was a proof attached and I clicked to open it, hardly recognising myself in the photographs they'd chosen. I looked radiant and happy sitting at this very desk, wearing a white blouse and indigo blue jeans, some turquoise crystal chip bracelets on my right wrist and my hair in a messy bun. There was a glimpse of the garden in the background and a mason jar of fresh flowers on the windowsill. It looked earthy and wholesome and a bit middle-class. I was pleased to say that the chat I'd had with the photographer about angles had been taken on board too. No one wants to have their *Sunday Times* debut with more than one chin.

Scrolling down, the additional photographs loaded, a picture that would usually make my heart melt, made me pause - Damien sitting with Mia on his knee and me by his side, family picture perfect in every way. We were laughing and I remembered the photographer cracking a joke to make us smile. Mia had misunderstood the punchline and made it even funnier, and here we are, captured in a moment of joy and connection.

I had been so careful about not allowing photographs of Mia on social media, knowing that I was setting myself up to be so public. I wanted her to choose what she shared of herself with the world when she was old enough to do so, and even more than that, I wanted her to be safe. There were people out there who didn't agree with my opinion at times, keyboard warriors who would pull me down publicly in a blink, and I never wanted my daughter in the firing line because of what I chose to do for a living.

I can't remember Jay ever reading the *Sunday Times*, so the chances of him seeing it were super slim. I'd end up being one story nestled in between an article on chalk painting furniture and summer mocktail recipes. The article would, however, be on social media, and this is where he was watching me.

The article screamed success and, for marketing purposes,

hinted at further works in the pipeline, which, to Jay, would spell out a pending payday. Something so lovely was now contaminated, and even if he never saw it and nothing came of this, it already had. I was viewing my life through a completely different lens, second-guessing everything, wondering if – no, *fearing* that - he was closing in.

Maybe I could email the newspaper and ask them to change the family photograph? I clicked reply, requested the amendment and asked if the references to Damien and Mia could be removed. It was about me and my journey, after all. I really wanted them included so they would pull the piece together, but I would lose so much face. This opportunity had been hard-won, and my agency had pulled so many strings.

Feeling a slight margin of reprieve, I opened my social media page to schedule some posts. I shared a poster from a page that I liked, and then I posted one of my own. A quote about life being a journey, with the text laid over a winding country road. My laptop pinged to announce an incoming email. The article wouldn't be adjusted because 'removing the references to family would lose the whole tone of the story', which was about new writers and working from home. What was the point in sending me a proof to look at if they were going to be so inflexible? Surely, this was my chance to have input on the finished article before the public saw it? It's my life they are splashing across their pages! My fingers flew across the keyboard in anger and I told the agency exactly that, my life – my choice. Their reply came back quickly.

Hi Stephanie,

We can, of course, ask them not to print, but please consider this carefully.

It's a golden opportunity to help get you out there, and we chased it for an age. It positions you as a successful writer and

*thought leader in your field, and in our experience, this could
lead to many more doors opening.*
We will have to know by close of business today please.
Kind regards

I felt horribly compromised. A couple of days ago, I'd have
been delirious about the article, and now I was completely torn.
My head started to throb and I felt nauseous. A sob caught in
my throat, fuelled by anger and frustration. How long was this
going to last? It had been one message. One threat. That's all.
I didn't need to escalate it to something extreme. In truth, I
could be making a mountain out of a molehill. I tried to think
about Jay's next move, but I didn't know him now and hadn't
even known him then.

Blackmailing someone was desperate and manipulative. I
needed to believe that to stop giving my power away and to stay
in the present moment so I could function and start to attract a
different outcome.

Thoughts are energy, remember?

The Universe sends you energy that matches your vibration.
You are literally creating your experience, thought by thought
and feeling by feeling. I needed to get back to basics and get
out of fear and worrying about what might happen. Instead, I
needed to focus on everything being ok.

This is done and all is well.

With that thought at the forefront of my mind, I took a breath
and emailed the agency back, saying that they were right, I was
just having a wobble, and to please proceed with the article as
planned.

There you go, Universe, it's business as usual.

I thought about responding to some of the comments on my
social media before signing off. People were kind enough to
connect with me about my work and I liked to let them know I

appreciated their support – gratitude is a magnet for goodness, after all. I scrolled through and started to drop a 'like' and a 'thank you' and a heart emoji, and then I saw it.

A comment from Jay The Taxi.

He'd written under the poster that I'd made about life's journey, something that no one would identify as manipulation but to me was fully loaded.

"Sometimes the cost of our happiness is to clear up the journey of the past."

The comment had been left moments ago - so this was stage two. My heart was racing again, and fear jumped back into the driving seat and hit the gas. What was I supposed to do now? If I deleted and blocked him, what would stage three be? And then someone started interacting with him on my page in front of my eyes.

"Totally agree!" a woman called Linda commented.

Jay was straight back with, "It's the only way – your past can come back and ruin your present!"

He knew I'd see this and he was baiting me to respond.

"I wish more people knew that then the world would be a better place!" Linda confirmed.

"We could all do with taking a good hard look at ourselves and what we've done. Until you own your actions the past will hold you hostage." Jay The Taxi.

"Preach!" followed by "LOL."

"Sounds like you have been on quite a journey yourself."

Linda would you just leave it?

"Haven't we all?"

Yes, you have, indeed, you spineless waste of underpants.

Heart emoji from Linda.

For fuck's actual sake.

I waited and watched, trying to control my breathing and calm down. The message was loud and clear and I'd absolutely received it. Jay wasn't going away. I felt panic and my heart rate was making me dizzy. I was home alone with Mia. I couldn't pass out again.

It's only fear. He can't hurt me.

Good old fight or flight reaction made my breathing too fast and shallow. I felt like there was no oxygen in the room. Jay may as well have been there in person with his hands around my throat.

Forcing myself to look out of the office window, I tried distraction, even though I was shaking. Tops of the trees swayed in the summer breeze, and a bird flew onto a branch. Clouds drifted and I deliberately battled with my thoughts until I could see some pictures emerge, just like I'd done when I was a kid. After a while, I started feeling less giddy. The fear was still there, but it wasn't gripping me as tightly.

Maybe paying him off was the smart thing to do after all.

How much he wanted was as yet unknown, and the last thing I wanted was to enter into any kind of dialogue to find out. I was overthinking and getting confused, which is probably perfectly normal when you are being stalked and blackmailed and shitting yourself about losing everything.

Perfectly normal but not at all helpful.

Slowly, I made my way to the bedroom, pausing on the landing to look through the gaps in the staircase spindles, seeing that Mia was still happy on the sofa watching kids' television. I dabbed lavender oil onto my t-shirt and breathed it in deeply; the undercurrent of Jay was still strong, but it wasn't going to pull me under and drown me.

I put my headphones in and made sure the volume was quiet enough to still hear the television downstairs, and then I clicked through to my go-to calming meditation. Thoughts of my current situation kept hijacking me and trying to drag me back into the land of fear and what-ifs. I told myself this was normal, and I had permission to observe the thoughts instead of fighting them. They flowed through me, and I felt their emotional burn, doing my best to breathe through and stay present. The meditation took me to the same mountain top it always did and asked me to look at the view. Expansive and awe-inspiring, it appeared in my mind's eye. Some features were familiar, and some weren't – it changed for me each time depending on what was going on in my life and what I needed.

This time, the sun was setting and the birds were chirping as they made their way over treetops and back to their nests. At first, it felt peaceful, but then, as the darkness descended, I was afraid. This had never happened on the mountain top before. I'd always been there at sunrise or in broad daylight, but the audio was telling me I was safe and whatever I experienced was right for me right now. I tapped the bed beneath me lightly with my fingertips and reminded myself that I was still at home. The darkness became absolute, and although it felt like it stretched to infinity, it also felt crushing and close. I focused on my breathing and allowed the fear to rise. From my core, it erupted, and I sobbed it out, staying as present as I could and with my eyes tight shut. It felt like each heaving breath was adding to the darkness. Finally, it slowed, and the sobs became softer. I wouldn't say that I felt ok, but I would say that releasing the fear, for now, had made way for more feelings of sadness and regret. In my mind's eye, I saw a scattering of stars in the darkness, tinkling above the mountain range, and I could just make out the moon as it rose high in the sky and brought a brief moment of serenity.

I breathed deeply and affirmed that everything was happening as it should be, knowing that my human self would struggle with this, but right now, in this consciousness, I could believe this was the case, although I didn't know why. I would do my best to hang on to this feeling; it would help me navigate and think more clearly. With that, I followed the usual instructions of sending out gratitude and listened to the reminder that being grateful was the same as sending out the frequency to The Universe of 'my life is full of goodness' and who doesn't want more of that?

Make it a rush order please.

Just as I opened my eyes, I heard the front door open and Damien calling for Mia. I needed to be really present now. I'd find some time later to think things through. Maybe it would all fizzle out and I'd never have to share the gruesome details. The truth was that unless Jay turned up at the door, I wasn't going to share anything today, so I could at least enjoy Mia showing off her new shiny shoes and have a lovely evening with my husband. No point in ruining that – who knows how many more I'd have if this all comes out?

CHAPTER 5

Damien and I shared a glass of wine on the patio as the sun went down. The heavens were soon ablaze and the dark silhouettes of the trees looked like they were drawn onto the sky canvas with black ink.

"You're miles away, Steph," he said softly as we sat underneath Mia's bedroom window.

"Just thinking about Mia starting school and how I'll cope." This was partly true.

Damien reached for my hand and suggested he could work from home that week if I needed him around for moral support.

"To be honest, it's as much for me as it is for you. I don't want to miss these moments either."

"I'd love that, and so would Mia," I said and squeezed his hand.

"Shall we go to bed?" Damien asked and raised an eyebrow.

I paused for a second before answering. Why did it feel like I needed to weigh this up? Because sex was the ultimate act of trust, connection and intimacy? It was a precious expression of love, and you gave all of yourself. I couldn't give all of me right now. There were parts of me lying and hiding in guilt, shame and regret.

He registered the split-second pause and checked himself. "Hey, don't worry if you aren't in the mood - I'm being a bit selfish, aren't I? I forgot you aren't feeling yourself." His comment hung in the hot night air and I heard myself answer,

"An early night sounds perfect to help me get my mojo back." And as easily as that, I slipped into someone I didn't recognise. I became a woman who is keeping heartbreaking and devastating secrets from her loving and devoted husband. This man will make love to her with passion and tenderness in the sanctity and safety of their marital bed and have no idea she's telling a lie that would break him and their otherwise solid relationship.

For the first time ever, I had sex with Damien on autopilot. Pushing my emotions aside and making something that was usually so intense and loving for me feel entirely physical. There were no complaints on his side. If anything, I did more of what he liked; maybe I was trying to prove myself worthy because I felt so far from it. In the afterglow, he lovingly stroked my hair, and I felt terrible.

I'd just shagged my husband like a one-night stand. Yes, we were a married couple and, with consent, could do whatever we wanted in the bedroom, but I'd deliberately deceived him. I'd had to cut off my feelings, or I wouldn't have been able to go through with it. I needed to make sure our sex life stayed active because the more he wanted me, the less likely he would be to leave – if ever it came to that.

What the hell was I thinking?

Was I trying to snare him and show him a good time so he wouldn't go? Damien would never think like that, ever. I was obviously losing the plot; the pressure was getting to me, and the peace I'd felt earlier that day had evaporated into oblivion.

"I love you," he whispered as he held me tight and breathed me in.

"Love you too," I mumbled and I truly meant it.

Although I was praying to hear his soft snores so I could have some head space to think about getting out of this mess, I was exhausted. As he drifted off, so did I, peacefully at first but waking with a start, tormented by shadows chasing me and a feeling of suffocating. Restless and shallow, the remaining hours of the night passed so slowly. As soon as I heard the birds singing their good mornings, I sat up, desperate to check my phone, and padded out of the bedroom, closing the door quietly behind me. Damien wouldn't be awake for another three hours - time enough for me to tie myself in a million knots.

I opened messenger with everything clenched – nothing. Emails – nothing. No new comments on my Facebook page from Joe The Taxi. I sat at the top of the stairs dumbfounded and checked them all again. Definitely nothing. Shouldn't I be relieved?

What a head fuck!

If anything, I was more anxious. The ever-present anxiety that was the background to my marriage to Jay was back, and this time it was on steroids. He knew there would be no price I wouldn't pay to make this go away, and in my heart, I knew that too.

CHAPTER 6

Thankfully, the next few days passed without incident, and I allowed myself to relax a little. Mia's excitement about starting school grew whilst Mel and I firmed up our school-run plan several times and reassured each other that everything would be fine, even though neither of us felt an ounce of the courage we were trying to project.

Where is that sense of freedom I've heard mothers speak of when their children start school? Right now, all I felt was anxious. Although I couldn't remember my first day at school, I could remember being the new girl at work several times and it being tough. Hopefully, things in the schoolyard weren't nearly as brutal.

I briefly worked in telesales, where the floor manager didn't like me and decided one day to isolate me for no reason at all, moving me away from all of my colleagues. She was a willowy, middle-aged woman with pinched features and longish brown hair that was desperate for a good trim. Haughty in her attitude, although she had no right to be, she would float around the sales floor like she owned the place, whispering her gossip and trying to look busy and important – of which she was neither.

After a while, I moved back to my seat and nothing was said, but I knew she'd voiced her opinion about me and it wasn't flattering. I needed the job, so I'd stayed for as long as I could bear it. I wonder who she's picking on now all these years later?

Yes, there were bullies out there, but I had to trust that Mia was in safe hands once those school gates were closed. As I pushed her on the swing in the park, I talked about sticking up for yourself, being kind to other children, listening to the teacher, and doing your best.

"Yes, Mummy, I know!" she rolled her eyes and asked if we could go to see Gran.

I agreed, reminding myself to take the sandals. "Do you want to take your school uniform and new shoes to show Gran?" I asked.

"Yes, and my lunchbox too." Mia skipped beside me, and the sun was warm on my face, my daughter's little hand in mine and her voice like a melody I wanted to hear over and over. This was one of those perfect moments you want to hold on to forever. I was so grateful for my life, and she was its crowning jewel.

"Right, Mummy, you get the shoes." Mia tumbled into the front door, started collecting school-related items, and piled them in the hallway.

"Are you excited to show Gran all of your lovely school things?" I asked as I gathered them up.

"Yes, I am super excited!" Mia jumped up and down and clapped her hands together.

"I'm so pleased you're happy about starting school. It's going to be great fun and a big adventure."

I'll miss you so much, and please, please stay safe.

"Yes, I'm going to paint you lovely pictures for the walls, Mummy."

"I've already made space for that." I also had a massive trunk to use as a memory box because I knew I'd never throw a thing away and part with even a tiny piece of her.

I helped Mia into her car seat and turned up the happy tunes. Today was a good day and I wanted to soak it up.

Mum was thrilled to see us, and after the school uniform parade, she made us lunch. Mia ate hers in the playhouse outside and Dad managed to fold himself onto a tiny wooden chair to join her while Mum and I sat in the kitchen. She asked me how I was feeling about Mia starting school and told me to go easy on myself.

"It's a big deal, Steph. I can remember being all over the place."

"Really?" I asked.

"Oh yes," Mum laughed. "I held it together when I dropped you off, but when I got home the floodgates opened. Your dad was at work and there were no mobile phones then to text anyone, so I just had to tough it out. I stripped the beds and cleaned, clock watching in the background and guessing what you'd be doing. I was wishing away the minutes until you were home, desperate to know if the other kids had been nice to you and you liked your teacher."

"So what I'm going through is normal then?" I sighed.

"Yes, love, really normal." Mum poured the tea and continued. "And it gets easier quickly, I promise. Once you have a couple of weeks under your belt, things start to feel better, and there is a new rhythm to your life. You'll find that you can settle into doing bits of work and even consider going out for a coffee because you'll know she's safe and happy."

"Really?"

"Yes, of course. Look at all the mums you know who are managing just fine. You're no different to them. They're just a few steps ahead and have some evidence that their kids are settled and working." She reached out and took my hand in hers.

"Of course there will be blips here and there - days when she doesn't want to go to school, or she's had a falling out with another kid, and there'll be days when you really miss her. But generally speaking, it's as much an adventure for you as it is for her, Steph. You'll always be a mum first and foremost, but you're many other things too, and you're allowed to be."

She was right and it was perfect timing to be sitting here today and talking woman to woman, mother to mother, with someone who had experienced exactly what I was about to go through.

My own mother was giving me permission to feel the way I did and also to step back and give both Mia and myself the chance to grow.

"She'll be ok, love, and so will you."

"Thanks, Mum," I replied and felt emotional but lighter.

"Actually, I've got something for you. I know it's your birthday soon, but you may as well have them now." I produced the second shoe shop bag that I'd brought in and passed it over the table.

Mum's happy smile at receiving a surprise didn't last long as she opened the box and stared inside.

"Crikey, Steph, are you kidding?" We both started laughing and she picked up one of the sandals up and looked closer. "I know I'm getting on, but I'm not ready for this much Velcro!"

"Actually, they are quite ugly now I can see them up close."

"Ugly? What possessed you to buy these? A blind man on a galloping horse could see they're hideous! I hope you got a gift receipt because these need to go back!"

I could hardly speak for laughing as I tried to explain how I'd been encouraged to buy them by Brenda, briefly recapping the boot saga, and yes, she did recognise me, and no, I couldn't say no.

"I only wanted Mia's school shoes. Honestly, Mum, I just don't know how things like this keep happening to me, it's ridiculous!" I laughed.

"I'll take them back," said Mum. "If there's nothing I want, I'll ask for a voucher and you can have it for the next pair of school shoes."

"I can't go back there, ever. Maybe I'd consider it if I knew Brenda had retired, but knowing my luck, she'd be filling in for holidays when I showed up."

"Actually, I agree with you," Mum said, and we both laughed again.

I stayed for another hour and we joined Mia and Dad in the

garden. Some of the leaves on the trees were starting to yellow at the edges, and although it was still hot, autumn was on her way. Dad gave me some courgettes and tomatoes from the greenhouse and gave Mia some pocket money.

"Mum, I'm in the paper on Sunday. It's the *Sunday Times,*" I said, feeling pleased with myself.

"That's amazing, love!" Mum said, and Dad was beaming.

"Can we order copies at the corner shop?" he asked and Mum nodded.

"I'll ring straight away," she said, counting on her fingers how many copies she'd need.

"It's only the magazine, actually, not the proper paper." I shrugged, not wanting to big myself up too much.

"Only the magazine? That's fantastic, love. We are so proud of you." I could hear the sincerity in his tone, and it brought a lump to my throat. I could see Mum was tearing up as she hugged me and told me to drive safely. They waved us off, and I could still see them in the rear-view mirror as I turned off their street. I could also see Mia starting to nod off.

STEPHANIE'S JOURNAL – LESSON 27
SURRENDER TO THE SEASON

*Surrender is the simple but profound wisdom of yielding to,
rather than opposing the flow of life.~ Eckhart Tolle*

Life is a series of seasons and cycles that are sometimes predictable and sometimes not, and just like the seasons of nature, they cannot be changed or held back; trying to do so can cause pain, resistance and challenge. Embracing the season or cycle you are in can help you cope, progress, and embrace life differently. Once we recognise this, we can adapt our expectations, mindset, and behaviour, and we can become present with ourselves and our situation, reclaiming our power.

This releases frustration and helps us to grow through the lessons that life presents to us rather than resisting them. It brings an acceptance that is not to be confused with defeat. There is strength in acknowledging where you are right now and how you can use the experience to your best advantage, healing and evolution.

Being in denial of where you are and trying to fight it is exhausting and wastes both time and energy that you could be using more productively. Each season can be honoured and enjoyed in different ways, as they are all a valuable part of our journey when we allow them.

CHAPTER 7

Early Sunday morning, I walked to the shop at the end of our street and bought a copy of the *Sunday Times*. I couldn't bring myself to open the magazine in the shop and check to see if I'd made the final cut. I scurried out after making a bit of small talk about the weather.

The house was quiet. I slid the magazine out of the folded newspaper and gasped. My face was looking back at me from the front cover. The headline read 'Mum's the Word' with a strapline underneath about 'Women Who Make Millions from Home'.

This was not what I signed off on, not at all.

And I didn't have millions in the bank, not now anyway. I'd heard loads of people say that you couldn't trust the media, and they printed what they wanted just to sell papers and here was the evidence. I frantically flicked through and saw a collection of women they'd given a share of the spotlight to, as well as me. I scanned my section and picked out the key points, most of which were true or 'massaged' to sound more interesting, but there were thankfully no out-and-out lies and no references to my bank balance, which I would never have discussed, just the leading headline, which quite frankly was more than enough.

There was a mention of pipeline foreign rights for my work and a healthy advance that I'd received. Both were correct, and both of which I wish I hadn't mentioned. The main article was true to the proof that I'd signed off, but my face splashed across the front page was a shock. I guessed it was a slow news week or maybe they wanted some diversity, so they picked someone chubby.

I hadn't seen or heard anything from Jay for days. Although

he was no longer centre stage, he was still lurking in the wings. The thought of him was like watching storm clouds roll in on a beautiful summer day that slowly darkens the sky. You're waiting for the rain to fall and you know when it does, it's going to be biblical.

This should be a happy moment, but thinking about him has stolen any of that.

He has seeped into everything and made a stain like muddy water or a sewage spill. The dirty laundry of my life was in his possession and could so easily be aired. Perhaps even the *Sunday Times* would document my fall from grace, and I'd make the front page of a supplement in the future, but in a totally different light.

Who was I kidding? Even if it got into the papers, it would only be the sleaziest gutter press that picked up a story like that, and once the cat was out of the bag, I'd have lost my marriage anyway, so the rest wouldn't matter.

My phone lit up with a message from Mum. She and Dad were so proud of me and they were going to visit Great Auntie Margaret in her nursing home and take a copy to show her this afternoon. I sent back some heart emojis.

Finishing my coffee, I scrolled through my social media feeds. The agency had shared the article. It had a few likes, and I would have to post it later. Maybe Jay was losing interest, and this was blowing over? I needed to get my life back. I couldn't keep second-guessing and letting fear control me.

I made my way quietly up the stairs and into the shower. Mia would be up soon, and the day would begin with a snuggle on the sofa and pancakes for breakfast, as was our routine on a Sunday. When I came back, Damien was sitting at the kitchen table beaming.

"I'm so proud of you, Steph. This is amazing." He squeezed me tight.

"Thank you," I mumbled, wanting to be happy but feeling

like a traitor.

"Hey!" Damien lifted my chin and looked straight into my eyes. I blinked back tears.

"It's just overwhelming. It's all coming together now and I didn't expect to feel this way." I looked away, praying that he couldn't see the guilt and shame written all over my face.

He put his arms around me again and rocked me gently from side to side. "It's ok, love, you're human and sometimes things feel a bit much."

I do not deserve this man.

After a few moments, he kissed my forehead and wiped a tear or two from my cheeks with his dressing gown sleeve.

"Why don't you take a coffee back up to bed and I'll make the pancakes this morning?" he suggested and clicked the kettle back on to boil.

"Thank you, I think I might." I smiled weakly.

"I'm worried about you," he said in a soft but serious tone. "You've not been yourself since you had that tumble in the office. Is something bothering you, love? You know you can talk to me about anything."

No I can't, not this.

"I think it's just Mia starting school. It's come around so much faster than I expected, and I don't feel ready. In fact, I sometimes feel like the world's worst mum..."

Uh, oh, the floodgates were opening.

Speaking the words out loud made my gut wrench, and I sobbed into my hands.

"Steph, you are a great mum!" Damien said all the right things in that moment, but everything he said was based on his own frame of reference, and he was missing the ultimate plot twist that I'd kept from him. He bundled me back to bed, tucked me in, kissed me again, and said he'd be back in half an hour with breakfast. He told me to get some rest and that we'd talk later - I knew this meant he wanted me to make a doctor's appointment, and I knew I'd have to go through the motions and phone up tomorrow. A pointless appointment unless they could help me turn back the clock.

Maybe I could go and see Robin and have some therapy instead? She'd helped me before. Surely she could help me again? I could tell her everything, and from experience, I knew that this alone would lighten the load. Even the thought of sharing with Robin made me feel slightly unburdened. I was able to close my eyes and allow sleep to settle upon me lightly, and for the first time in as long as I could remember, I had a Sunday morning lie-in.

CHAPTER 8

Monday came far too quickly. Due to teacher training days and a staggered intake of the new reception children, our start day was Wednesday.

I had two days left at home with my baby, and as her excitement was building, so was my sadness. I noticed the way the sun shone on her hair, making golden highlights, and my heart was so full of love. Her first adventure into the real world was only moments away and it was so hard to think of her growing up. The first step of many in her life – each one taking her a bit closer to independence and a bit further away from the safety of the nest we'd built for her. It was the way of things and perfectly natural, I knew that, but it didn't mean I didn't ache.

There had been a flurry of messages yesterday afternoon about the press release that I needed to reply to, but they could wait. They'd be a good distraction on Wednesday morning once I'd dropped Mia off and I had half a day to fill.

We met Mel and George in the park for an hour. As the kids ran riot, Mel and I sat on a bench and sighed in unison.

"How are you doing?" I asked.

"Probably the same as you," Mel replied.

"We can do this," I said, trying to project some kind of confidence for us both.

"We have to," Mel replied. "Or we'll have to home-school them."

"Now there's an idea!" I said in complete seriousness.

"What?" Mel looked horrified and I burst out laughing.

"I'm joking, for goodness sake!"

"I should bloody hope so!" she joined in and the mood

lightened… until she changed the subject.

"Anything from your troll?"

I came back down with a bump. "No, nothing," I answered truthfully with a big sigh. Here he was again, the thunder cloud on the horizon of my life.

"What a relief. I hope he's pissed off and leaves you alone for good. You could do without being anxious about that this week, and as long as it all blows over, you don't have to tell Damien. I think you're right about that, by the way. If there's nothing to tell him, why upset him as well as you?"

"I've been so conflicted by it, Mel." Not quite the whole truth, but a close enough version. "I really wanted to tell him, but like you said, if it goes away, there is no point in burdening him. I can talk to you and feel better, so I've got what I need."

"Always here, you know that."

"It's triggered so much fear and anxiety. I hope that goes away soon as well as him," I said.

"Maybe you've got some kind of PTSD response happening or something? Is there stuff in your past that this could have picked a scab on?"

Mel, you will hopefully never know how accurate you are on that one.

"Maybe. I thought about going to see that therapy lady Robin again for a couple of sessions if I don't feel like myself again soon."

"You told me when you were married the first time, you had loads of stuff to deal with. Perhaps that's not as resolved as you think?"

"Maybe not."

"Regardless of what happens next, I think it's smart to get some therapy, Steph. It's obviously really affecting you. Who wouldn't need help if they were going through this kind of thing? And having to keep it to yourself must be super stressful."

I agreed, and we sat in comfortable silence against the background of birdsong and the happy sounds of our children playing. After a few moments, we heard footsteps approach and saw a park regular walking past with her Yorkshire Terrier whom we'd gotten to know as Tuppy (short for Tuppence, the name of the Yorkie Gemma, her owner, had owned as a child). We exchanged hellos and fussed the dog, who was around a year old and still jumped up too much and barked at anything that moved. Gemma swiftly put her hand in her deep pockets and pulled out her new secret weapon, a small water bottle that delivered a fast and targeted squirt at the back of Tuppy's head.

"No barking!" she commanded, and the dog stopped in her tracks, looking at Gemma defiantly but no longer making a racket.

Mel and I were impressed.

"I bet you wish you'd had that when she ruined that picnic," I said, and we all burst out laughing as Gemma rolled her eyes.

It had been a hot day in August when a mum and her two children arrived with their wicker picnic basket and rug and sat down to enjoy a 'light lunch before visiting grandma'. We knew this because the mum spoke slightly louder than usual. Subtext - look at me. I'm such a good parent.

Picnic Mummy unpacked the basket nicely and laid out the breadsticks, chopped carrots, pepper batons, and houmous. There was fresh fruit, baby plum tomatoes on the vine and some elderflower cordial to use with the sparkling water.

The girl started to faff about and scratch her thigh, nearly knocking over her drink.

"Stop that. You are not allergic to the picnic rug, sweetie – it is organic, fair trade, unbleached and ethically sourced. Stop scratching and have some food please."

Mel and I had sniggered.

Sweetie scowled and reached for some carrot sticks – some picnic. The boy was slightly chunky and went all in on the breadsticks. Unfortunately, he didn't like houmous, and they were so dry on their own that they made him cough and shower the rug with crumbs. Sweetie didn't like that, and neither did Picnic Mummy, and they both scolded him for "being greedy". Poor kid was just hungry and would have probably loved a straightforward sandwich. He was nearly my size and I wouldn't want to face the afternoon running on half a packet of breadsticks and a couple of sips of fizzy water.

"Uh oh, here comes trouble," I'd whispered to Mel as Gemma had trotted up with Tuppy, who was only just being allowed off her lead.

Tuppy was delighted to see the picnickers and showed her appreciation by running laps around their blanket and barking her tits off. Then she claimed the rug as her own by peeing all over it. Sorry, Picnic Mummy, it's definitely going to need bleaching now.

Picnic Mummy stood up and frantically tried to shoo Tuppy away.

Gemma had managed to huff and puff her way to the edge of the scene and tried to calm things down. She told Picnic Mummy to keep still and that Tuppy would soon lose interest.

"She thinks you're playing!" Gemma shouted over the commotion. "Keep still and stop flapping around!"

"I'm not flapping. I'm protecting my kids' faces from your hairy piranha!" Picnic Mummy shouted back as her kids cowered, sitting in dog pee. "Fuck off, you savage!" Picnic Mummy shouted and by the look of her sensible shoes and the expression on the kids' faces, she was not usually Sweary Mummy. On reflection, those shoes may have indeed been from Brenda's comfort range. Picnic Mummy most definitely had set out with the intention of a smart day and was being served up with something quite unexpected.

No amount of reassurance from Gemma that she was "just a baby" and "not bitey" would wash, and threats of calling the police started to fill the air.

The final straw for Picnic Mummy was when her expensive sunglasses fell off her head and she stood on them.

The final straw for Gemma was when Picnic Mummy shouted that Tuppy was a hairy c-word and that they were fucking prescription lenses and not knock-offs from a Turkish market like the ones Gemma was wearing.

"That bloody animal is trying to steal our food and savage my kids!"

More flapping, and Tuppy was living her best life. She went for a victory lap with one-half of the sunglasses in her mouth.

"No one wants your shite food! Not even the dog!" Gemma shouted back. "That's not a picnic. It's a fucking punishment!"

Picnic Mummy packed up quickly after that.

Gemma turned towards Mel and I and shook her head. "Well, I've seen it all now!" she said.

Mel and I had finally managed to compose ourselves, and Gemma stood with her hands on her hips, watching Tuppy chase leaves and bark some more.

"Yes, now you mention it, I do wish I'd had the water spray back then," said Gemma, barely able to speak for laughing.

"I wonder if she'll ever come back," snorted Mel.

"I seriously doubt it." I giggled. "Poor woman."

"Silly woman, you mean!" Gemma was indignant. "If only she'd stopped flapping around, everything would have been fine. And anyway, she's trained now, aren't you, Tuppy?"

Gemma spoke to the dog like you'd talk to a toddler, and then she bent down to pat her cute little fur baby in a checked jacket. Tuppy bit her index finger hard, then ran around her in circles, tangling her up in the lead and barking the place down.

"You little shit!" Gemma shouted, grappling for the bottle but confined by the ever-tightening lead that was wrapping around her waist.

"Stop flapping. She thinks it's a game!" Mel said through

fits of giggles, and we were both helpless again.

CHAPTER 9

Wednesday was here at last. Mia was up with the larks, no fear of being late for her first day at school. Everything looked too big for her and all brand new.

"Wow, Mia, you look really smart!" said Damien. "Are you excited?"

She nodded and talked about playing in the yard and painting pictures in the classroom.

"And Mummy?" Damien asked and cuddled into me.

"So far, so good, but I've just opened my eyes."

"You need coffee, Mummy," said Mia.

I thought about other firsts that we'd been through: her first steps, her first tooth, her first time in her own bed. Each one had felt huge at the time, but after a few weeks, it had quickly merged into the fabric of normal family life. Hopefully, going to school would be no different. As long as she was happy, the rest would follow, and right now, she was happy to be going, and that was the best possible start to today, that and coffee.

After breakfast, we left the house for our first-ever school run.

George and Mel were waiting at the designated meeting spot. George was hopping from foot to foot, which was much better than his cling-on routine. We took photos of the kids before we set off, and Damien took one of the four of us despite Mel and I objecting that we looked a mess.

"You're gorgeous, the two of you, yummy mummies or whatever they say these days. Stop picking your nose, George. Everyone smile!" The memory was captured forever in the cloud, as well as my heart.

Damien asked Mel how she was doing, and she answered in

a way that I could only describe as formal. I shot her a sideways glance, and she blushed slightly. Damien was oblivious to all of this, being dragged ahead by Mia.

"What the hell?" I whispered.

"I don't know what happened there. I'm so sorry. I just can't keep secrets, Steph. I'm so awkward."

"There is no secret."

"Has he gone then?"

"Come on, you two slow coaches!" Damien spoke over his shoulder, George in one hand and Mia in the other.

"We're coming!" I shouted back in an overly cheery school-run mummy voice.

We joined the congregated parents in the yard, between the newly painted hopscotch and the freshly cut grass of the games field. George let go of Damien's hand and started to limpet on Mel's leg. I shrugged sympathetically in her direction. While she talked him through it, more parents and kids arrived. Mia stood between us both and soaked up the scene, waving now and then to familiar faces from nursery, including that horrible woman Rosie the childminder.

There she was, all tall and aloof, with her hair piled up on top of her head. Even with her back to me, I recognised her silhouette, like one of the witches from Roald Dahl. She had two children with her. Both girls were huddled closer to her than I guessed the real her would have liked – but she wouldn't want to appear anything less than loving and caring in public. The last time I'd seen her was in the restaurant when she'd called me a doormat in front of everyone and then qualified it by saying if *her husband* had been shagging someone with big tits and ten years younger than her, she wouldn't have taken him back. Evidence that confirmed my doormat status, in her opinion. Her very loud opinion, which turned out to be the first domino that fell for me, years ago, on that fateful night.

Causing trouble was a hobby for her, along with making

other people feel small. Poisonous whispers and covert put-downs were her usual style, but in my case, she'd added in a full-on public performance. I disliked her intensely, and Mel did too. She was the last person I wanted to speak to this morning, well, second last. Luckily, she was too busy to notice me, performing for the audience of parents around her and making sure she showed what an excellent childminder she was.

"Now, girls, remember to have a lovely time and make lots of new friends," Rosie adjusted her volume to draw in as many people as possible. The girls looked up at her the way she liked the adults in her life to look up to her too, and they nodded in agreement.

"Annie, I'll see you tomorrow morning. Your mummy is coming to collect you, and Bella, you are stuck with me this afternoon while *your* mummy is still at work." Bella hung her head slightly as Rosie's putdown landed perfectly. Now she could be the hero, the good egg who stepped in when Mummy didn't bother. I was probably the only one to notice it and imagined that Bella's mum got a version of the same at both pick-up and drop-off.

"Is that Rosie?" Mel muttered in my direction.

"Yes, and from what I can gather, she hasn't changed a bit. She's still a spiteful cow," I replied. Scanning faces, I recognised a handful of others from nursery and smiled in their direction. I also noticed that the space around Rosie was unoccupied. She was being avoided by more than just us.

The teachers came onto the yard, nursing cups of coffee and chatting amongst themselves, smiling widely at the parents and children and then making a line. I crouched down and hugged Mia tight before holding her at arm's length to take her in completely.

"Have the best day ever," I said, bracing myself for her to say she wanted to go home instead.

"Be good for Mrs Miles." Damien patted her head and straightened up her backpack. He was starting to tell her that it would be brilliant, and he couldn't wait to hear all about it, but his words floated after her as she skipped towards her reception class teacher.

Mrs Miles smiled and waved reassuringly. She was a mum of two and knew the ropes. It was clear she was very well-liked and had a lovely way with the children, which gave confidence to the parents. Mia turned and waved too, full of happy, and we waved back, full of goodness knows what.

Mel was joining the line with George attached to her leg, and the lovely reception classroom assistant came to reassure him. We'd heard on the grapevine that Mrs Barrie ("please call me Lisa") had recently become a grandmother, but she didn't look anywhere near old enough. She was gentle but firm; exactly what the children needed and the parents wanted. Good boundaries and consistency, along with a hug when needed.

I saw Rosie smirk. She looked me up and down and then did the same to Damien, smirking again and turning on her heel.

"What was that about?" Damien asked.

"She's horrible, that's what." I shut the conversation down as Mel joined us. We could all hear George crying in the background and Mel was about to cry too.

"They said they would call me in half an hour with an update," she sniffed.

"I know it's going to feel like forever, but it's not all that long, Mel. We can do half an hour." I tried to reassure her, but I could feel her turmoil that could have easily been mine this morning. "Let's go to that coffee shop around the corner. We'll be really close to school and can be back in a blink if needs be," I suggested, linking her arm and pulling her closer.

"Yes, let's do that." She smiled weakly. "Mrs Barrie, sorry, Lisa, is so lovely, I feel terrible for her."

"But why? This is what they do and she'll know exactly how

to handle things."

"It's not that, Steph. Did you see the size of her? She obviously shops in the petite section and she's George the limpet's new rock."

"Ouch," said Damien. "That's a slipped disc by hometime."

"I hope not. We'll be red-flagged on day one."

"I'm sure George will be a pet limpet by the end of the first week, or maybe he'll feel more secure by then and just be George." Damien smiled.

"Let's hope so, or she'll need crutches." Mel managed to smile back.

"At least she will have something to fight him off with," I said as we turned onto the main street and the smell of coffee and sound of traffic filled our senses.

"I'll leave you ladies to it," said Damien and leaned in to kiss me.

"See you later, Mel. Hang in there," he said as he walked towards the car.

"It's 9:12am already, Mel. You're nearly halfway there, and the coffee is on me." We settled into a booth and counted down the minutes over our cappuccinos.

When the phone rang, we both jumped, and Mel answered all fingers and thumbs. George was completely fine, and they would call if that changed. Apparently, he'd settled within a few moments of carpet time when the teacher had asked each child to share something that made them happy, and she'd strategically picked him first. At first, he was shy, but once the teacher coaxed him into telling the class more about his dog Benji, he'd become quite animated and made everyone laugh with the story of the stolen sausage from Grandad's plate and how Grandma had been blamed for giving him less than his share. When he was asked how big Benji was, he had to release his death grip on Lisa. She'd gracefully sidestepped out of reach but stayed close enough for him to still feel safe. Everyone's a winner – apart from Grandad.

"That's a relief." Mel sighed and her hunched shoulders relaxed. "Only two hours left to fill before we pick them up."

CHAPTER 10

We were a week into the school run before I knew it, and full days were happening now. When I say full, it was until three o'clock, which, when you are only five years old and there is no more afternoon nap, is definitely a full day. I was starting to relax into the routine more and trust that Mia was safe and happy. The first pictures had been stuck onto the fridge and there were scuffs on her shoes already. Life was finding a rhythm and I was able to turn my attention more to work, and that meant writing again.

Writing feels like you're living a secret double life no one else knows about. Things that usually go unnoticed by the majority spark ideas and make connections like you're painting a three-dimensional canvas in your mind's eye all of the time. Filling in a little here and there, highlighting, connecting, smudging. An ever-present backdrop only you know about. Mia being at school would give me time and space, and I needed to use it wisely.

The *Sunday Times* story had sparked a couple of interview enquiries and book sales had spiked the following week. There was also a pipeline opportunity to appear on Radio 4 and talk about writing as a career. I'd have to weigh that one up as I'd literally fallen into it – both career and the interview.

I'd spoken to the agency and felt more focused. Things were on the up. Sitting at my desk, I wondered if I could start writing the draft my publisher was expecting soon.

A new collection of wisdom, lessons, insights and guidance for real life - but where to start? I'd been journalling a little, but the situation with Jay was both a distraction and an energy drain. In the past, I'd written about what I'd been going through. My current experience was certainly very different. Maybe I should try writing about parenting? I was going through a whole lot in that department. Perhaps there was something worth sharing.

My fingers tapped across the keyboard. Parenting could be something I can write about. After about an hour, I'd written over a thousand words. This was exciting! I ended with my final thought and stretched. If I kept producing around one thousand words a day, I'd have a first draft within a couple of months and be ahead of the deadline. I wanted to tell someone I'd started, but at the same time, I didn't. After a bit more progress, I'd tell Damien, but for now, this was a secret between me and my laptop.

It looks like I'm getting good at keeping secrets.

School pick-up time arrived in a flurry, and I left the house feeling good. Pulling up and unclipping my seatbelt, I waved to Mel, then gasped out loud and ducked behind the dash. A silver saloon drove past with a phone number along the side. It was gone in a blink, and Mel tapped on the glass. I pretended to rummage around the passenger footwell, looking for something. Who on earth was I becoming? It was just a random taxi. I had to get a grip.

"Sorry, just trying to find the phone charger," I said as I got out.

"It's already there, you silly moo!" said Mel, pointing.

"God, I think I'm losing it!" I said and forced a laugh.

"You lost it ages ago," Mel jested, and we walked towards school.

I smiled at a few parents while Mel struck up a conversation with Beth from toddler group. Her daughter was quiet and softly spoken, just like her mum. Beth was a single parent. I didn't know the full story, but I knew she'd had to get a protection order for her and her daughter because of her abusive ex and she had counselling once a week as standard - maybe it was time for me to book some therapy and stop hiding from taxis.

Children came tumbling out of the building and scattered across the yard like ants. Noise filled the air, and Mia's sticky little hand grabbed mine. She excitedly told me about glue, tissue paper and making a collage for the classroom wall. Life felt good, with an undercurrent of anxiety, but good.

Just a little psychological mopping up to do and I'd be sorted. The past can stay in the past, and no one gets hurt.

CHAPTER 11

Mum and Dad called in on their way back from visiting Great Auntie Margaret. Mia took centre stage, showcasing her reading book and the first painting stuck on the fridge. Once she was all talked out, Mum and Dad updated us on the cul-de-sac news, three doors up, the teenager was learning to drive and the L-plates went on the car at least twice a week. The Avon lady had packed in and next door were thinking about solar panels. That's the round-up, folks. I asked how Auntie was and Mum's mood changed.

"She's ninety-two now, you know, Steph. That's a good innings, but she's slipping."

"Could go anytime now then," said Dad.

"For god's sake, stop that!" Mum snapped.

"I'm right, though, if you ask me, once you get into your nineties, you're on borrowed time."

"I don't think anyone did ask you, though, did they?"

Mum turned and spoke directly to me as Dad huffed and puffed.

"You should go and see her, love. I hate to admit it, but your dad's right. While she's got most of her marbles, you should go and visit. You could take Mia."

Mum was right; I felt guilty for not visiting, but I hated the way the place made me feel. It was cheery and bright, and the staff were always friendly even when they were obviously exhausted, but there was something you could feel - all gathered up and cold, lurking, like fog does at the bottom of a valley. It was God's waiting room, and no one wanted to say it. The residents were well fed, watered and cared for, but most had lost their spark when the fog moved in, which could be a blessing as it blurred the memories of who they'd once been. I always left feeling so sad, and that's what made me avoid going.

"I will, Mum. You're right, I should go," I said. "What did you mean when you said she was slipping?"

"Just little things, love. Nothing really bad, but you'll notice that she's different. She used to be as sharp as a tack, but she sometimes needs prompting with someone's name or what she's done the day before. Her long-term memory is great, and she can talk for ages about travelling when she was younger, holidays and family gatherings, but it's the present she struggles with."

"Oh, ok. I'm sorry I've left it so long." I sighed, feeling bad that Mum was shouldering most of this on her own.

"Nothing to be sorry about, love. It's not my favourite place to go either. I want to see her, but crikey, it's bleak. Just think about it, and your dad is right, go sooner rather than later."

"She couldn't even remember who you were married to," said Dad. "She said you were married to Jay and how much she liked him."

I took a sharp intake of breath. "Wow, that's a blast from the past!"

I can't get away from him.

"I know, love, that's what I mean. She's living in the past. She always did like Jay, though, didn't she? I can remember him making a big effort with her at Christmas and the two of them having a sherry together after we'd eaten." Mum half smiled at the memory, and although I wanted to tell her that he'd done that to spite me and avoid the mountain of washing up he'd promised to do, I didn't want to steal any happiness she felt.

Jay and Christmas, I remember the combination well. I was anxious about any kind of occasion, but Christmas was the biggie. I couldn't pinpoint why or when it started being this way. It just kind of happened. Even a Friday night with the girls gradually became harder until socialising was so tricky that I stopped it. I probably had an undiagnosed social anxiety disorder or something after I met Jay. Who knows.

I always felt wound up before a family get-together, drinking my way through it to numb the nerves.

Jay found it exhausting, and I would often drive him to be nasty with me before we even arrived.

He'd say that if going out caused that much anxiety, we should have stayed in, and we'd always have to leave early before I got pissed and embarrassed us both. The awful truth was that often he was right; it started and ended with me, and usually the ending was bad. I used to be so carefree and confident. Maybe this just happened as you became an adult; life got harder and you felt it.

In the early days, it was subtle. I told myself the butterflies were excitement, not nerves. But then I began to question whether I should go or not. Nothing felt right about my clothes or hair, and I'd constantly ask Jay for his opinion, which I knew deep down meant his approval. I hated that I needed it and hated myself more for asking. I had no idea why either was happening.

He was always supportive. I didn't have to go out with friends if I wasn't feeling it. Jay would remind me that it was usually a drama-fuelled gossip fest, and staying in with him and watching a movie was a better idea. He was right, of course, and the thought of staying home brought relief. Couples needed time together. I wasn't letting anyone down, and if they didn't understand, maybe they weren't the right friends for me anyway. Those movie nights often led to early nights, and by the time Jay had talked me down and convinced me I'd done the right thing, I couldn't wait for bedtime to show him how much I appreciated him.

Hang on, what was I thinking?

My marriage to Jay ended as a nightmare, and I needed to remember that. I was confused and wearing the thickest pair of rose-coloured glasses to look at the past. Could I possibly still have feelings for him?

Stop it!

Even if there were any residual emotions, they had quickly evaporated when he turned up the heat and tried to blackmail me.

But had they?

I'd just felt them again. What on earth was going on with me? I really needed to get some therapy. I was actually, possibly, and legitimately losing it.

"Steph, you're miles away, love," Mum's voice brought me back to reality.

"I was just thinking about Christmas," I answered honestly. "And visiting Auntie Margaret, of course."

"She'd love to see you, but be prepared for her to go around the houses a bit. The best way is to just go along with it, whatever she tells you. There's no point in distressing her and trying to correct what she's saying." Mum smiled and I knew she was right.

"Maybe I'll go on my own first and get the measure of her before I take Mia," I said.

"Good idea. Explain to her again that you are married to Damien."

"She even told us that Jay had been to see her!" Mum laughed and Dad snorted. He had only been half listening and was thumbing through the newspaper he'd brought with him.

"Wow, that's quite a story." I tried to sound casual and dismissive, forcing a laugh myself.

"Yes, they'd had a lovely chat, apparently," Mum stage-whispered, only just audible above the sound of the television programme Mia was absorbed in. "She said he was just as handsome but that he had some grey hairs now and he had to wear his glasses to read her the television guide." She shook her head. "Old age catches up with us all, love."

"I'll go as soon as I can, Mum, I promise." Mum patted my knee and smiled. I made an excuse about checking something in the oven and escaped to the kitchen, fanning my face and fighting back tears. Panic was setting in, and I couldn't let them see. This was ridiculous. Mum was completely right. Auntie Margaret was in the early stages of dementia and she was making things up. She didn't know what day it was, never mind who had been to see her. I was being triggered. The trip down memory lane had brought old feelings into the now and mixed them up with what I'd been trying to ignore. Robin had talked me through this before and explained that my thoughts were creating a physiological response in my body, and I could choose different thoughts and feel a different way. I needed something else to focus on because all my mind wanted to flash through were future images of my life in ruins because of Jay.

Breathe, Steph, breathe.

I was pacing up and down the length of the countertop, with the back door wide open, trying to calm and cool down, when I heard Damien open the front door. My parents small-talked and asked him about work. Mia was interrupting and telling him about the collage and tissue paper. I closed my eyes and tears fell down my cheeks, streaking mascara across my hot and blotchy face.

I heard Mum tell him I was in the kitchen, and I made my way to stand on the back doorstep.

"What's wrong, love?" he said and rushed to me. "Are you feeling faint again?"

"I just felt all panicky." He wrapped his arms around me, and I sobbed into him as he rocked me gently.

Could I tell him the truth?

Look what it was doing to me. I couldn't hold it in much longer. Even the mention of Jay could totally derail me; it felt like a net closing in, and no matter which way I moved, I was trapped. My great auntie was old and getting confused – that was the truth of it. I was filling in the blanks incorrectly and scaring myself stupid into the bargain. Never mind *her* losing the plot. It was actually me.

Was this what a breakdown felt like?

"I can't face Mum and Dad like this," I whispered.

"Let's get you sat down with a glass of water." Damien released his hold on me slowly and carefully, checking I had my balance. He guided me to the kitchen table and ran the cold tap.

My breathing was slowing and I sipped the cold water.

"We're off, love," Mum shouted. "Your dad's program is starting and we want to get home and settled for it."

I sighed with relief when Damien shouted back on our behalf.

"Steph's just taking some rubbish out to the bin. I'll let her know you've gone. Good to see you both."

"See you soon, love. We've got to dash."

I heard them saying goodbye to Mia and then the front door closing. Tears reappeared, as well as my chance to come clean. Damien sat next to me and held my hand, looking deep into my eyes with worry and concern. I was doing this to him through cowardice, dragging him through torment to save him from torment. I needed to believe that for better or worse meant just that.

"Steph, please go to see the doctor," he said quietly. "Something isn't right here."

I hung my head, unable to make eye contact.

"I'll come with you," he continued. "We're a team and you're my best friend. You have always been there for me and now it's my time to support you."

Kindness - something I needed but didn't deserve. I wasn't who he thought I was or who I'd thought I was either.

"Ok, I'll go," I heard myself say. "I'll be ok on my own, I promise."

"You don't have to go alone," Damien reiterated.

I was falling deeper and deeper into a hole I'd dug for myself, and it was getting darker and narrower and harder to climb out. One day, the light at the top might be so small I can't see it anymore, and the hole will swallow me up.

"I'll make the appointment, I promise." I heard myself say.

Damien squeezed my hand and kissed me on the forehead. "Is there anything you're not telling me?" he asked, and the question hung in the air between us like the blade of a guillotine.

Yes, yes, there is, and I'm so ashamed and scared.

"I mean, you haven't found a lump or anything, have you?" he asked.

I breathed out and shook my head. "No, no lumps, I promise," I said, knowing the door of opportunity to speak the truth was still ajar. I raised my eyes from the table and blinked back more tears.

"Oh, Steph, I'm so, so sorry!" Damien reached for the kitchen towel on the countertop and ripped a sheet off. "I didn't mean to accuse you of lying, Steph. I know you'd never lie to me." He fussed around me and dried my tears. "I'm so sorry if that felt loaded. I'm just a bit, erm, scared and cancer-centric. I can't lose you, Steph. You and Mia are the whole world to me."

He hugged me tight and I cried tears of regret and self-reproach. He kept telling me he knew I would never lie to him and he was so, so sorry. What an awful thing to say, and then the kicker – could I forgive *him*?

And with that final heartbreakingly ironic request, I let the door of opportunity slam shut. Instead of speaking up, I clammed up. After muttering a weak "of course" and thinking about how low I'd sunk in that moment, there I was again, trapped in my web of lies. A web I might never escape from.

CHAPTER 12

After a broken night's sleep, I braved the school run and made three phone calls. The first one was to the nursing home to see Auntie Margaret, as I'd promised Mum. Then I rang the doctors to book in for the well-woman clinic as I'd promised Damien. And then I rang Robin the therapist, as I'd promised myself.

Robin's couch was a familiar and safe space. I knew that was what I needed. I was surprised to hear she had a cancellation and could see me later in the day. I guess the power of intention was still something I could harness at times. If only I could use it to get out of the mess I was in with Jay.

I filled in the rest of the morning with housework and angst, and when the time came to leave, I'd tied myself in as many knots as last year's fairy lights. I couldn't face anything to eat, and although it's not a diet I'd recommend to anyone, I fleetingly thought my nausea might help me shift a few pounds. Silver linings and all that.

Robin hadn't changed, and being with her felt comfortable. I allowed the armchair to envelop me as she made coffee. As before, there was a low-level table between us with two coasters, a box of tissues, a tray with two empty glasses, and a water pitcher.

"I think it's white with no sugar?" she asked.

"That's right, and yes, please." I smiled and fidgeted on my chair as I wondered where to start.

"It's lovely to see you again," she said as she passed me a mug full of coffee. "What brings you here today?"

"Can I check something first, please?" I asked.

"Of course." She was just as reassuring and kind as I remembered.

"Anything I tell you is really confidential, I mean *super* confidential."

She smiled and confirmed everything that was said between us was kept in the strictest confidence – unless I was going to hurt myself or someone else and then she had an obligation to involve other agencies.

"I thought so," I said, considering where to go next.

"You can start anywhere you want to, Steph. Just relax. This is your time and it's a safe space."

"I just don't know where to start," my hands were on my lap and I started fiddling with my wedding ring, turning it round and round and remembering the never-ending circle of love it was supposed to represent, a circle I'd broken.

Robin waited a few moments and then spoke softly again. "Just start where you are today. How are you feeling right now?"

"There's just so much to say. There really is." I took a breath, knowing deep down I couldn't be selective. I had to go all in if I wanted help. Things were so muddled I had no hope of clarity if I didn't confess everything.

"I need to know that you really, really won't tell anyone." I started to cry.

"I absolutely promise that I won't, Steph. I can tell that trust is a massive thing for you at the moment and I want you to know that whatever is said in this room stays between us."

I reached for a tissue and stared into space. Whether Jay ever got in touch again or not, the damage was being done and I needed to find a way to cope, move forward and possibly even forgive myself. Deep inner work and transformation, if it's even possible when you carry this much guilt. And all without my husband finding out.

No pressure, Robin.

"And you won't judge me?" I asked.

"I won't judge you; I promise," Robin answered, "You can

share whatever you want to, whatever you need to."

"I'm so anxious all the time. I'm having panic attacks where my heart starts racing. I get too hot and I want to cry. I've even passed out once."

Robin listened, then asked if I had seen my doctor.

"I've booked in for some well-woman clinic thing in a couple of weeks, but I know it's pointless and I've only done it to pacify Damien." I shook my head and shrugged. "It's something I need to work through and get some coping strategies or something. I really don't know, but it's definitely nothing that can be fixed with a pill."

"Sometimes it's a good idea just to rule things out, though?" Robin needed to make sure I was being responsible.

I nodded and blew my nose.

"Now, can you talk me through what happens when you feel anxious, Steph, perhaps when you're triggered, maybe give me an example?"

"That's easy. I had a meltdown in the kitchen just a few days ago."

"Ok, just so I can understand exactly what happened, can you let me know what was happening just before the feelings kicked in? Was it anything specific?"

"My mum mentioned my ex-husband, Jay," I said and didn't elaborate.

Like the good therapist she was, Robin asked more about the context and my reaction.

"I can tell you are really uncomfortable talking about this," she said and told me to take my time.

"I just need to stop overreacting when I hear his name," I said, frustrated. "Why can't I just get over it and move on with my life? What's wrong with me that I'm so stuck in the past and feel panicky and confused whenever he's mentioned?"

"The past probably holds feelings that are unresolved or unhealed for you, and that can be painful and scary to revisit."

"I just need it to stop happening." I was crying angry tears; anger at myself and the situation I'd created, anger that I couldn't tell Robin the truth and ultimately angry at Jay.

She gave me a moment to catch my breath and then she leaned in. "I can't help you if you don't tell me what's really going on here, Steph."

"I know you can't." I kept crying. "I'm so confused. I want to tell you, but I'm so scared," I said through snot, tears and tissue.

"What are you scared of?" she asked.

"That you will think I'm a terrible person, that you'll tell someone, that therapy won't work and I'll keep drowning. All of that and more. I feel sick, I can't sleep and every now and then, I'm so panic-stricken I shake and cry and feel like I'm being choked. I need to pull myself together, Robin, please help me."

"Of course I'm going to help you," she said. "Let's start at the beginning, though. I want to understand why it's happening before we look at what we can do, and it could be a really quick process, but I have to know more, Steph otherwise, it's like putting a band-aid on a broken leg and hoping for the best." She smiled at me and I smiled back weakly.

"Where shall I start?" I asked.

"At the beginning. What was your relationship with Jay like?" Robin sat back and listened as the floodgates opened, and I talked about my former life. I didn't know what she wanted, so I mentioned just about everything, and before I knew it, our time was up, and we were booking another appointment for the following week.

"I feel so much better for talking, thank you," I said as I made my out. Although I hadn't learned anything to help me cope, I left feeling lighter and less burdened. This is a win. I was back in therapy and it was working already.

I had time to drive to the nursing home before the school

run, another box ticked. The Manor had been purpose-built and had a modern, maybe even corporate feel to it, lots of wood and glass. The double front doors were open and flanked with colourful flowerpots, leading to a vestibule and an intercom. Once I'd given my name, I was buzzed through and asked to sign the visitors' book. Curiosity niggled, and I flicked back the pages silently – scanning names and dates for Jay Slater or any variation. But there was nothing.

I am a basket case – confirmed.

Like Mum and Dad said, it was dementia creeping in and nothing more. I was just about to convince myself for a final time by looking at the week before when I paused.

Stop this now – you are making yourself anxious for no reason.

Fighting the feeling of going back further, I stopped myself. That's better; I was moving forward and didn't need to be scared because it was over and done. I needed to bring my best self to visiting my great auntie and stop fretting over something that wasn't worth my energy.

I remembered the way to her room. The door was partly open. "Hi Auntie, it's me, Stephanie," I said loudly and approached the old lady sitting in a high-winged back chair near full-length patio doors.

The doors looked out onto a courtyard filled with wooden planters and benches. It was tiled beautifully so that no one would trip and pushing a wheelchair would be easy. A couple of people were sitting out and enjoying the autumn sunshine; birds were singing and easy-listening music drifted into the room on a light breeze.

"Stephanie?" her voice sounded frail as she turned to look at me and outstretched her hand to hold mine. "What a wonderful surprise! I can't believe you're here."

I pulled up a chair and we started to talk about anything and everything, past and present. She seemed in fine form. Maybe she was just having a good day. I showed her some pictures of Mia and said I'd bring her to visit soon. A carer brought two cups of coffee and, thankfully, some biscuits. I needed a snack now.

The conversation naturally turned to my writing and I talked about starting the new book and how it was good timing that Mia had started school. Auntie mentioned Mum and Dad visiting and finished her coffee.

"Next time you come, we'll have a sneaky sherry," she winked.

"Just a sip for me. I'll have the car." Usually, I wouldn't touch a drop if I was driving, but I could accommodate an old lady and literally have a thimble-full if it meant a lot to her.

"I'm waiting for new sherry glasses, or you could have had one today." She went on to tell me.

"You could always use a tumbler. No one would know."

"Oh no, dear! That's uncouth!" she laughed. "Proper glasses for sherry, always. I was so cross with myself when I broke not one, but two in one fell swoop."

"That will teach you to drink one glass at a time!" I laughed and she joined in.

"No, dear, I had company, and I reached over to pick up my glass, but I was wearing a cardigan with fluted sleeves – totally impractical and vain of me, really, but I've had it for years, and the colour suits me, it's a sage green. I went to pour a second glass for us both and the sleeve scooped both glasses up and they toppled over. One shattered completely and the other sort of snapped. I was so cross with myself. I won't be able to get the same glasses again and I loved them."

"I remember those glasses. You brought them to my house one Christmas," I said. "I was so scared of breaking them, I washed them by hand and gave them straight back to you."

"Well, thank you for taking care of them back then, but they're broken now anyway. I'm glad it was me who did it in the end. I'd rather be furious with myself than anyone else," she sighed. "They weren't worth anything really, but they were my mother's and they held a good measure of sherry!"

"Maybe we can get some more the same?" I said. "I think I can remember them. Were they like this?" I opened the eBay app on my phone and showed her a set of six vintage sherry glasses.

"Exactly like that!" she exclaimed and clapped her hands together. I enlarged the picture for her to see more detail.

"I can make an offer on them if you like them?" I asked.

"I don't know how all this stuff works, but you young people seem to have the idea, so yes, please do what you need to and I'll settle up."

"It's ok, I'll get them as a gift, and I'll put this address in for delivery so next time I come, we can raise a glass instead of a mug. I could even get Damien to come along and I could have more than one glass if he drives."

"Now that sounds like a plan. I'd love that." She patted my knee. "You've been lucky in this life, Stephanie, and I'm not going to pry about how things went bad the first time, but as far as I can see, you've had two lovely husbands."

And just like that, the perfect chance arose for me to ask about Jay. I hated myself for even considering it, but even amid my self-reproach, the devil on my shoulder whispered to me to find out more.

"Ah yes, well, life happens, doesn't it." I looked at my watch and noted I had to leave in a few minutes.

"It does, Stephanie, and like I said, I don't know what happened, but I really liked Jay, and I still do."

Don't tempt me, please don't.

I couldn't remove those rose-coloured glasses she was viewing the past through; that would have been cruel. I tried to respond in as neutral a way as I could. "We did have some happy times, but things just didn't work out in the end."

"It's a shame, but like you say, life happens."

"I hope he's happy now because I am," I said, inviting in the past and not knowing if I should.

"Oh, he is. He's got a new love interest, I believe. We all have to move on, don't we?"

"Oh?" I couldn't help it. Curiosity got the better of me.

"And a new job as a taxi driver, can you believe that? I hope those sherry glasses come before he drops in for a tipple. I'll be sure not to wear that cardigan next time. It's a good job it didn't spill all over him just before his night shift."

I froze to the spot, my words catching in my throat. I just managed to splutter something about the time and needing to make tracks, and made for the door.

He HAD been here.

Striding down the corridor towards the exit, I grabbed the visitors' book. With a shaky hand, I turned back time, a page at a time, until I saw it. In black ballpoint pen and block capitals, three weeks ago to the day, Jay Slater had been here just after five o'clock and he'd stayed for an hour. Just long enough to begin rebinding those old family ties, to share a sherry and a short trip down memory lane, which I had no doubt would be continued in the very near future when he returned. Two awful thoughts came to me as I stared at his name and blinked back tears. The first was that my auntie had no idea she was being used; the second was that the net was even tighter than I thought, and there was nothing I could do.

CHAPTER 13

The short journey to school was a blur. My mind and heart were racing. I felt giddy, and I knew I should have pulled over. Someone honked me loudly and I jumped. The lights had changed and I hadn't noticed, and now I'd stalled and there was more honking. Trying to restart the car made me panic even more. It roared into action and lurched forward, straight into the path of a white van that had to do an emergency stop—cue shouty drivers, me crying and absolute chaos.

Confirmed – I should not be driving.

I pulled in and sobbed. My heart was still pounding and my face was all red and puffy. There was no way I could go to school looking like this.

I needed a plan.

Who was I kidding? I was screwed.

The only *plan* was to come clean or pay up. Even just thinking about contacting Jay made me feel sick. I opened the car window, retching twice. Sipping from a water bottle on the passenger seat, I closed my eyes. After a couple of minutes, the giddiness had made way for a full-on pounding headache. I had to get home. Driving carefully with the window down and the radio off, I talked myself through it just as I had as a learner. I reminded myself to indicate, check my mirrors and give way. Soon, I was turning up my street, home sweet home and Mel had agreed to pick up Mia.

My advance from the publishers was my nest egg, our nest egg. I'd been living on the royalty payments that landed every month, and I had no intention of touching this until I'd made good on my contract. Otherwise, I was spending money I hadn't earned yet. I had agreed to keep it safe on behalf of us both, of us all. I'd been trusted with it, and I couldn't be trusted. Lies had built upon lies, but surely I couldn't steal from us as well? Would it be stealing, though? I'd earned this money, so it was technically mine.

Stephanie, no!

Whoever I was becoming I didn't like her and she needed to get a grip. This was OUR money and I had been *trusted*. I needed to deserve that trust, keep it safe. And keep it safe I absolutely would, because if I ever needed to use it for something really, really, important I'd be taking a loan from the pot, not stealing it. Once the next book was finished, I'd have more royalties coming in each month, and I'd be able to replace what I'd borrowed and no one would ever know.

This was a responsible plan.

The only plan.

The only option.

I would even write IOU slips and keep them in my purse so I knew exactly what I needed to pay back. Because I could be trusted, I could definitely be trusted.

I could mostly be trusted.

I opened up Facebook and searched for Jay's profile. Scrolling through the posts he'd shared over the last few months, it became abundantly clear he'd hoped I'd end up here. Each one was a surface level lol or meaningful meme, unless you knew the lines to read between.

Our wedding song was first, posted of course on the anniversary of the big day with a message about regretting the things you have done rather than those you haven't. Friends and family members sent love and hugs and told him to keep his chin up, that he is a good person and there is someone out there for him. Posts about karma, getting what you deserve, and how letting other people see you succeed was the best revenge. I was obviously *other people*.

I clicked to send a message and started to type. Then I

stopped and deleted it. I had no idea what to say. Anyway, he'd no doubt screenshot the conversation and send it to Damien along with the pictures. I had to be careful. There had to be as much damage limitation as possible.

I just needed to pay him and fuck him off – fact.

Therapy could save my marriage. I'd be the best wife ever and totally make it up to Damien. The money would go back into the bank and this would all go away. I needed to focus on the outcome I wanted and not the mess I was in. But how on earth do you open a dialogue with a blackmailer? Where do 'negotiations' even start with shit like this? Maybe I'd start by telling him that I knew about him going to the nursing home, but why would he care? He wants me to know that. He's been leaving a trail for me to follow and guess what? I'm right where he's led me. Scared, confused and completely at his mercy.

The cursor blinked at me in the empty message box and I blinked back. Maybe I should make him an offer? But leave myself some wiggle room to go up a bit?

Oh, Steph. Listen to yourself! This is blackmail, not a second-hand car.

Standing up, I opened the window, paced around and felt sick again. Reminding myself to take deep, even breaths or as close to them as I could get, I sat back down. He might not even see the message straight away, or ever. My fingers hovered over the keyboard again and I could see them trembling slightly. I typed one character and pressed send. A question mark, which in my head meant what the actual fuck are you doing, how much do you want and can you please just fuck all of the way off and leave me alone?

Then I stared.

And stared.

And stared.

The message had remained unread for five minutes – which felt like five years - and I was even more anxious now. What had I done? Even if I deleted it there would be a notification to say I'd done just that and then it would be even worse – if it could get any worse. And then, just like that, a tick appeared, he'd seen it.

Yes, things could get worse and they were just about to.

Nothing. No response at all. Maybe he was driving or busy or couldn't message me back. Ten minutes, then twenty. Still nothing. The radio silence was torture. How was I going to cope? Half an hour.

I needed a distraction and I needed to calm down. Adrenalin was coursing through me at a rate of knots and I was full-on shaking. I made it to the bathroom and dry-heaved. After five minutes, my stomach ached from the effort and I wasn't sure I could stand back up. Shuffling to the side of the bath, I sat upright with my back against the panel and my legs flat out on the floor. The tiles were cool. I laid my palms flat and closed my eyes. There was nothing I could do until I heard from him, and I could suppose that now he'd seen my message, there wouldn't be any point in him sharing the photographs. He had me exactly where he wanted me; his cat-and-mouse game was about to begin in earnest, and the stakes had just gone up. The dice was rolled and I had to let this play out.

Place your bets, ladies and gentlemen, stick or twist.

Dragging myself to my feet, I saw myself in the mirror. The state of me would have secured a scarer's position at a Halloween event. I needed to lie down. Heading for the bedroom, I surrendered to the exhaustion and somehow drifted off to sleep.

"I'm home!" Damien shouted, slamming the door behind him.

I woke with a start and quickly checked my phone. Nothing. "Up here," I replied.

He appeared at the bedroom door, looking concerned. "Where's Mia? What's wrong?"

"I'm ok. I just had a migraine, that's all. Mel was taking George out after school, so she picked Mia up too. They'll be back soon," I said.

"A migraine? It's ages since you've had one of those." He stroked my hair and asked if I needed a glass of water, headache tablets, food.

"I think it's lifting a bit. Hopefully I've caught it in time and it won't be a belter."

My phone pinged and Damien reached for it. I held my breath and tried to remember the Facebook name Jay used. Would it be blatantly obvious the message was from him? Jay The Taxi could be anyone. Damien didn't know his occupation and Jay's profile picture was a landscape. Depending on the content, I might just be able to fluff over this.

Please God, don't let it be the pictures.

"It's Mel, she's heading here now," he said and put the phone back on the nightstand. "Hey, what's up? You look terrified! Were you expecting a message from your secret fella?" he laughed and kissed my forehead. "I'll get you some water and start running Mia's bath. You stay here and rest."

I exhaled.

Too close, way too close.

CHAPTER 14

The days that followed were blurry. Sleep alluded me and even if it came, my dreams were nightmares filled with the fear of being caught and losing everything. I blamed the deadline from the publishers for the lost car keys, the tiredness and generally dropping the ball. Writing was all but impossible. My head was full of Jay and what might unfold next.

My next appointment with Robin thankfully came around quickly, and I took my seat while she made the coffee.

"How have you been, Steph?" she asked.

"I don't know where to start. I'm still confused, emotional, anxious," I said, knowing I should tell her everything.

"Well, that's understandable," she said, pausing.

I looked up at her and her expression was one of empathy, the same way you look when you give someone bad news. The 'sorry for your loss' face.

"Steph, I listened really carefully to what you were telling me last time, and I took loads of notes because I wanted to refer back to them, and I did." Another pause and a quiet sigh. "Have you ever heard of gaslighting?"

"Erm, no," I replied, wondering why she was giving this so much gravity.

"Well, let me explain. It's a phrase used to describe a type of manipulation that gets you to question your own reality, your memory and your perception of the world and yourself. It comes from an old movie back in 1944 called *Gaslight*, where a husband convinces his wife to think she is mentally unstable and unwell so he can steal from her." Robin explained carefully, waiting for my response.

"Ok, but what has an old movie got to do with me?" I asked.

"Well, based on what you told me about your relationship with Jay, there are indicators that you may have been a victim of gaslighting," she paused to see what I'd say, but I had nothing. "My gut feeling is that this was for the duration of your relationship."

With that, I shook my head. "Surely I would know if something like this had been going on, Robin, and anyway, I know Jay wasn't good for me; that's why I'm not married to him anymore. I honestly don't see what this has got to do with anything." Robin was usually on point, but not this time.

"It's got a lot to do with what you are going through now, Steph. We need to talk more and dig in with the past and the present, but in essence, I think you might have complex PTSD because of your relationship with Jay and I think it could be playing out now and sabotaging your current life with Damien."

"But I'm happy with Damien. I'm just anxious – that's what I need help with."

"I know that, but I also see a lot of confusion, a lack of self-worth, a struggle to make decisions, anxiety, people-pleasing, and that's just based on our first session. All of these would indicate you have been in an emotionally abusive situation and that it's affected you hugely, and you've given me obvious examples of when Jay used gaslighting to manipulate you and make you question your reality so he would have the upper hand and be able to control you even more. I know this is a lot to take in, and I also want you to know that we can work on this together, but the anxiety and confusion you feel could well be the legacy of this abuse. In order to help you, we need to heal the past."

"Robin, he was a bastard. But he never abused me." My frustration showed in my tone. I couldn't believe she'd missed the point.

"There are different kinds of abuse, and from what you've told me, there is evidence of emotional, psychological, and financial abuse here. None of which are your fault and all of which would leave a legacy, a toxic legacy that would contaminate future relationships."

"I'm sorry, I just don't think this is right." Maybe I should have chosen someone else for therapy this time. Maybe I still would.

"What makes you feel it's not right?" she asked softly.

"Because I would have known if I was being abused. He was selfish and a liar and yes, there were times when I compromised, but that's not people-pleasing or being abused, for god's sake; it's just being married." Tears of anger were welling up. "I just need you to help me stop feeling so anxious, Robin. This stuff that you are raking up from the past is where it belongs – in the past."

"I hear you; I really do." She nodded. "I'm going to have to ask you to trust me with this, and I know it's going to be hard because initially, this will feel like I've got it wrong. You'll feel frustrated and confused and probably angry with me at times. I get that."

"You're going to tell me all this is normal, right?" I threw in a little sarcasm.

"Yes, perfectly normal." Robin was treading carefully.

"Well, give me some examples then." I crossed my arms and let out a deep sigh. Let's see if she could back this up.

"I'm not trying to be right here, Steph. Believe me when I say I would rather you weren't going through this, and you absolutely don't have to go any further if you don't want to. It's a big thing for someone to suggest to you, and it's normal not to believe it and to look for evidence," she said, scanning through her notes.

"Here we go. Remember when Jay told you that you'd upset his colleagues at a works night out, and the following day he'd had to text everyone and apologise for your behaviour?"

Which night was she talking about?

There were several examples of this, until I literally stopped going out with that crowd because I always ended up having way too much to drink and feeling dreadful the next day - a dreadful hangover and dreadful about my behaviour as Jay filled in the blanks.

"The night of the birthday party and the alleyway?" Robin prompted me.

"Yes, I remember that night – parts of it anyway."

"Great, you mentioned a couple of things that raised red flags to me in your last session. I'd like to hear more about the evening if that's ok? Starting with the lead-up, the few days before. How did you feel, what was happening and how did Jay seem to you?" Robin asked.

"You want the whole thing?" I asked. "Warts and all?" I rolled my eyes at her. After all, I had nothing to lose now. It's not as if I'd be coming back after this.

"Yes, please, just as you remember it. I'll let you talk and I might make notes, but I won't interrupt. Please explain as if you're telling me a story and don't leave anything out, even if you think it's unimportant. You're my last client of the day, so if we run over a little, it's fine by me. I want to hear it all."

"Ok then," I sighed. "But it's not pretty in parts, so please remember that it's forever ago and I'm not like that now. Yes, I'm anxious and struggling a little bit mentally, but I'm nothing like the mess I was back then."

"I'm not going to judge you, Steph. I want to help," Robin said. "I've done loads of stuff I'm not proud of, so has everyone else. But it's who you are right now that matters, and this is a huge step in owning your story and healing it."

I sat back, tucked my feet up underneath me, and stared into the coffee cup. In my heart and mind, I travelled back to that time and allowed the feelings and past experiences to wash over me. I talked and talked and she listened.

As I shared the story with Robin, I felt several steps

removed, watching the movie of my life in my mind's eye and describing it to her. The birthday in question was one of Jay's colleagues. She was twenty-five and worked in accounts. No big deal, you could say, just show up and have a good time, but I remember I felt on the back foot weeks before the event.

Jay wouldn't tell me anything about the party, and it made me anxious, although I kept my feelings to myself, which made it worse. I wanted to know what to wear and if we needed to take a gift. I'd asked more than once and had nothing back, and now I was stepping into territory that would anger him, tip-toeing around emotional landmines.

As the date drew closer, I got more anxious. Facebook pictures of the work's Christmas party had shown everyone looking fabulous - heels, handbags and not a bingo wing in sight. There was no way I'd fit in. Desperate, I bit the bullet and asked him again what he thought I should wear, if there were a dress code and where the venue was. I can remember the relief and almost crying when he kissed me, telling me I looked nice in *everything* and to stop fretting. I had to pull myself together and stop self-sabotaging.

With a couple of days to go, my anxiety peaked again. There was just enough time to find something to wear if need be. I didn't want to show Jay up by looking out of place - so I asked again. My timing was out. I should have known he'd be tired after work, so when he told me to chill the fuck out and be normal for once, I knew he was right. I was forever spoiling things for us both. There was nothing wrong with a bit of tough love from him; it kept me grounded.

Eventually, I decided to get some smart jeans – the ones with the control panel tummy, so I felt less chubby - and some bling and a black top because it goes with anything. Why hadn't I just trusted myself in the first place? Jay was right when he said I created drama out of nothing.

The big day came. He said there would be food there, so I'd

eaten nothing since lunchtime. Going with the flow more and not prepping the life out of everything was my new way. I could do this. Normal people doing normal things, and tonight, I was on the normal bus. In fact, I was driving the normal bus – that's how normal I was.

Before we left, Jay looked me up and down and said, "You'll do", which could have made me wobble, but then he laughed, and I told myself to stop being so sensitive. Normal people wouldn't overreact to a joke like that, so I didn't. Being close enough to have this silly couplesy banter without anyone getting offended was lovely. What a relief and how totally normal.

So why did I feel deflated?

I knew not to crack a joke in return. He'd already pointed out I should be grateful he was willing to drive. Agreed, but I knew the real reason. He wanted his colleagues to see his new car, his pride and joy. I'd managed to juggle things financially to make the monthly payments. Switching to a dry trim at the hairdressers every eight weeks and a supermarket box dye was saving us a fortune, and I'd been able to cut other corners too. Marriage was about compromise, and I was all in. If a new car made him happy, that was good for me too.

My stomach rumbled. I'd tried to make some toast before we left, but Jay pointed out that bread bloated me. He might have even looked at my tummy when he said it, and he was right. The control pants and the lift and sculpt jeans were helping, so why spoil it now? I didn't need any toast or any extra bloat. Thank goodness he had my back.

We pulled up and before he cut the engine, Jay asked me not to get shit-faced and embarrass us both.

"You know you go too far, Steph, and these are my colleagues," he said.

A couple of girls stood in the doorway, shivering and wearing next to nothing. Perfect figures, golden curls, looking like movie stars at an awards ceremony. Then there's me, with my chubby trotters forced into my strappy black high heels and I wondered what on earth I was doing here.

I was being a good wife and doing normal couplesy things, that's what.

Those two were probably having a cocktail or two here and then heading to a nightclub; they were certainly dressed for it.

"I won't," I said and smiled, desperate for a large glass of wine or two to calm my nerves. I'd definitely stop at two, enough to take the edge off but stay in control.

One of the girls waved and Jay waved back

"You know them?" I asked.

"Yeah, that's Sarah and Meghan. They work in the office."

"Oh, I've never heard you mention them," I said.

"Because I have to tell you the name of everyone I work with now?" His defensive tone made an early appearance. I could have kicked myself for sounding so needy and insecure.

"Of course you don't!" I laughed and patted his thigh. "I'm just curious!"

"Well, don't be, Steph. Stop being so weird and insecure. We haven't even walked in yet and you're already pissing me off."

"I'm sorry, I just…"

"Well, just don't. Can we have one night out where you act normally, please? Is that too much to ask?"

"No, of course not."

"Good."

Cue heartsink.

Jay went to the boot and pulled out a suit bag. He adeptly fastened a black bow tie and threw on a dinner jacket before coming round to the passenger side to open the door for me. I'd been so preoccupied, I hadn't noticed the winged collar on his shirt or the black satin stripe on his trousers. He was James Fucking Bond, and I was wearing jeans and some cheap mail-order earrings.

"Wow, you've pushed the boat out," I muttered.

"Darcey sent an email saying the dress code was black tie."

"Why didn't you tell me?" I blurted out before realising he'd probably forgotten – I mean, his job is really stressful - and feeling myself shrink with embarrassment.

"I was going to, but I know you get stressed out about these things, and you'd settled on your new jeans, and they look alright with your heels, so I thought it wasn't worth making you *even* more anxious and needy."

I could see his point, but it didn't make it any better. "I can't go in with jeans on, Jay," I said and stayed put in the passenger seat.

"Yes you can, Steph. Some people aren't going to bother getting dolled up. You won't be the only one."

"But they'll think I haven't made an effort."

"Look, I'll say that I forgot to tell you," said Jay. "I'll say it's my fault." He leaned over and kissed my forehead. Nice Jay was back. If I behaved myself, then maybe he would stay all night.

"Are you sure?" I asked, still awkward but relieved he'd have my back.

"Of course, we're a team, aren't we?"

"Yes, yes, we are," I said, thinking about that first glass of wine and pulling myself together. So what if I wasn't wearing something designer and figure-hugging? Jay loved me as I was, and I was walking into the party with my handsome husband, and people could think what they wanted.

He was greeted like a celebrity when we entered the room, high-fiving guys and kissing girls' cheeks as I stood like a spare part, waiting for an introduction. It wasn't his fault; it was noisy, and he was hijacked as soon as we walked in.

Thankfully, one of the women shuffled closer and asked, "You must be Stephanie?" She looked like she'd stepped straight out of a magazine. Her black dress was beautifully cut and accessorised with silver and sparkles. I wanted to cry.

"Yes, that's me – I didn't get the memo about the dress code," I shrugged, scanning the room and feeling my face flush with humiliation. Everyone looked amazing. I wanted to leave – this had been a terrible mistake.

"This is Steph, everyone," he turned and slipped his arm around my waist, finally drawing me into the conversation. "I'm afraid she didn't get the dress code memo." He laughed, pulled me closer and kissed the top of my head.

"She's a bit ditsy, but I love her." Laughter rippled through the group, and Jay went on to elaborate by telling them the story of when I was at the passport office and argued that I was actually a year older than I was. More laughter, and I joined in through obligation, remembering that day very differently - Jay yelling at me in the foyer and me crying and asking him to stop. It was ridiculous that I couldn't remember my birthday, but Jay had always mixed me up every year as a silly game and told me I was a year older than I'd thought. I'd often have to go and check my driving licence to make sure I had it right. It confused the shit out of me, and he knew it, but still found it funny.

Once he'd finished being the centre of attention, he turned to me and smiled, but I didn't smile back. He'd leaned in and kissed my cheek, whispering that he'd had no choice but to make a joke. It was painfully obvious that I looked different to everyone else and the best way to handle the stares and giggles was to tackle them head-on and save face – for me. It wouldn't matter when everyone was drunk in an hour or two. But the truth was it *did* matter. I felt like I'd been set up and couldn't say a thing about it.

Why couldn't I speak up?

Because it was probably a misunderstanding, and I had promised to be normal and not spoil the night as usual, so I needed to let it go and get on with having a good time.

Asking if I wanted a drink, he pushed a twenty into my palm and nodded to where the bar was.

"Pint of lager, thanks." He turned his back on me and kept talking. This was the kind of thing I'd usually be oversensitive about, and I caught myself starting to feel upset – but for what? He was buying me a drink and I was going to the bar. I needed to get a grip. Returning with the drinks was uncomfortable. I stood behind him as he wrapped up the punchline and made everyone laugh again, remembering my time as a waitress and thinking that, at least back then, I got tips.

It's good to see Jay in the mix and having such a good time.

I needed to rein in my own insecurities and not spoil everything. The first glass of wine was heaven and didn't last long enough. I kicked myself for giving him the change along with his pint. Now I'd have to ask for more money. Why hadn't I just brought my own? He'd told me to leave my money at home, that tonight was on him, so of course, I complied.

Right now, though, I wished I hadn't spent the emergency tenner I usually kept in the back of my phone case. But it was an emergency last week when I was hungry and passing a McDonald's, but too far into my overdraft to use my debit card. My stomach rumbled. If I'd been offered another glass of wine or large fries in that moment, I'd have faced a huge dilemma.

"Can I get you another?" the woman was back who had spoken to me initially.

"I am mortified," I said, looking her up and down. "I had no idea it was formal dress. I can't believe you're even speaking to me, never mind offering me a drink."

"Didn't Jay tell you? To be honest, I'm really uncomfortable. I'd never usually wear a dress and I'd far rather be in jeans. Anyway, you look lovely, don't give it another thought, it's just a stupid birthday party. We don't have to impress anyone." I liked her and clung to her offer of a drink like a life raft.

"I'd love another if that's ok, and we'll buy you one back once my husband has stopped talking, and no, he didn't tell me – at least I don't think he did," I said, fake smiling, which I'm sure she picked up on.

"I'm Jeanette," she said. "I don't work here either. I'm married to Gary, he's one of the drivers. We're coming up to twenty-five years, if you can believe that!" she smiled and I imagined that in a different time and place we could be friends. She was my kind of person. "You're lucky you didn't have a full month of stressing about what to wear. When the invites came out four weeks ago and I saw the dress code, I was so stressed. This little number belongs to a friend of mine who is thankfully the same size and far more glamourous than me. I'm more of a jeggings and messy bun kind of girl. Was it chardonnay or sauvignon blanc? I'm a bit of a wine snob, and I don't like to mix my grapes."

"Sav blanc please," I said, wondering how on earth Jay could have forgotten to tell me about the dress code when he had remembered.

He was trying to protect me from the anxiety of it all because he cares about me and loves me.

The second glass of wine was much more enjoyable with company. Jay was still loving the spotlight. A couple of girls had joined the group, and I noticed one of them seemed to be standing a little too close to him, or maybe insecurity was fuelling my imagination. The way she curled her hair around her finger and licked her lips when she spoke to him made me uneasy, and he was running his fingers through his hair and leaning in to whisper to her. She giggled and blushed and her hands fluttered up to her throat. She looked around – was it to see where I was? Then Jay looked around and totally missed that I was sitting on a bar stool, not that far away but obviously far enough away to blend in and become invisible.

"Did you see that?" said Jeanette.

"I'm glad you saw it too. I thought I was being paranoid," I said back quietly.

"Well, you can't unsee *that*," she said as Jay cupped the girl's backside with his beer-free hand and she fluttered her eyelashes, making a big deal of opening her red lips slowly and sucking her straw.

"Are you going to sit there and take it?" she asked me.

"It's ok, it's just flirting. There's nothing in it." I fluffed over my humiliation and drained my glass.

"Well, you're a better woman than me," said Jeanette and beckoned the bartender, ordering the same again with some shots this time.

"Thank you, but I can't have any more," I said. "I promised not to have more than a couple."

"Promised who? Casanova there? I wouldn't listen to a word he says, love."

"Honestly, they are just being friendly. I've asked him before and he promised me there's nothing going on with anyone and it's just me being a bit of a basket case."

"You're married, right?" she asked, and I nodded. "Well, it's not ok. Wouldn't be ok in any kind of committed relationship, but especially not when you're married. This has got nothing to do with you, apart from you being the injured party. It's all on him. Oh, and her, of course." She raised the shot glass and downed it and I reluctantly did the same, enjoying the sweet taste of peach schnapps on my tongue and the warm burn as it trickled down my throat.

"I've got to go, Stephanie. It was nice to meet you." A man was waving from across the room and she waved back, and then, in a swirl of sparkles and with a kiss on my cheek, she was off, and I was alone at the bar, feeling like my life raft was deflating fast.

The girl Jay had been speaking to had gone too, and I saw my opening, shuffling to the edge of the bar stool, I stood tall, my confidence returning. I was secure in my relationship with Jay, and his talking to other women was allowed. I'd slip in beside him and be all normal and charming.

Sucking in my tummy, I walked his way, but he was gone. Scanning the room, I saw him heading towards the exit. That must be where the loos are. I followed his footsteps into the foyer but couldn't see him. Damn! I shouldn't have had that schnapps. He was probably back inside looking for me. The night was young, and it still had time to come good.

A cooling breeze drifted through double doors that opened onto the street, and along with it, I heard Jay's voice. Was he laughing? Inching forward quietly, I wondered why I was sneaking around. This was ridiculous. I was looking for my husband and there was absolutely no need to be so weird about it. Another laugh, this time a woman's. The odd word drifted my way, nothing I could tie to a definite context, but enough to stir up feelings I didn't like. Another step forward, another breath held.

I could hear a bit more clearly – "massage", "happy ending", "wouldn't mind". All followed by more laughing, then even more disturbing - silence. I stepped out of the building and took a deep breath, looking down the alleyway, expecting the worst. It was pitch dark apart from the glow of a faraway streetlight. I could only vaguely make out two silhouettes tangled as one. The deep, groaning sound I heard from Jay was one I was all too familiar with. I knew that she probably had her hands down his pants, and he was probably grabbing a handful of her silicone tits as my world started caving in.

I braced myself, ready to confront them. How dare he call me insecure and needy? Just how far would this have gone if I hadn't caught them red-handed? Well, the game was up. I braced myself and took a step towards them.

Then a cough, a splutter and another cough followed by a "Fuck me, Ken, you need to give up those tabs!" The moment slipped through my fingers.

"Sorry, love, did I scare you?" Ken's friend asked me way too loudly for my liking.

Emotion betrayed me, and my voice faltered as I muttered back the standard default answer of, "I'm fine." I was anything but fine – furious, confused and drunk would work, but most definitely not fine. Jay would have to make an appearance soon, slinking out of the shadows. I didn't know what I would say to him, what I felt, or anything in between.

What the hell is going on?

He walked in confidently, looking surprised to see me.

"Steph! I thought you had made a friend. You looked like you were having fun so I left you to it."

"I didn't make a friend, I got rescued because you were ignoring me and then you fucked off into the alleyway with Miss Happy Ending." I spat the words out and didn't care who heard.

"Steph, stop!" he got hold of my arm. "How much have you had to drink? You promised me you wouldn't get shit-faced again, you're such a bloody embarrassment. We need to leave – *now.*"

"Oh, so it's all my fault, is it? You're taking some woman down an alleyway for a quickie and *I'm* an embarrassment? Get a grip, Jay. This is on you, you're a liar."

"And you're pissed out of your head and making shit up. Yes, I was talking to her, but we were talking about a guy that she was dating and, as usual, you are super insecure and making this all about me having a thing with another woman. Time to go. Now!" He reached for my arm again and I swerved. Unfortunately, the swerve made me trip, and I landed on my backside, with my head hitting the wall.

Ken and his friend ran over, stinking of smoke to ask if I was ok.

"She's had one too many, that's all," Jay said, unflinching.

"I'm going to throw up." I managed to say before I did. It turns out that a combination of too much booze, emotional trauma and a bump on the head makes you vomit and infuriates your husband.

"I knew I couldn't trust you." He spoke through his teeth as he dragged me to my feet.

"It's me that can't trust you," I said back as Jay secured an arm around my waist and started to march me outside towards the car.

"Don't you dare puke in here," he warned as he fastened my seatbelt.

I'd started crying now and couldn't stop, even though I knew it would just make him angrier.

"Stop fucking snivelling, this is your own fault, Steph. As usual you've gone too far and ruined it for everyone. I was just talking to her about her weird boyfriend, and you've gone all psycho as usual. You won't let me breathe. I can't talk to anyone without this kind of reaction, and I'm sick of it."

He flicked on the radio to drown out my sobbing and drove like a maniac all the way home. No further words passed between us as he slammed the spare bedroom door, leaving me kneeling in front of the toilet, hoping that if I was sick again, the room might stop spinning.

The next day, I woke up around lunchtime with a banging head and dry mouth. I'd slept in the black top and sparkly earrings, but my jeans lay puddled at the foot of the bed, along with my shoes and phone. Fragments of the night before started collecting in the corners of my mind, and shame flooded me as I realised the picture was incomplete. A shot of peach schnapps, and then the edges got blurry. Feeling angry and shouting at Jay, being on my hands and knees and vomiting. Crying in the car all the way home.

He'd been comforting a girl about her boyfriend and I'd got it all wrong because I was drunk. I'd let us both down and he would be furious with me, so furious he wouldn't speak for days – I deserved it. Yes, he was a flirt, but that was all. I didn't have to join up the dots every time and create an outcome that just wasn't true.

Why was I so insecure?

I didn't want to move but knew I had to. My mouth tasted vile and I desperately needed to brush my teeth. I flashed back to being sick in the toilet, hoping I'd flushed it all away and it wasn't there for me to face, along with the carnage I'd created in my marriage and Jay's career. Hauling myself onto the edge of the bed and then my feet, I wobbled and sat back down – listening for clues that Jay was in the house. I steadied myself and went to the window, parted the curtains and breathed a sigh of relief. His car had gone.

Time to check my phone and face the music, there it was - the text envelope. Dread stopped me from opening it straight away. Vomit started to rise, and I ran to the bathroom. Ten minutes later I'd managed to wash my face and brush my teeth and drink half a glass of water. Nauseous but ravenous at the same time, I hadn't eaten since lunchtime the day before. I'd start with a biscuit and see how that stayed down, but not before I'd read the message.

CONGRATULATIONS STEPH YOU REALLY HAVE OUTDONE YOURSELF THIS TIME. I'VE GONE TO THE VENUE TO OFFER TO PAY FOR CLEANING UP YOUR PUKE AND I'VE HAD TO TEXT ALL OF MY COLLEAGUES TO APOLOGISE FOR LEAVING EARLY AND FOR WHAT THEY OVERHEARD YOU SCREAMING AT ME. HOPEFULLY I'LL STILL HAVE A JOB NEXT WEEK.

I couldn't have felt any worse. The ground opening up and swallowing me would have been amazing.

Anything to escape the horrendous cocktail of guilt, shame, self-reproach and fear that were both shaken and stirred by the text I'd just read.

Why did I keep doing this to myself?

And even worse, why did I keep doing it to Jay?

Two simple questions I couldn't answer right now, and maybe not ever. It was as if I was on a self-destruct mission. Whenever we went anywhere, I always ruined it, and it ended in this familiar morning-after regret and misery, followed by at least a week of trying to make it up. Thankfully, he'd always allowed me to get away with it.

But this time felt different. It was the worst so far and especially with his work colleagues, I'd never be able to go to anything work-related again. I was an absolute liability. Who knows how long it would be before he'd acknowledge me? Some would call it the silent treatment, but I knew through many years of experience that this was the time he needed to think and recover from whatever had happened from my stupid actions. The least I could do was afford him that, even though it was excruciating.

By enduring this, I was accepting what I deserved, and perhaps it would help me learn to stop being such a let-down. After a week, he usually reached out, and I always made sure I gave him what he wanted and needed to make amends and show how much I loved him. Many times I'd cried with relief after we'd had make-up sex, silently, of course. I'd never expect anyone else to understand the intensity and passion that Jay and I shared. I was so lucky that he loved me enough to stay after everything I put him through.

I wiped my eyes with the scrumpled-up tissue in my hand. "That's it, the whole thing," I said to Robin.

"Thank you for trusting me with that, Stephanie. It's really helping me understand how I might be able to help you," she said softly, closing her notebook. "How do you feel after sharing all of that?"

"Lighter but sad. An emotional hangover, I suppose." In

fairness to Robin, I did feel better. Even if I disagreed with her and initially found it a bit pointless, I felt like I'd unburdened myself.

"Yes, I'd say that's perfectly normal."

"I'm worried that you think I'm really toxic and screwed up." I cast my eyes down towards my lap. "I was hard work, and I know that I didn't deserve to be cheated on and dumped, but quite honestly, I'm surprised it didn't happen sooner."

"Steph, I don't think you are toxic and screwed up. I really don't," Robin paused and sighed. "I think you were trapped in an abusive relationship for years and it's left a legacy that you're doing your best to deal with now. You're doing amazing, considering what you've been through."

Silence filled the gap between us.

"Steph? Stephanie?" she said softly.

"I heard you, Robin, and I respect you, but you've got this all wrong. There might be a legacy, as you call it, but I'd call it guilt and shame for my shitty behaviour, my neediness, and constantly letting myself down – until I met Damien."

"And what changed when you met him?"

"I can't explain it, but things were so different and I just managed to behave so much better, I suppose. I'd calmed down and didn't drink as much. Maybe I grew up."

"Do you go to family gatherings together and other social events?"

"Yes, and it's lovely. Life is much easier, and I don't suffocate Damien. I'm not as needy and I don't feel like I need to drink whenever we are out together. Apart from the undercurrent of anxiety, I'm generally very happy."

"That's interesting." Robin made another note in her pad. "And how do you feel in the run-up to an event or a gathering?"

"Excited, happy and looking forward to doing something lovely together."

"That sounds very different." Robin's observations were

obvious.

"Can I ask what you're getting at?"

"Of course you can. I'm convinced that you've been in an emotionally, psychologically and financially abusive situation with Jay for many years, and I think if you're ready, it's time to unpack that experience and do what we can to help you heal."

"But you're wrong, Jay was a dickhead at times, and no doubt he still is, but making me a victim isn't going to help me. I need to own my part in this."

I hated what he was doing to me in the present moment, but I wanted to be honest, at least with myself. Otherwise, what was the point of being in therapy? But I wasn't being honest. Robin might know some of the past story, but she didn't know the current chapter. Maybe I should spill the rest and see what she could help me salvage. I'd shared some of my shame today, and she'd been there for me – perhaps it was time to give us both the best chance of working through this.

"Stephanie, I'm going to tell you now that this was not your fault, and there are clear indicators of abuse in what you've told me. Gaslighting, baiting, future faking and more. We can go through what this means, but I'm being honest when I say that it's common for people who have been in your type of position to struggle with confusion, anxiety, low self-worth, depression and more. Being in a relationship like this is similar to being in a cult, but more harmful because it's wrapped up as a marriage, and that makes it so difficult to see what's happening, including you."

"But you're wrong." I started to cry. "A lot of it was me."

"No, it wasn't you." Robin handed me another tissue. "It was a really harmful situation and you've done brilliantly to get out of it and go on to build a happy life. This is just some mopping up."

"If what you say is right - and I'm not buying into it yet, even though I do trust you - can you help me?" Maybe one more session would help. She had touched on a couple of things that could possibly make sense, definitely the fear of making decisions and poor self-worth. I was open to giving her one more chance if she could show me how the past was affecting the present, and for that, I'd need to come back.

"Of course I can help you. Together, we can work on this, I promise." She smiled. "I want to go through what you've told me today at our next appointment if that's ok? Between now and then, I'll read through the notes and highlight all the examples I think will help you see what was happening. You can then weigh up what you think and see if you want to keep going. But at least you'll be able to piece things together more clearly and hopefully start letting go of the self-reproach and shame. It's honestly not yours to carry because none of this is your fault."

"I'll have to borrow your belief in me for now," I said with a shred of hope in my voice.

"That's all I ask, Steph. One session at a time, and you are always in control." Robin stood up and asked one more question. "Between now and next week, can you start to think about what might be triggering anxiety in the present? If you could try to be aware of what's happening around you when you feel anxious, that might help."

"I can tell you that right now, and I'm sorry I didn't earlier," I said, and within two sentences, I'd gone all in. "Jay has some very compromising photographs that he took of me a while ago when I went back to his flat for a one-night stand and passed out. He's recently started to blackmail me with them."

Robin's face was a picture. "Scrap what I just said about triggers, Steph. We've found them, and we need to act fast."

STEPHANIE'S JOURNAL – LESSON 28
SHARE YOUR SHAME

Shame cannot survive being spoken. It cannot tolerate having
words wrapped around it. What it craves is secrecy, silence
and judgement. ~ Brene Brown

Shame is a feeling that is underscored by the belief we are
unworthy in some way, unworthy of belonging, connection,
taking up space or even of love. Shame brings up so many
uncomfortable emotions that we avoid speaking about it, which
is where it gains power over us. When we hide our shame, it
lives in the shadows and can influence destructive thinking and
behaviour, poor choices and decisions, and force us to live in
fear.

Shame is usually connected to past or present situations that
we have no control over and it drives fear. The fear of someone
judging us or finding out we are flawed and not good enough.
As well as feeling all the discomfort of carrying shame
energetically, it is a very low-vibration emotion that will
prevent you from manifesting into your life all the goodness
you deserve. It creates immense resistance.

We all experience the feeling of shame. This is important to
remember because part of the experience can be a stream of
self-talk that tries to convince you that you aren't as good as
others. That is not helpful and undoubtedly not true.

Shame can be disarmed and even dissolved completely,
when shared and met with empathy. Empathy can shut shame
down, and you can only experience this if you bring your shame
from the shadows and into the light of sharing. In that moment,
it is no longer a secret, and you gain evidence from someone
else that they have also felt this way and experienced shame in
some way.

This starts to lift the burden of carrying shame and allows

for healing and worthiness.

Choose someone conscious, trustworthy and empathic to share your story with, and ask them if they can listen to you without judgment, keeping the conversation confidential. Sometimes, a therapist is a good choice, or even phoning a helpline.

You are worthy of living without the burden of shame, as are we all.

CHAPTER 15

That night as Damien watched television, I Googled 'gaslighting'. Although I was seeing the words, this couldn't really be what had happened to me, could it? Surely I was smarter than that? I scrolled on and looked at some real-life examples, and the more I read, the more I saw my past self in the stories of others.

Countering – this is when someone questions your memory and asks if you are sure about something. Did you really say that, or did that really happen? They might blame you for being forgetful or stressed or anxious or simply getting mixed up.

Denial – refusing to take responsibility for what they have said or done, blaming a situation or their behaviour on someone else.

Trivialising – when a person belittles or shuts down how someone else feels, perhaps accusing them of being too sensitive or overreacting even though they have reasonable concerns or points and want to raise them.

Lying by omission – not giving you the entire truth about a situation and then turning it around on you when challenged because you didn't ask. Blaming you for not having the full picture and making you feel stupid for not knowing all the facts when they were deliberately withheld from you.

These strategies can all be considered under the broader heading of gaslighting, and the more they sank in, the more I remembered. The way I'd stopped seeing friends in favour of staying home with him had led to isolation. Anxiety in case I said or did the wrong thing was ever-present, and my self-worth had definitely been in short supply.

But why hadn't I felt controlled at the time?

I'd been a willing participant. I'd wanted to please him and make him happy because that's marriage and compromise.

Hello, confusion, apparently you are part of the package, too and will be for a while yet.

But there were times I'd felt loved and wanted and happy. How was that being controlled? I did what I wanted to - I wanted to be with Jay. He'd never told me not to spend time with family and friends. I'd chosen to.

To avoid consequences.

Even if the truth was hard to face, it was still the truth.

CHAPTER 16

The following day came with familiar feelings of anxiety, but at least now I was starting to understand more of what I'd been through and the legacy I was living. Maybe once I'd had more time and therapy, I'd feel more normal.

Once I had escaped from Jay once and for all.

After the school run, I had coffee with Mel. Trying to be present, I put my phone in my bag. Constantly checking it for a response from Jay was making me even more edgy. Although I didn't want to hear from him, perhaps it would be better if I did.

He's in control ... making me more anxious.

No shit.

"How's George settling into school?" I asked.

"He's doing great, he really is. No more swinging on the assistant's leg, and he's a lot more talkative with other kids in the class, coming out of his limpet's shell, I guess you'd say. And Mia?"

"Yes, she loves it. She's always chatty in the car with her news about who did what in class. I know about Jessica's guinea pig and Sam's football boots and the rip in the green story carpet that no one will own up to," I smiled and so did Mel.

"We're bossing this parenting thing now, Steph!" she said and I agreed. "Speaking of all the news, did you hear Beth has a boyfriend?"

"No, I didn't. Spill the beans."

"Last week when I picked Mia up I was there early and she came over to chat. Well, it turns out she's been seeing this bloke for a couple of months and apparently he's lovely! He's super considerate and kind, spoiling her rotten and already he's saying he loves her and thinks she might be *the one*." Mel was grinning from ear to ear. We both knew that Beth deserved someone lovely after what she'd been through.

"Wow, that's fast – *the one!* I really hope it lasts and she's happy."

"She certainly seemed to be *and* I asked her about the bedroom side of things!"

"No you didn't!"

"I couldn't help it! I didn't ask for details, of course, I just said how are *things* and she knew what I meant because she blushed and giggled and said that *things* were fine, thank you!"

"You're terrible," I laughed and hoped Beth had found Mr Right. Maybe even Rosie could find it in her heart to be happy for her? I doubt there's room in there for any genuine good wishes for anyone else. I reached into my bag for my phone, berating myself but compelled to check I hadn't missed a message from Jay – nothing. Should I contact him again? Silent treatment was one of his favourite things to do in the past, and it seems he's still good at it.

"Any more from you know who?" Mel asked.

"No, nothing," I said and shrugged, deliberately looking away.

"That's good. Maybe he got the message when you didn't respond. I've noticed you keep checking your phone, though, so it must still play on your mind?"

"Yes, I suppose it does," I threw her a half-truth. "But the more time that passes when I don't hear from him, the better I'll be."

"And if he gets in touch again you have to tell Damien and the police, Steph. This is so stressful for you." Mel said with great kindness but even greater naivety.

"If I have to, I will, honestly. But for now, as you say, it seems like it's all blown over, so maybe I'm in the clear."

"Let's hope so. There are some crazies out there. Sorry, that's not helping, but you know what I mean."

"Yeah, I know what you mean. Don't worry. The only crazy person I hang out with on a regular basis is you!" I opened the messaging app on my phone again. Nothing. Maybe I should block him? But then he might turn up at the house. He was ballsy enough to go to the nursing home, after all. I'd give it another few days and then decide what to do. Now Robin knew the truth, I could ask her for advice. She was the only one I could talk to, so I'd give it a shot.

The time had come to part ways, and I headed back home to write. I needed to contact my agent to let her know this book might end up more niche than the last one and ask her to check it would be ok with the publishing house that had me under contract.

The type of emotional abuse that Robin was explaining to me was called 'covert'. It lived in the shadows and usually couldn't be named or seen. Covert abuse is introduced gradually, so you lose your sense of self and confidence slowly, becoming more isolated from healthy references and people and more reliant on your abuser.

It can be so subtle that it's easy to turn the tables around to everything being your fault when you question it. Because your self-worth is being chipped away, and it's gaslighting galore, you think you are the one at fault. You even start to forgive your abuser and put them on a pedestal as they are 'always there for you', and they are someone who keeps you on the straight and narrow every time you mess up.

I'd started writing about the anxiety that results from emotional abuse, or rather, I'd written about myself. There was still no message from Jay and my emotions were a coiled spring. Things were falling into place as I read more about emotional abuse and my past, even though it might never make sense to me that I'd been oblivious. Two hours had flown by and it was time for the school run. I met Mel as usual. She spotted Beth and said we should get an update. As we made our way towards her, the strangest thing happened. She turned away slightly and patted her coat pocket. Then she pulled out her phone, gave a theatrical swipe and started talking a little too loudly and a lot too weirdly.

"Yeah, that's what I thought too," she said and gave us a half smile over her shoulder before stepping away to lean over the fence with her back to us, her super important conversation ongoing.

"Wow," I said to Mel. "What was that about?"

"I have no idea. She was fine with me earlier, but she's clearly not now." Mel shrugged.

"It must be me then!" I said.

"No it's not you. Remember, she's lovely but also a bit up and down with her mental health after what happened before. She's probably just having a day where she can't be peopley."

"She could just say that instead of making up a phone call and acting all weird."

"Agreed."

Mel leaned in, which was unnecessary since Beth was still giving it large to Mr Nobody and wouldn't have heard a thing.

"She told me earlier that her ex was a narcissist, whatever that means. I don't know if she meant actual narcissist or if she just thought he was one, if you get what I mean? I didn't ask if he was *diagnosed,* and to be honest, I felt a bit stupid because I could tell she was trusting me and it was a big deal to be sharing, and yet I didn't know what she was on about. I Googled it and loads of really disturbing shit came up and I felt really sorry for her. Whatever she's been through, it's not good and no wonder she might have lost a marble or two. Apparently, they do this thing called gaslighting that screws with your reality and isolates you and makes you really anxious. It can literally steal your sense of self and all of your confidence, and here's the kicker – you don't know it's happening."

"Wow," was all I could manage to say. The Law of Attraction really is working all of the time.

"I know, right? Imagine someone is brainwashing you, and you don't even know it's happening. Like I said this morning, there are some crazy people out there. I don't mean Beth, by the way. I reckon she could still pull off a good game of marbles. I mean her ex."

"I know who you mean, you silly moo," I muttered, "Sounds like a cult."

"He does, but I thought you didn't say that word," Mel said, and we both laughed as Beth threw us another over-the-shoulder glance and went back to telling Mr Nobody she was at school waiting for her child.

The Universe definitely wanted to bring my attention to this, and finally, I was listening.

CHAPTER 17

That night I read up on narcissistic abuse and everything fell into place. My past was starting to make sense, and the haziness was lifting. I could see now how I had become a shell of my former self, how I'd been isolated, worn down and controlled – and it was scary, to say the least. I was reviewing my history through a totally different lens, feeling sorry for myself and even more guilty for allowing it to happen. Guilt and shame were cited frequently as emotions that would surface both during and after an emotionally abusive situation. It was so common to beat yourself up for not seeing what was going on and for staying far too long.

Part of recovering was understanding that you didn't have the awareness you have now and you were isolated from family and friends. Being so reliant on your abuser means you live in the narrative they'd provided, a false reality. You don't have people around to show you any different. Even if people tried to reach you, in most cases, the victim would get defensive and not want to listen; such is the strength of the trauma bond.

I really wanted to speak to Beth about what she'd been through; it could help us both. Sharing your story in a safe space means you can heal the guilt and shame, bringing them out of the shadows and into the light of your conscious awareness.

The following morning, after drop-off, Mel and I had coffee and I suggested Beth join us. "Shall I just message her? If she's having a better day, she might want to come and have a catch-up?"

"Of course, message her. To be honest, I don't think she's got many friends and she's lovely, so I don't really know why."

I do. It's because her ex isolated her from them.

Maybe we could be her new friends. Perhaps The Universe was lining things up.

"There, all done."

"Brill. Oh, by the way, did you see her Facebook post this morning? It was all about finding real love and being happy - one of those lovey-dovey posters, all hearts, flowers and soul mates. I'm really glad for her."

"No, I missed that. Let me look now before she gets here." I clicked and swiped. "It's not there. She must have deleted it. I hope everything's ok still? Maybe that's why she hasn't messaged back. I hope they haven't fallen out?"

Mel opened her phone and scrolled down her feed. "This one, see?"

"But I can't see that on my phone." I showed Mel.

"Strange because it's definitely there." Mel took my phone and laid it side by side with her own. "I don't get it. I can see stuff that you can't when she posts it. You're still on her friends list, but it's like you can't see everything. It's probably an update or a glitch or something."

She gave me my phone back and the penny dropped.

"I'm on a restricted list. That's what she's done."

"What's that?" asked Mel.

"It's where you filter your posts so only specific groups of people can see them and others can't. It's a privacy setting you can customise."

"But why would she do that to you? I don't get it. There's nothing on her timeline that looks secret or private or anything. It's just all school uniforms, fundraisers for mental health charities and stuff about being in love and happy."

"That's the stuff I can't see," I said. "I seriously have no idea why she'd do that. I could kick myself for messaging her now. Why would she not want me to see that she was in love and happy, for god's sake? I know you said she had most of her marbles, but I'm not so sure. I'm not judging, but wow, what a weird way to behave."

"I can't say I disagree. When you put that crazy fake phone call into the mix as well, maybe she isn't doing as well as I thought. Why don't you just unfriend her?"

"Because if she is mentally unwell, that might upset her or trigger her."

"Good point. Unfollow her then. That way you won't see anything she posts, and *you* won't get triggered."

"I'm hardly going to get triggered by the school jumble sale or a sponsored walk, Mel. That's all I can see, so it's not exactly riveting or inflammatory, is it? I think I'll cope with that."

"Yeah, not exactly the life and times of Little Miss Interesting."

"Little Miss Odd Ball, if you ask me."

"Exactly. And don't worry if anything juicy pops up, I'll be sure to screen shot it and send it to you anyway!"

So much for wanting to help her and be her friend. I couldn't work out what was going on, but this certainly wasn't helping my anxiety levels one bit. And Jay was still ghosting me.

CHAPTER 18

My next session with Robin started with the obligatory small talk and then I dived straight in, asking about the information I'd read online.

"Steph, it's easy to get overwhelmed at the beginning of this journey when you start to see what was happening, and it can bring up a whole spectrum of emotions. Most people are desperate to find out as much as they can so they can try to make sense of it all. What you are going through is very normal, and we will work through it together piece by piece."

"I just can't believe how complex and common this is," I said. "It's happening to people right now and we have no idea – even worse though, *they* have no idea."

"You're right and that's what makes it so hard to identify and then try to help victims. The abuser will do everything they can to maintain a public image of them being a good person and a good partner. They groom everyone around them to buy into this and then the victim is labelled as a troublemaker or damaged if they ever try to speak up. These people are charming and kind in public and behind closed doors, they are chipping away at who you are but making you think it's your fault and not theirs. It's seriously the stuff of breakdowns in some cases, and then they simply move on to find their next victim."

"Because they need supply."

"Yes, it's like oxygen to them, and once their primary source realises what's going on and they shut down supply, they have to go looking for it and secure it really quickly," Robin replied.

"So that's why they end up in new relationships as soon as old ones break down."

"Yes, but because supply is so important to them, they usually have some background people they keep on the boil, just in case they need to promote them to a primary source."

"And those people have no idea that this is going on," I said.

"No idea at all. They just think this person is kind and charming and nice to them. They often don't even know the person they speak to or meet up with is in a relationship. It's common for them to be living some kind of double life or even have more than one potential source of supply that they are warming up just in case. They are likely to have experience of this; if you ever get to look back over the life of a narcissist, you are probably going to see a collection of broken relationships and a series of moving on, and they will blame everyone else but themselves. The truth is that they have been exposed as being abusive, and the victim has finally been able to escape them. However, there was no relationship breakdown – the victim finally got away from their abuser. And this happens repeatedly in their life, sometimes in short relationships where they are busted quickly and sometimes in longer ones. Sometimes even a lifetime of abuse where the victim is so worn down and compliant that they couldn't ever imagine leaving, even though they are desperately unhappy."

"I can't imagine a lifetime of that," I said sincerely.

"Luckily you don't have to. It sounds like you're becoming more aware of what you went through, but with your permission, I wanted to review your account of the birthday party and point out some things that might help you get more clarity. Would that still be ok?"

"Of course, and thank you for this. I'm sorry I was so defensive at first. I can see now that you're helping me. I should've trusted you."

"That's perfectly alright. It's a really common reaction and actually confirmation that you probably have been in an emotionally abusive situation – victims tend to defend their abusers because of something called 'trauma bonding'. We can talk about that soon."

"Ok," I nodded and shuffled in my seat as Robin pulled out some notes and started to dissect my history with compassion and cold, hard truth.

Starting with the lead-up to the event, Robin took me back to the moments when I was asking Jay about what to wear. Immediately, a feeling of shame washed over me. I started to feel that I'd been needy and hadn't been able to decide for myself like a proper grown-up – no wonder Jay was irritated.

"Now you know about gaslighting, Steph, can you see that Jay deliberately withheld details from you to make you anxious and feel like you were displaying behaviour that was needy? That he used this to belittle and humiliate you?" Robin asked.

"Maybe a little," I said, mentally reviewing it myself too.

"Just sit with that as a consideration and I'll keep sharing my observations, ok?"

"Yes, ok."

Robin pointed out that the gaslighting was making me more and more anxious before the occasion and Jay was deliberately making sure I wouldn't show up feeling confident and self-assured. He wanted me on the back foot so he could control me by being the person I relied on for guidance and support. The mean and barbed comment about my appearance just before we left, disguised as humour, was a technique known as baiting. I had to admit that I'd been hurt, and it made me feel even more self-conscious of the extra weight I was carrying, which I'd thought was an embarrassment to him.

"He said it in such a way that you were unlikely to challenge him. It was abusive and mean and you know full well that if you came back at him there would have been a consequence or a punishment. I'm guessing, based on what you've told me, that he would either have had a meltdown or given the silent treatment. Maybe even both. He seems to use the two in sequence."

"You're right. I did know that I was hurt and that it was a mean thing to say, and I also knew that I wouldn't dare stick up for myself, or I'd ruin the evening."

"He ruined the evening, not you. But he wanted you to think that it could be you because by keeping you in that fear of consequence, you are more compliant and easier to control. So now you're going to a social event, and he has made you super anxious about it for days beforehand. His comment confirms that you aren't looking your best, so you feel even more anxious and unworthy. This is a perfect scenario for him. Can you see that?"

"I'm starting to think I can."

Robin then went on to ask about the food and why Jay might have told me not to eat before the party. What might he gain from that? As I thought back, I remembered watching him from the bedroom window as he shoved a McDonald's bag into the bin. I presumed it was because he wanted the car to look super clean and tidy, but actually, it was always super clean and tidy, and he never left any rubbish in it. The house, on the other hand, was a totally different story, but then again, that was my responsibility.

"So you think he had already eaten? Why do you think that?"

I told her what I'd seen from the car window and explained that sometimes he didn't get a chance for lunch, and maybe this had been a late lunch.

"You're covering up for him, and this is totally normal," said Robin.

"Am I?" I asked, genuinely confused.

"Yes you are. I think he had something to eat and he lied to you about the food at the party so that you'd get drunk faster, and he could make a drama out of it and belittle you."

"Do you think he thought it through like that and did it

deliberately?"

"I don't know if he consciously planned it and strategized it, but I do think he was aware this was likely to happen and that he could use it to shame you. You told me that just before you got to the event, he started to bait you again with this exact idea, telling you not to get drunk and embarrass yourself and him. He's setting you up for it by making you anxious, not allowing you to eat and then reminding you that this is what you do and it's a pattern that he is expecting."

When I looked back, I could see that Jay had used this strategy many times over in different contexts.

"He said this was why we didn't really go out much."

"What did he mean by that?"

"That I was a let-down, I'd get drunk and stupid and humiliate him."

"Can you see how he was using this to isolate you and stop you from having fun and connection with other people? How he made you feel like the cost of doing anything social was just not really worth it?"

"I guess so. When I look back, it seemed to happen a lot, but why would he want to isolate me?"

"Because you would buy into what he was telling you more if you had no healthy references around you. In simple terms, you become a lot easier to control. He becomes your go-to person, and you start to cut out friends and family who are trying to help you because, in trying to help you, they are criticising him. It's tough to wrap your head around at first, but emotional abuse follows a clear cycle and once you see it, things start to make a lot more sense."

"What do you mean a cycle?" I asked.

"You remember the feeling of walking on eggshells and tension building? Usually, you can't put your finger on it, but you know you have to start being more careful and not trigger them. Something is brewing, and there's going to be a flashpoint." Robin raised an eyebrow in my direction.

"I know that feeling, yes. It happened to me every four to six weeks, I'd guess. I used to blame my hormones at first and think it was around the time I was pre-menstrual and super sensitive, but I started to mark my period dates on the calendar, and it wasn't related. If there were any kind of occasion or social event, the tension would start to build about a week before." My mental fog was lifting.

"It's so common to blame yourself when actually it's a tactic the abuser is using to maintain control," Robin spoke kindly but firmly.

"Another one?"

"Sadly, there are many, and the abuse cycle adds in a lot of confusion and compliance."

She went on to explain that the abuse cycle could last for any length of time, depending on the dynamics between the people involved and how much supply and control the abuser needed at that time. It could all happen in a day or be drawn out for months. A typical cycle starts with tension building, and this elevates anxiety within the victim. It also triggers patterns of people-pleasing and placating the abuser to try and avoid the incident that is looming. The incident could be a full-on meltdown, argument, a huff or anything else. The victim has no idea that they are people-pleasing. They think it's normal and that they are compromising in their relationship. Ironically, it feels like healthy behaviour. Because they are isolated and have no healthy references, and the cycle has become part of how they live, they don't see the toxicity or destruction it causes.

God, I could remember that feeling. The subtle shift in Jay where he'd start to detach emotionally and filter in how stressed he was at work, how he thought he might be depressed. He'd tell me at weekends that he'd been around people all week and couldn't cope with seeing anyone, so any plans I had to see my parents or friends were shut down fast. I always felt terrible when I had to call things off, and after a while, people stopped making plans with me anyway. Robin was right about the isolation.

My parents once dropped in unannounced; you could have cut the air with a knife. They obviously felt it because they didn't stay long. Mum sent me a flurry of texts over the days that followed, asking me how things were. After interrupting dinner for the second night in a row, Jay took my phone and put it out of reach. He told me I was a grown woman and didn't need my mummy and daddy to suffocate me. I knew my own mind, and I could eat my fucking dinner in peace. I should stop pandering to them and spend time with my husband, who had been out at work all day. Part of me though that he was right, and I was so lucky to have someone who loved me so much they wanted to connect with me over dinner and be fully present. The other part of me missed my parents and thought he was being mean. This part wanted to stand up, get my phone back, and call them. He was helping me to be an adult and independent of them, but my phone was on top of the dresser and I couldn't reach it, and every time it pinged, I wanted to cry.

He ignored the notifications initially and kept eating, forcing conversation about my day and eating his favourite food that I'd made a big effort to cook just right. It felt like an elastic band was being pulled tighter and tighter between us, and any second, it would snap. And then there was one ping too many. He slammed his knife and fork down and shoved his chair back from the table, reached up higher than I could and grabbed the phone.

"Just fucking call her!" he said through his teeth and threw it at me. My glass of wine spilt and I stood up, too, trying to grab hold of his arm as he stormed out of the room and left me in tears.

"Just call her, Steph. They won't leave us alone for half a

fucking hour to eat after we've been out all day at work, it's not normal!"

Mum knew we ate at about six every night, but now it was half past seven. I'd cooked a full roast dinner with all the trimmings, and it had taken longer than usual. I could hear Jay moving around upstairs, and I knew this meant he was going to sleep in the spare room, confirmed by the final door slam and the sound of the television.

Yes, I knew about tension building leading to a flashpoint.

Thinking back, I'd been walking on eggshells all that week and been in full people-pleasing mode. The housework was done, and there had been no nagging about discarded coffee cups or the pile of dirty laundry in the bedroom beside the basket. We'd even had sex when I was far too tired, and I'd faked my way through it, making him feel like a hero. He thought he'd put in some hard shifts that week, but he hadn't worked as hard as me.

After the flashpoint, I'd typically get the cold shoulder for a few days. There would be some surface-level communication, but he'd be distant. He'd stay late at work once or twice and not call me, so I'd fret over making dinner, trying not to call him and look needy. Sometimes, he'd eaten at work and didn't let me know, so I'd just grab a bowl of cereal before bed, starving but never daring to say so.

After about five days, things usually thawed a little, and I'd find a way to get back into favour. I'd start with something small and see how he reacted. When I knew he was moving towards forgiving me, I did more.

Once, I managed to book us tickets for an exclusive gig and get front-row seats. The lead guitarist from a rock band he loved was doing a stripped-back acoustic set as a one-off on a Friday night, and I happened to see it on my Facebook feed. Another time, I booked a city break. Once my credit card was maxed out, I'd have to rely on a cosy night in with the promise of bedroom fun that I knew he'd love. It didn't matter what I did or the cost as long as things got back on track.

The relief I felt when we were back in sync was heavenly. It was like falling in love again, and Jay would sometimes even apologise for being stressed out and reactive. He'd tell me he loved me, and he was so lucky that I was patient and understanding and the best wife ever. Sometimes, he would make bedroom time about me, too.

During the happy times, I told myself I had to stop spoiling things. Things could be great between us if it weren't for my behaviour or lack of boundaries with other people. I wanted to maintain this honeymoon feeling so badly, and I'd get annoyed with myself because even in the good times, I was still worried things would go south and I'd mess up somehow.

If only I could be a good wife all of the time and give him what he needed, things would be on an even keel, and I'd always be on honeymoon. As long as I was on the ball, I could maintain things being good between us. Yes, I worked full-time in a demanding job, but I could easily get up early and do some housework to get a headstart.

And if I was super organised, I could cook up a storm in the kitchen every night too. I'd make sure Jay was settled in front of the television with a lovely glass of wine, and I'd clean up like the brilliant wife I was, and then I'd join him for a snuggle on the sofa. The only thing I had to work on was not falling asleep too early. I was exhausted by the end of the day. Jay had said a couple of times that he'd been in the mood for love and I'd let him down. Damn you, early mornings, you ruined my early nights!

I took to drinking a cup of coffee when I was cleaning the kitchen after dinner every night to help me stay awake longer, and it did the trick. The only downside was that Jay often seemed to have gone off the idea of a shagathon, so I was usually lying there at eleven o'clock listening to him snore and getting wound up that I had to be awake at five to get a load of washing in and mop the floor. I knew, though, that the first time I wasn't willing, able and awake, he'd want to do it and then I'd be a let-down. I shouldn't complain. I had a husband who wanted me! I was putting us first and that's what a good wife should do.

Had this been control?

He'd made me feel guilty for not having enough energy to have sex once, making me vow to always be available. I was medicating with caffeine every night just in case he felt like it, and usually, he didn't.

"I feel so stupid for not seeing it happening," I said to Robin. "No wonder I was always anxious."

"You don't see it when you are in it, Steph. It's classic for victims to have no idea this is going on. Remember, you were isolated from your family and friends and your self-worth was being decimated. You'd become reliant on your abuser and he knew that, so he turned the screws more and more to get more control over you. As I said at the beginning, it's like being in a cult. The gaslighting stops you from thinking clearly and gives you a load of distorted references, and you are subjected to intermittent punishments that make you adapt your behaviour to try to avoid triggering someone. Before you know it, you are seriously losing who you used to be and feeling nothing like your former self. But you don't know why. Yet you have someone telling you that they love you and you can rely on them."

"And do people who do this kind of thing do it on purpose?" I asked.

"People do what works for them, and when you get a result that pleases you, you do it again. They know they are being harmful and unkind. However, these people lack empathy, and even if they know this, they don't necessarily care."

"But I can remember Jay helping loads of people, so how

can that be lacking in empathy?" I wasn't defending him; I just needed clarity.

"What was the context of him helping?" asked Robin.

"There are loads of examples! He'd always be offering people a ride to work if he was passing that way. He bought cakes when it was someone's birthday at work. He'd always sponsor someone if they were doing something for charity, and he tipped everyone from the hairdresser to the Chinese delivery driver and often went way over the top to the point they were a bit embarrassed. When he took his car to the garage to get new wheels fitted, he bought lunch for everyone, and he was always super generous with his assistant and the other girls who worked in the office. Fancy lunches here and there and flowers for their birthday. So you see, he really was kind, and that shows empathy, right?"

"I hear you, and I don't want to burst your bubble, but narcissists can display empathy if there is a social advantage. In other words, they know how they should behave and what they should say to be considered a good human, which is super important to them. They have worked hard at creating a fake persona with everyone. They want to be seen as a kind, generous and charming individual and they act this out with everyone so it's bought into and believed. It sounds like Jay got a lot of supply from work colleagues and invested a great deal into maintaining the fakery there."

"But why would he?" I asked.

"Because there were probably women there that he was grooming as a potential primary supply if he ever needed it. He got a whole load of secondary supply from them thinking he was such a great guy, and when things went sideways with you, he could rely on telling them a story about it not being his fault and they'd buy into it without question. Their experience of him was that he was a nice person. He'd bought his way into their favour. So later in the game, when he starts to spin a victim story and poor me narrative, they all get behind him and believe it."

"Do you think he told them it was my fault?" I asked quietly.

"I'd say it's very likely, yes," Robin said gently. "These people take no responsibility for anything they have done and seek to blame others. The other people in his life were also being manipulated, just in a different way, and they didn't have any idea it was going on either. They'll buy into everything he says about you hook, line and sinker. This is a challenging part of breaking up with a narcissist because you just can't defend yourself." She paused and pressed her lips together in a sympathetic smile. "They tell everyone a version of events that paints them in a good light and makes you look like the problem, elevating themselves to hero status by saying they tried hard for so long but couldn't put up with your behaviour anymore. People who were manipulated to buy into the fake persona buy into this too and start to feel sorry for them, thus giving them more supply."

"That explains why his colleagues unfriended me on Facebook," I muttered.

"And there is nothing you can do because if you ever did reach out, you'd be playing right into his hands. He'd say you were unhinged, crazy, jealous of his new relationship, and couldn't move on, and everything else that people like him use to maintain their fake public image and get you off the scene fast in case you blow their cover. They need supply so badly they can't have you spoiling any new opportunities by showing up and telling the truth of what happened, so they cut you out quickly and set you up to look like a basket case, even if you did manage to be heard."

"That's horrendous." I shook my head.

"And it's way more common than you'd ever realise. Then they start the cycle with someone else. In fact, in many cases, it's already started before the existing relationship breaks down.

They are so desperate to secure supply there is very often an overlap," Robin said.

"It sounds like they can't bear to be alone."

"Correct, because when they are alone, they have no supply – no one to stroke their ego, to big them up or admire them. Although they come across as confident and charming, they are masking a deep insecurity and lack of self-worth, and they never take any responsibility for themselves. They never acknowledge it or get help because it's not their fault. The string of broken relationships, friendships and bridges burned has nothing to do with them in their inflated opinion of themselves and everything to do with everyone else." Robin underlined something in her notes.

"So they pretend to be someone they aren't just to gather all praise and admiration?" I asked. "And they get it from controlling their primary source of supply?"

"Exactly. They might spoil your night out with friends by making you think you look chubby in your new outfit and then rescue you with a movie and a takeaway, so they are the hero. They might play the poor me card and say they've had a tough week at work and can't face seeing your family this weekend. This leads to lots of TLC from you, and you cancel everything else. They might use stone walling or huffiness to make you anxious about what you could have done wrong so that it triggers a people-pleasing behaviour in you and you pander to them. And of course you notice none of this while it's happening." She paused for a minute before continuing. "Can I ask you about Jay's former relationships? What did he tell you about them when you first met?" she asked, looking up from her notes.

"He had just come out of a really bad situation and was hurt. She had taken him to the cleaners financially and he was a bit of an emotional wreck. He said she'd bullied him and all he'd try to do was love her, but in the end, it got too much. He said she had mental health problems and drank too much. He just got sick of making excuses for her and reluctantly, he had to leave. She refused to go for any kind of couple's counselling even though he begged her to. To be honest, she sounds like she was pretty toxic herself."

Robin looked at me without comment but drew a breath and waited.

My aha moment arrived with a bump. "Oh," I said and shook my head. "He made that up, didn't he?"

"Although we can't know for sure, he likely did. He managed to get a load of sympathy and supply from you," Robin said, adding that if Jay's ex had approached me, I would not have believed her.

"I guess back then, I'd have told her to leave me alone," I answered the rhetorical question honestly.

"Would you have been open to hearing anything she said?"

"No, because I believed her to be unstable and a troublemaker," I said slowly, realising this is exactly what others would have thought of me after our breakup.

"And that's how it works, time after time. Then they move on to the next victim, leaving the last one wondering what the hell happened and how they can piece their life back together. It's nothing like a normal breakup. In a healthy relationship, there is processing, understanding, and compassion for each other. This is sudden and brutal, and you're stripped of any dignity, confidence or worthiness you once had, totally isolated from friends and family members and feeling crazy." Robin confirmed and sighed. "It's awful."

"And they just start over as if nothing happened?" Although I was starting to see the truth of how this all played out, it was still unbelievable that people like this existed.

"Yes, as I said, they've often got their next victim ready."

"Yes, of course." I agreed and wondered if anyone in the future would contact me to ask if what they had been told was true and how I'd feel about responding.

The session was coming to a close, but before we parted ways, Robin asked me about the blackmail. "I can't let you go without asking, Steph, are you in any physical danger? I know I told you I wouldn't involve any other agencies, but if you are being threatened physically, then I would have to."

"No, I'm honestly not in danger physically. To be honest, he can harm me far more by ruining my reputation and my marriage than he ever could by physically hurting me."

"You know that contacting the police is an option though?"

"But all he's done is send me the pictures and a threat to share them, which I deleted straight away, so I don't even have any evidence. The only thing I have is a whole lot of anxiety that he'll follow through with it and I'll lose everything."

"I'm sure that's both harassment and a cybercrime," she said as she stood up.

"If it escalates, I will. I promise, but right now, I just need to process what you're telling me and cope. That's it right now."

"Ok, I hear you," she said and passed me a sheet of paper. "Here is an exercise to help you with unravelling the effects of gaslighting. It helps you to look at the way you are thinking and look at where those thoughts have come from. After you've been emotionally abused it's common to have some beliefs that aren't yours."

"Thank you, if you think it will help I'll have a go." I folded the sheet and pushed it into my handbag.

"Same time next week?" asked Robin.

"Yes please," I replied, leaving with a head full of questions and a heart full of regret that I'd ever met Jay at all.

CHAPTER 19

At the school gate, Beth was telling Rosie all about her new man. We weren't eavesdropping. They were talking loud enough for everyone to hear. The odd word reached us along with a lot of giggling, and before long, we'd established that Beth had a sex life now and was very happy about it. Mel rolled her eyes. It seemed like her new man was quite the romantic; an expensive French Bistro in town was mentioned, and a new black dress. Rosie turned and looked me up and down, leaning into Beth and whispering something, and they both laughed. I felt my face flush. So Facebook wasn't a mistake after all.

Shame threw me back to the last time I'd spoken to Rosie. Each time I replayed that awful scene in the restaurant from years ago, I hated myself more. She'd spat her words at me like venom, a quick-acting poison making me shrink into myself and run, right into Jay's back seat and a world of regret. I know who you are, Rosie. You suck the goodness out of people and situations to fill your own darkness. You're a happiness vampire.

Watch out, Beth, you might be next.

The ring of the school bell brought me back to the present moment, and soon Mia's hand was in mine as she talked about a trip to the seaside. I could still hear her talking about rock pools and crabs, but her voice faded a little and reality started to tilt. I froze as I watched Beth and her daughter climb into a cab and pull away. Other parents and children walked around me as I stood rigid in the eye of the storm.

It's just a trigger.

Taking a breath, I shook my head. It could be any taxi with anyone driving it, and I was telling myself it was Jay because I was anxious and scared – that's all. Dread was welling up inside of me. Could they be in the same taxi that had taken my whole life on a ride up shit creek? I couldn't see the driver, but I desperately wanted to.

"Mummy," Mia tugged at my sleeve. "Mummy, are you alright?"

"Yes, my love," I said automatically. "Mummy is fine. I was just wondering what to eat when we get home." I started walking again, my heart beating twice as fast as my feet were pounding the pavement. But this time, I wasn't scared. I was furious. How dare he come to my daughter's school? Was he using Beth to get to me?

It wasn't him!

I needed to calm down before I could drive, so I asked Mia to tell me more about the seaside and tried to breathe more evenly. Fastening my seatbelt, my fingers trembled with rage. I opened the window and concentrated on driving slowly and deliberately, a smouldering dormant volcano of emotion getting ready to erupt.

As soon as Mia was settled with a snack, I sent Beth a text, asking if her new boyfriend was driving the taxi and if he was called Jay. Too impatient to wait for a response, I spilled my guts and told her if it was him, he was a snake, he was using her, she was in danger, and so was her daughter. Before I hit send, I paused and read over what I'd typed so furiously. Two or three deep breaths later, I tentatively wondered how she might feel, receiving something so out of the blue and perhaps shocking. But surely she needs to know? I changed it a little, softened the edges, added three kisses, and clicked send.

The message was marked as read straight away. I held my breath and wondered if Jay was with her. Three dots appeared, she was messaging back and I had everything clenched.

HI STEPH, GOOD NEWS SURE TRAVELS FAST. THANK YOU FOR

MESSAGING ME AND FOR YOUR CONCERN, BUT YOU REALLY
HAVE NOTHING TO WORRY ABOUT.

WE ARE HAPPY AND IN LOVE AND JAY IS TREATING ME LIKE
A PRINCESS, EVERY RELATIONSHIP IS DIFFERENT AS I'M SURE
YOU'LL APPRECIATE. JAY TOLD ME THAT THE PAST WAS
CHALLENGING FOR YOU BOTH, AND I WANT YOU TO KNOW
THAT HE WISHES YOU WELL. HE IS HAPPY YOU MOVED ON AND
HE WANTS YOU TO BE HAPPY FOR HIM. IF YOU'RE STRUGGLING,
I CAN GIVE YOU THE NUMBER OF MY COUNSELLOR, SHE IS
BRILLIANT AND HELPS WITH ALL KINDS OF THINGS INCLUDING
MOVING ON IN LIFE, COPING WITH JEALOUSY AND MORE.

I fucking knew it was him.

I read it in disbelief – disbelief that this was happening and
that she was ignoring my warning. This one message could save
her from a lifetime of misery and therapy and she thought I'd
sent it because I was jealous and 'struggling' because I'd seen
Jay with another woman.

BETH, I'M NOT JEALOUS I'M TRYING TO HELP YOU. HE IS NOT
WHO HE SEEMS TO BE, HE'S A MANIPULATOR AND HE'S ONLY
IN A RELATIONSHIP WITH YOU TO GET TO ME. HE'S DANGEROUS
AND CRAZY, HE'S BEEN STALKING ME AND NOW YOU'RE A
PART OF THAT!

STEPH, THIS IS MADNESS. AND ACTUALLY QUITE DISTURBING
IF I'M HONEST. I KNOW THAT YOU AND HIM WENT THROUGH A
REALLY AWFUL BREAK UP BECAUSE OF YOUR MENTAL STATE,
BUT IT'S NOT FAIR FOR YOU TO MESSAGE ME LIKE THIS AND
MAKE UP SHIT ABOUT OUR RELATIONSHIP, WHICH ACTUALLY
IS NONE OF YOUR BUSINESS.

BETH, PLEASE LISTEN TO ME – HE'S USING YOU TO GET TO ME
AND HE'S GOING TO USE YOU AND THEN SPIT YOU OUT, I'VE

GOT NO REASON TO LIE TO YOU.

YOU'VE GOT EVERY REASON TO LIE TO ME. YOU'RE JEALOUS BECAUSE HE DIDN'T WANT YOU AND HE IS HEAD OVER HEELS IN LOVE WITH ME. HE LEFT YOU STEPH BECAUSE YOU WERE A FUCKING BASKET CASE AND YOU STILL ARE.

BETH, NO! HE'S LYING TO YOU, PLEASE LISTEN TO ME YOU ARE IN DANGER. PLEASE DON'T BELIEVE HIM THAT'S NOT WHO I AM, HONESTLY.

IT IS WHO YOU ARE RIGHT NOW THOUGH ISN'T IT? I THINK THE BEST THING HERE IS FOR ME TO BLOCK YOU TO BE HONEST, YOU'VE GOT NO BUSINESS MESSAGING ME WITH YOUR NASTINESS AND TRYING TO RUIN WHAT I'VE GOT BECAUSE YOU'RE SCREWED UP AND JEALOUS, SO FUCK OFF NOW AND HAVE A HAPPY LIFE IF YOU ARE EVEN CAPABLE OF THAT! OH AND ONE MORE THING BEFORE I GO, KEEP AWAY FROM MY MAN. I KNOW THAT YOU THREW YOURSELF AT HIM THE NIGHT OF THE WHOLE RESTAURANT MELTDOWN, I ACCIDENTALLY SAW THE PICTURES THAT YOU'D ASKED HIM TO TAKE OF YOU AND I WAS DISGUSTED. THE WAY YOU LIED TO HIM ABOUT YOU BEING DIVORCED AND REELED HIM IN WAS DISGRACEFUL, ESPECIALLY SINCE HIS DAD HAD JUST DIED AND HE WAS SUCH A MESS. YOU'RE THE MANIPULATOR AND LIAR NOT HIM, I SERIOUSLY DON'T KNOW HOW YOU CAN LIVE WITH YOURSELF – A DISGRACE OF A WIFE AND A MOTHER AND A JUDGEMENTAL WHORE IF YOU ASK ME. I'M GOING TO BACK UP THE PICTURES FOR SAFE KEEPING IN CASE YOU EVER GO NEAR HIM AGAIN AND I'LL BRING YOU DOWN BIG STYLE. AND THEN YOUR PERFECT LITTLE FAÇADE OF A WORLD WILL BE RUINED, JUST LIKE YOU RUINED JAY WHEN ALL HE DID WAS TRY TO LOVE YOU AND HELP YOU. I'LL BE FOREVER GRATEFUL THAT YOU ARE SUCH A FUCK UP BECAUSE IT MEANS THAT HE CAME TO ME AND HE CAN

FINALLY BE LOVED PROPERLY. LEAVE US ALONE.

I sat shell-shocked, staring at the screen. Robin was right. I cried for myself and I cried for Beth. She thought I was some sex-depraved manipulative bitch who had cheated on her husband and risked everything for a filthy one-nighter with her ex.

Maybe I should go to the police after all?

I felt sick and scared, angry and ashamed. Jay had me cornered and he was advancing. I'd have to pull myself together, Damien would be home from work soon and I had to get back on the normal spectrum somehow.

A notification pinged, and I clicked it: a friend request from Jay The Taxi.

Are you fucking kidding me?

STEPHANIE'S JOURNAL – LESSON 29
WE LISTEN IN DIVINE TIME

We cannot force anyone to hear a message they are not ready
to receive. But we must never underestimate the power of
planting a seed. ~ Uknown

When people don't listen, it could be for different reasons. Maybe they are in their ego, stuck in old ways of thinking, closed to change or not living consciously. We can perceive this as being very limiting, but we need to remember that that they are on their own journey.

Maybe listening to someone's advice would change the direction of their life that is not in alignment with where they need to be. They might not be at a stage in their personal and spiritual development where the timing is right for change or opportunity. There could be lessons that they need to learn and integrate first, aspects of self they need to heal, unfinished emotional business that needs clearing up or something else that needs to fall into place in their life.

Missing an opportunity and experiencing the disappointment and knock-on effects of being so closed, could be the lesson that they need right now. This experience may help them to be more open in the future, get out of ego and listen to people that are trying to help them.

By not listening initially, the consequences or outcome could hold amazing epiphanies and teach them about themselves and others. In this way, not listening could be helping them, even if it brings challenges that could have been avoided. Perhaps these challenges are what they need for their Highest Good.

CHAPTER 20

The following day, things felt worse. I'd had no sleep and I was pretending to be ok in front of my lovely husband and child, but actually, I was unravelling at a rate of knots and feeling like I might lose it any minute. Calling Robin in desperation, I briefly told her what had happened.

"He is making his presence felt to scare and control you, just like before." As always, the voice of reason.

"Well, it's working," I said, thanking her but still refusing to tell Damien or the police.

In my mind, I circled back to the idea of paying up. It would get me out of this nightmare and give me my life back – or would it? I was getting desperate. Maybe I could get him to confess on messenger that he was blackmailing me? Perhaps I could lure him in and he would get arrested? I could screenshot the message and Mel could show Beth.

What was I thinking?

I was obviously on the verge of making some terrible decisions if I was even considering egging him on. I was losing it here and needed some common-sense advice and help.

I decided to call Lizzie, my long-term friend, *and* she's a lawyer, double win. She also knows what a snake Jay was because he'd manipulated her years ago. Luckily, our friendship survived after their very brief fling, and she went on to rebuild her life after the trauma he'd caused. Lizzie was the perfect person to reach out to, and she would be bound by client confidentiality. Thankfully, she had space, and an hour later, I was waiting in reception to be called up to her office. The elevator whirred, and double doors opened to reveal Lizzie, looking amazing as usual, as she walked over and hugged me tight.

"It's been too long, Steph. Now show me some pictures of Mia before we get started." I flicked through the recent ones, including the picture of her in her too-big uniform and could see that Lizzie was genuine when she said she was gorgeous and a credit to me.

"Now you're going to have to put me out of my misery, Steph. What is so urgent?" she asked as we stepped into the lift and she pressed for floor three.

"You're going to think I'm crazy, and I don't want you to be offended at all, but I need to know that you will keep this super confidential," I said. "Not just two friends telling each other their secrets, I mean in a businessy and legal way. I've got myself into a stack of trouble and need some help."

She looked straight at me with a million questions written all over her beautiful face and worry underscoring her tone.

"Yes, I promise you it's confidential." The doors pinged open and we walked across the hallway to her office. "Let me call my assistant to bring us two coffees and you can tell me everything."

An hour later, we'd looked at the situation from every different angle. Lizzie was heartbroken for me and for herself. I could see her lightbulb moments as I spoke about emotional abuse and manipulation. She still carried some guilt about what had happened between her and Jay, which was validation that she might have made some bad decisions but she was another of his victims too.

"I hate to say it, Steph, but you don't have enough evidence here to do anything legal. I agree that involving the police would mean Damien finding out, and he might even be questioned as part of an investigation. I think, unfortunately, you have to wait and see how it unfolds for now. If Jay gets in touch, let me know, and we can see what he might want. Take a screenshot of everything. Even if your instinct is to delete it, take a picture and then send it to me and I'll keep it all in a secure folder until we know what's going to happen."

"I was afraid you'd say all of that," I said with a sigh.

"He might just be getting some kind of sick satisfaction from playing mind games and scaring you. Maybe the best thing is to try to ignore him unless anything else transpires."

"It's just all so unfair. It feels like he's getting away with ruining lives."

"I agree, but if we can get you out of this with your sanity, marriage and bank balance intact, I think that's winning. Let's tread carefully. We don't want to trigger him. Ignore him, I say, and try to get on with your life. It might all blow over."

I said I'd try, but at the same time, it felt impossible.

CHAPTER 21

JAY: SO YOU'RE STARTING TO SEE SENSE?

It was happening; we were in dialogue. I had to be careful what I said to him. Lizzie had warned me not to bait him or look like I was leading him to make any kind of confession. If things escalated and went legal, we needed it to be clear that I was the victim.

STEPH: JUST TELL ME WHAT YOU WANT.

JAY: I LIKE YOUR DIRECT APPROACH, BUT I'D RATHER SEE YOU IN PERSON TO DISCUSS.

STEPH: JUST TELL ME.

JAY: I WILL WHEN WE MEET UP.

STEPH: I CAN'T DO THAT.

JAY: YES YOU CAN, NO ONE WILL KNOW.

STEPH: JUST TELL ME WHAT YOU WANT.

JAY: ARE YOU BEGGING ME STEPH? (LAUGHING EMOJI)

I stood up and began pacing around the room, trying to stay calm and collected but failing badly. He was goading me, trying to get a rise. I needed not to react, so I picked up a pillow and punched it three times, then stuffed my face into it and yelled.

STEPH: JUST TELL ME WHAT YOU WANT AND LET'S PUT AN END
TO THIS.

JAY: THEN MEET ME.

STEPH: JUST TELL ME WHAT YOU WANT.

JAY: NOT ON HERE, MEET ME LATER AND I'LL TELL YOU. TWO
O'CLOCK AT THE PARK NEAR THE SCHOOL I'LL WAIT AT THE
BANDSTAND.

I didn't reply; instead, I sat with my head in my hands and
rocked back and forth. This was either the beginning or the
beginning of the end, and I had no idea which.

CHAPTER 22

I arrived five minutes early and parked across the street, in full view of the weathered bandstand with autumn leaves dancing around it.

I can't believe I am doing this.

Five minutes seemed like forever. Wired and hyper-vigilant, I scanned the street and checked the rear-view mirror for his approach. No taxi so far, and it was three minutes past. Maybe it was a trick? A trap, and he was watching *me*? Panic and paranoia started to rise and I opened the window a little, gulping in cool air and telling myself to calm down.

The familiar silhouette of a man approached the bandstand and lit up a cigarette. Show time. Hopefully this would end up being both the first and final act rolled into one, and as brief as possible.

I gathered myself and got out of the car, hugged my coat around me and made my way towards him, trying to walk confidently and feeling anything but. He turned towards me and looked me up and down as I approached.

"Well, well, well, you look a whole lot better than the last time I saw you," he said, raising an eyebrow and smiling.

I didn't know if I wanted to slap him or kiss him. Those old emotions sure knew how to cling on, and the confusion he had worked hard to create now held me hostage.

You know why you're here, so get on with it.

"What do you want from me, Jay?"

He took a drag from his cigarette and flicked ash onto the pavement.

"Isn't it obvious, Millionaire Mummy?" he asked.

"It was a headline they used to sell papers, that's all," I said.

"Well, even if you're not, you're a whole lot closer to being one than I am, and I'm sure you're not going to miss the chunk you're going to give me."

"And what makes you think I'm going to do that?" I snapped, angry but still pulled in by those eyes.

"Because you don't want your life to implode?" He let the question hang between us like the smoke in the air.

Part of me wanted to call his bluff and tell him to get the hell on with it, turn on my heel and walk away. But he knew me well enough to know that I wouldn't roll the dice where my daughter was concerned. Blackmail hid in the shadows like the coward it was. To survive, it needed secrecy and shame. I had two options here - pay up or tell Damien everything.

"How much, Jay?" I asked, and he smirked.

"You're opening negotiations. I like it. Now let me think." He drummed his fingers on the balustrade.

"Stop pissing about and tell me, or I'm out of here, and you can do whatever the fuck you like with the pictures. This is a one-off meeting, Jay and I'm not messing about here. And by the way, I'm thinking about going home and telling Damien everything anyway."

"You're not going to do that, Steph," he said with a wry half-smile.

I was being his supply. I couldn't help it. But he mustn't see me cry. "Just tell me what you want, Jay, or I'm leaving." I managed to sound relatively controlled.

"Well, I think fifty is reasonable."

"There is fuck all reasonable about any of this, and fifty grand is not happening. You've got me confused with JK Rowling if you think I've got that much going spare. I told you the headline wasn't literal. It was to sell papers. And you're deluded."

Jay held his position. I *was* lying about being able to get fifty thousand; there was more than that in the next egg, but it was just that – our nest egg. The truth is, I possibly wouldn't need the marital nest egg soon… if I had no husband. Maybe it was more chicken and egg than nest egg. He was confusing me again. Why, oh, why had I agreed to meet him?

"I'll give you five."

He laughed and then lit up another cigarette. "Five grand is pocket money for you, Steph. I can't believe that your marriage and daughter are only worth the price of a second-hand car. What an insult."

"Don't talk to me about insults. You're a walking insult. I'll go up to ten and that's it."

"Let's say twenty." He took another drag and waited.

"I. Fucking. Hate. You." I said slowly and deliberately to his face before turning and walking away.

I sat in the car, trying to compose myself and watching him finish his cigarette. He sauntered back down the road he'd come from with arrogance in every step, the cat who got the cream. I didn't want to cry anymore, not over him. He wasn't having any more of me after this. I closed my eyes and tears stung my cheeks. If twenty thousand pounds was the cost of me getting my life back, then I'd pay it all day long. Now I just had to withdraw the cash and get it to Jay, and that was the end. And the beginning of a new life for me, a life where lies would never be told again.

CHAPTER 23

It was obvious I'd been crying, but I could fix that with make-up and go straight to the bank.

I was borrowing it, investing it.

The return on the investment was me getting my life back, Mia keeping her mum and Damien staying blissfully unaware. The interest on the loan might be a lifetime of guilt and fear that I'd be found out, but right now, I'd rather take that than have everything ripped away from me.

All you can ever do is the next right thing.

And in a crazy, messed up, trying to cling on to what mattered way of things, giving twenty thousand pounds to my ex-husband seemed like that next right thing.

I dabbed with my concealer, added some blush and lip gloss, and felt more presentable and plausible. Did I even have to appear plausible? I was drawing out my own money from my *own* account. I didn't need to be bloody plausible, I could shut down the account and piss off to Las Vegas and it would have nothing to do with anyone at the bank.

I pep-talked my way there, and by the time I pulled into a parking space, I was quite indignant that I wanted my own money out of my own account, and that was that. This version of me was the one the bank teller would meet, and we might even have a giggle about the Las Vegas thing and me walking around with an envelope full of fifties. Scared and anxious me was going to step back and let ballsy-businessy me handle this brilliantly. I took a deep breath, walked in and joined the queue.

In front of me was a youngster paying in a whole load of change and an old lady asking about a nice crisp twenty-pound note for a birthday card. Coin boy finished up and I stepped forward.

"How can I help you today?" smiled Sally, according to her badge.

"I want to make a withdrawal, please." I smiled back but felt panic creeping in. I reminded myself that this was my money from my account and I could do anything with it. There was nothing shady going on here, and I could absolutely calm down.

"Great, have you got your debit card?" Sally pointed to the card machine to my right. "Just put it in and follow the instructions please."

I did as she said, and entered my PIN, followed by the amount I wanted to withdraw after mentally counting the zeros and deliberately tapping them one by one into the keypad. I didn't want to go through it again because I'd withdrawn two thousand by mistake. Pressing the green button, I exhaled and faked a smile.

"There, I think that's done," I said and felt my shoulders relax a little.

Nothing back from Sally at first, apart from looking at her screen and raising one eyebrow, so I said it again to make sure she'd heard. "I think that's done."

"Yes, sorry, I'm just going to have to ask you to step into our meeting room for two minutes if that's ok. It's standard procedure with a larger amount of money."

Panic stopped creeping and started running. "But why? It's my money?" and my whole life is depending on me getting this.

"It's just the bank's policy when it's a large amount, that's all. There's nothing to worry about, honestly. Please don't be concerned."

"I'm not concerned because I know it's my money." I was speaking through my teeth, and if there hadn't been a glass screen between us, I'm sure I might even be accidentally spitting a little in her face.

"If I could just ask you to hold on for one moment, please.

Everything is in order; we just need two minutes. I'll buzz a colleague. Luckily, we have one of our relationship managers here from the city, so it will be fast and easy to process. Would you mind taking a seat, please?" she smiled and I tried to smile back.

There were two blue bucket seats next to a rack of leaflets about pensions, mortgages, savings accounts and life insurance. I sat down and sighed audibly; I could feel myself getting stressed.

Why did I feel like I was doing something wrong?

Because I was.

"Steph?" I heard a familiar voice and there was Ryan looking sharp in a navy-blue suit. My face smiled, and my heart sank in tandem. Of all the people I didn't want to see, it was him. He opened a door marked private and gestured for me to follow him. I made my way towards a windowless office with an artificial plant in the corner and a standard landscape print on the wall. There was a computer on the desk, as well as pen and paper, and the strip light buzzed quietly in the background.

"Take a seat," he said. "How are you?" small talk while he booted up the computer.

Damien and I had known Ryan through the bank for the longest time, and he and his wife Jenny had become our friends, not besties but friendly enough to have round for dinner once in a while, to invite to a summer barbeque and the like. Friends I was about to involve in a web of lies and deceit. I really couldn't sink much lower.

"Yes, we really should get together soon," I kept up the small talk as he stared at the screen, wanting to keep things as fast and surface level as I could, but Ryan definitely put the relationship into relationship manager. After we'd covered kids, holidays, the school run and his neighbour's planning application, he finally mentioned the money.

"So you want to make a withdrawal today? Let's see." He

tapped on the keyboard in front of him and raised an eyebrow in my direction. "Twenty thousand in cash?"

"Yes, that's right," I tried to maintain eye contact, but as any liar knows, that's nigh-on impossible.

"Ok," he nodded, professional mode engaged. "This will feel really intrusive, but it's banking policy to ask you what or who it's for. I'm sorry, but it's to protect against money laundering and to see if you are at risk of fraud."

"Oh, well, sorry, I can't tell you, Ryan." I was floundering, drowning, not waving. My face flushed and I cleared my throat twice.

He looked at me and his eyes narrowed slightly. His tone was near neutral, and his voice was calm. "Steph, has someone asked you to come and withdraw this today?"

I dropped my gaze and looked at my hands in my lap, turning my wedding ring on my finger and saying a silent prayer. The game was up. There was no way I'd be able to convince him that I needed the money for something else, something I hadn't even thought of yet. Maybe I should come clean and tell him? Maybe he'd be bound by a code of ethics and he wouldn't be able to tell Damien, but I bet he'd have to call the police, and then the shit storm would commence in earnest.

I swallowed, took a breath, raised my head, and looked him in the eye. Starting to speak, I noticed the landscape over his shoulder and wished it was me on the open road, driving off into the rolling hills in a camper van, anywhere but here, lying to a friend and probably about to be found out anyway.

"It's a surprise for Damien." I heard myself say. "A camper van."

Ryan's expression changed from suspicion to surprise.

"Oh, wow!"

He'd taken the bait. Now I had to make something up on the

spot and reel him in.

Piss off guilt and shame, I'll deal with you later.

"Yes, he has no idea." A temporary breathing space opened up.

"He's going to love that!" Ryan smiled from ear to ear. "Are you going with something retro or newer? The old ones are charming, but you seriously can't fault the newer Volkswagen transporter vans. They are the business. Have you found one yet? Of course you have or you wouldn't be wanting the money." He chuckled and I joined in, sounding as genuine as the canned laughter from an eighties gameshow.

I wanted to stop digging myself into the hole I'd created, but it seemed there was nothing to do but keep going. "Yes, I've found one for sale. It's a friend of a friend," I said. "A new one, well nearly new."

"I'm not interfering here, but why did they want cash, Steph? It's a bit of a red flag if I'm honest. I don't want you to get ripped off." He looked at me and I tried to hold his gaze.

"I think they just need some fast cash and don't want it to be visible or something. I'm not too sure."

"Hmm, well, that's a concern." Ryan leaned back in his chair and looked thoughtful.

"Honestly, I'm sure it's ok. I know what you mean about it looking a bit suspicious, but I really don't care as long as I'm getting a bargain."

"But what if it's stolen or been involved in anything illegal, Steph? I don't want this coming back to bite you or Damien. We really should check it out properly. I'm not trying to take the shine off it or anything; I just want you to be safe, and there are all kinds of shady people out there who lie about anything and everything." He leaned in and asked if I'd like him to come and see the van with me.

The imaginary van. The van I had completely made up. The unicorn of vans.

"Honestly, it's fine. I'll make sure I check everything before I give them any money."

Ryan looked at me and shook his head.

"But I can come with you, Steph. This is looking pretty sketchy, to be honest, and I don't want you to lose your money or buy anything that's not safe or roadworthy. People fake documents and all kinds every day of the week. I'm not saying this is the case here, but honestly, it's really important to check it out." He sighed. He was getting frustrated with me and couldn't understand why I wouldn't let him, our friend, help me.

Because it's all a pack of lies, Ryan, that's why.

"I'll check it all out properly, I promise," I said, wondering if he could withhold the money if he thought something illegal was going on.

"I feel super uncomfortable about this, Steph. I seriously wish it hadn't been me sitting here today. Anyone else and I'd have to insist on a transfer or a banker's draft." He shook his head again. "It's not just about you and Damien. If this goes shits up and you lose that money, I need to show that I advised you not to take it in cash." He tapped his pen on the desktop and breathed in, his final consideration occurring.

"I understand, of course," I said, clinging to his every word and smiling broadly. I even nodded in encouragement.

"Ok, well, sign this," Ryan passed a withdrawal slip and pen across the desk. "I'll go to the safe and get the cash, but please, Steph, call or text me if you need me to help you and please make sure you don't get taken advantage of. I don't want to explain this to head office, or worse, to one of my mates."

He came back five minutes later with a paper bag filled with notes that were bound by paper strips.

"Doesn't look like twenty thousand, does it?" he said as he counted it in front of me. "Last chance to reconsider?"

"I'm fine, thanks," I said, standing up and taking the bag, hoping he didn't see any telltale nervous shaking. I was, of course, far from fine, as far away from fine as I could be. I may as well have gone to Las Vegas. I was literally playing life roulette.

CHAPTER 24

Doing the school run with twenty grand in your handbag does nothing for your nerves. I went through the dilemma of leaving it in the glove box but then thought about the car being stolen. My metallic green, battered mummy mobile, a toy box on wheels, was hardly a target. It was the Nokia brick of cars, standard mummy transport, a good height for a car seat and enough boot space for a *big* food shop. The money would be safe in the glove box, surely? My nerves talked me out of it, and I stuffed it in my bag.

I rounded the corner and Mel looked me up and down, then asked if I was ok. My face was blotchy and I was wearing my handbag 'messenger style', which I had hoped would look something like the models on the style edit program I'd caught a snippet of last week. But judging by Mel's expression, I wasn't exactly pulling it off.

"Wow, Steph, do you think someone is going to mug you for half a pack of wine gums and a clean tissue?" she sniggered. "Can you even breathe?"

"Yes, I can breathe," I mumbled. "I was just trying something new I'd seen on the telly."

"Oh, that style edit thing they do in the mornings? I saw that too." Mel was full-on laughing and I was trying to get out of my bag. "They were thinner than us, Steph, and the bags were a lot smaller. You're trying to do it in a big coat with a bag you could carry a toddler in."

If I wasn't hot and bothered before, I certainly was by the time I'd finished bag aerobics. Yes, over-the-shoulder was still the way to go. Thank you, style edit, you bunch of wankers. I made the decision there and then to edit them out altogether.

Never again would I watch their shite - they've lost a loyal viewer in me. I once even participated in a phone-in about shops no longer catering for women who loved jeans with a proper waistband and who wore full briefs.

"Oh god, there's Beth," I whispered.

Mel smiled at her, and I glared at Mel.

"What?" she mouthed.

"I haven't had time to tell you this, but shit has most definitely gone down." I turned my back to Beth in case she'd learned how to lipread in the last twelve hours.

"Shit's. Gone. Down. You've been watching American box sets on Netflix, haven't you?" Mel giggled.

"I've got something to tell you, but you must not react when I do. Don't let Beth know I've told you. She'll probably know anyway, but just don't gasp or anything, ok?" I was all stage whispery but for bloody good reason.

"Ok, this better be good. It's getting quite a build-up."

"It's anything but good, Mel, it's really bad. And I'm going to have to ask you not to tell Damien or mention anything about it in front of him."

"Steph, what the hell is going on?" The giggling had stopped and made way for concern.

"You know I told you ages ago about my ex, Jay?"

Mel nodded and waited for more.

"Well, he's the new boyfriend."

"Oh, wow!" Mel said.

"Yes, but there's more, a whole load more and I can't tell you now, but I think she's in danger. I've been going for therapy and it's dredged up a lot of stuff from the past that was abusive and I didn't know it was happening."

Mel leaned in closer.

"Beth is so lovely and she's been through so much," she said. "What the hell did he do to you, and what do you mean - you didn't know?"

"It's a long story, but I need to tell you because Beth has blocked me altogether. Last night, I messaged her and tried to warn her, but she's so caught up in him that she accused me of being jealous and a bit psycho."

"He's got quite a hold on her already, I think," Mel said. "The flowers and the nights out, she's never been treated that way before and she's loving it. I know it's a silly thing to ask, Steph, but you are sure, aren't you?"

"Sure about what?"

"That he's dangerous? People change, you know, and you're bound to be wounded by what happened in the past, so it's natural that you'd hate him."

"Mel, I'm telling you that man is dangerous. He's a manipulator; he bleeds people dry and Beth is next."

"I believe you, I do. But you might not believe me." Her eyes were wide. What the hell was she about to say? I'd had more than enough for one day.

"What do you mean? I'd always believe you, Mel," I asked, bracing myself.

"Don't turn around, Steph. Look right at me." She smiled in a way that was completely out of context at first, but then I realised she wasn't smiling at me but over my shoulder at Beth.

"There's a man with Beth."

CHAPTER 25

Truth be told, I wanted to walk right over to him and stuff the money into his smug face. I was furious, anxious and confused all at the same time. I wanted to turn around and glare at him. Conflicted and cornered, tears threatened. Was I jealous he was with someone else?

Fuck you, gaslighting!

I couldn't escape what I'd done or from the grip he now had on me. Why couldn't he just stay away?

Because he wants to make you feel like this.

"What should I do?" I whispered to Mel.

"Nothing. When the kids come out, I'll keep them occupied for a couple of minutes and that will give them time to leave. We'll get back to the cars without any drama, and tomorrow, we'll regroup and you can fill me in properly."

"Ok, you're right."

Fight or flight was tightening its hold.

"Keep looking at me, Steph. The kids will be out any minute. You have to keep it together."

"What are they doing?" I hissed.

"They are fawning all over each other just like you'd expect," Mel confirmed what was playing in my mind. I was desperate to turn around.

"That's called love bombing," I said, knowing it was a performance they both wanted me to see for different reasons.

"Whatever it's called, it's yuck. I swear to god there's a time and a place for it, and the school playground it is not." Mel reached for my hand and squeezed it.

"Mel, I'm hyperventilating," I said and puffed out my cheeks.

"No you aren't. Just focus on me and keep breathing. Slow it down if you can. That's right, breathe in and then out." She spoke calmly and I felt anything but. Perhaps I should make my way back to the car and wait there? Mel could bring Mia to me and I could say that I'd been running late. I was just about to suggest it through the fog of blind panic when I heard the sound of children's voices, and the yard started to fill with brightly coloured coats and bobble hats.

I didn't want him to see Mia with me. I never wanted him to set eyes on her and know she was mine. The man was a monster and I didn't know what lengths he'd go to in order to make me pay up. That's why paying up was the right thing to do. There was no amount of money in the world I wouldn't pay right now as my daughter's hand slipped into mine and her voice filled my senses about her day. I wanted to scoop her up and run far away from him, keeping her perfect little face pressed into my coat so he couldn't see her. I sidestepped a little and crouched down to her level, blocking his view and looking straight at her.

"Mummy, have you been crying?" she asked.

"Yes darling, yes I have. I've had a terrible headache and it made me cry, but Mel has given me some of her headache tablets and it's almost gone now," I said, trying to keep it together. I looked up at Mel for a clue on their movements. She gave her head a slight shake.

Time felt like it had slowed down and Mia wanted to go home. My thighs were starting to object to me crouching. I stood up shakily, still standing in any line of sight that would give him a clear visual of her. My tiny act of trying to retain her anonymity seemed like I was somehow offsetting some of the bad things I'd done. Maybe I was overreacting and unravelling, but this was all the power I had at the moment. The instinct to keep her safe above all else, even though I was the one who put her right in harm's way.

George ran towards us and started to limpet on Mel's leg,

and for the first time ever, I was pleased. He latched on and refused to tell her what was wrong when a teaching assistant joined us. She invited Mel to come back into the classroom to talk for five minutes, and George, to my surprise and horror, agreed.

"Can my friend come?" asked Mel. "We car share."

Yes, yes, I can come, and I can hide my child and regroup.

"You can come and wait in reception if you like?" the teaching assistant said to me, and Mia pulled on my coat sleeve. The safety of reception had never been so appealing. We were saved.

"I want to go home, Mummy," she said and I wanted to throw my head back and scream. I felt like the cork in a supermarket's own brand of Prosecco that was being shaken to death, and the pressure was building. People would want to duck and cover their eyes any second now. There I was, smiling at the teaching assistant and nodding, yet feeling like I should have been sectioned weeks ago.

I could hear Jay's voice but couldn't make out any words.

Beth was laughing.

Mia was tugging.

Mel was asking.

The classroom assistant was waiting.

Reality was slipping.

And I was imploding.

All at once, in one mad split second of time and awareness.

I had nothing to cling on to. Although I could see, feel and hear it all, I was like an invisible extra in the movie of my life. A life that was happening around me and to me but felt so tenuous and finely balanced that at any moment, it might all be finished, and the credits would roll.

Despite Mia's objections, I tightened my grip around her fingers and hoped my grip on reality would last too. A deep breath with a forward step, and I was heading for reception, walking away from the threat and hoping my heart rate would soon cotton on.

The hand on my shoulder came from nowhere.

Fuck my actual fucking life!

I gasped in horror and air filled my lungs, ready to scream.

The hand spun me around with a strength greater than mine, and we were suddenly eye to eye. Fear and love rushed through me at the same time. He could still do this to me after all these years.

Damien, thank god you're here.

CHAPTER 26

"Daddy!" Mia squealed with delight and jumped into his arms.

"Hey, Princess," he said as he lifted her up.

I forced a smile and dared to look across the yard for a split second. Jay and Beth were walking away with her daughter holding a hand each. He wasn't watching me at all.

Pull your bloody self together, fast.

His control was the invisible prison that held me captive now and had done, unknowingly, for years. If I didn't lose my marriage and my daughter because of him, I'd lose my mind in the process anyway. His poison has permeated my whole life now, even the school yard. My world was getting smaller by the day – and he knew it. All I wanted was to get home, double-lock the doors, close the curtains and hide.

"Steph, are you ok?" Damien asked and reached for my hand.

"I think I've got a migraine coming on, to be honest. Your timing couldn't have been better." I smiled weakly and Damien leaned in and kissed my forehead.

"You do look a bit washed out, love. Let's get you home and I'll see what I can rustle up for dinner. Are you ok to drive?" The care in his voice and the thought of what I was doing to him were almost too much. I wanted to be in the car on my own so I could cry all the way home.

"Yes, definitely ok to drive, but can you take Mia please? I don't think I can cope with the teeny-bopper music today."

"Sure, I'll see you at home. Please stay safe." He kissed me again. "You're precious to us."

I drove the long way back and let my tears flow throughout the journey. This was the last lap. I had to dig deep. Before I walked up the path to the house, I typed a message to Jay.

I'VE GOT WHAT YOU WANT. I'LL MEET YOU TOMORROW.

I stared at the message and shook my head.
Who had I become?
I quickly pressed send before I could change my mind. Twenty thousand felt like a lot and a little bit, both at the same time. Under different circumstances, it would have been a life changer, but right now, it was a life *saver* and if it could make this go away, it was the bargain of the century. My phone pinged.

FOUR SEASONS 8PM

I'd presumed that the drop-off would be in the morning. Going out on an evening was out of character for me to say the least.

MORNING IS BETTER

NOT FOR ME

THIS ISN'T ALL ABOUT YOU

OR YOU EITHER
I'VE GOT WHAT YOU WANT JUST LET ME GIVE IT TO YOU

8PM TOMORROW

This was the final step in a dance of deceit that had consumed me since it started. I needed to pay up and move the hell on. Somehow, tomorrow night, I would lie to my caring and devoted husband and meet my ex at a local hotel, give him a whole load of cash, and then come home and pretend it had never happened.

CHAPTER 27

The next morning, life ticked over in an ironically typical fashion. Coffee, toast, packed lunch, radio playing in the background. The thing I had learned about ordinary, though, was that its anything but. People write it off as boring, but in my experience, there is a lot to be said for a day that doesn't include the high drama of blackmail and off-the-scale anxiety. There's a whole lot to be said for ordinary, and I wanted it back really badly.

After the school run, I met Mel for coffee, and she was all ears.

"I can't believe he's your ex, Steph!" she was wide-eyed and waiting for me to fill in the blanks.

"Yes, that's him," I said, stirring and considering how much to share.

"What you said about him being abusive, I'm so sorry you went through that." Mel's reply was more of a question, so I drew a breath and told her the back story. Her eyes grew even wider in disbelief.

"And you didn't know it was happening?" she asked after listening carefully.

"No, I really didn't know, and that sounds ridiculous, but it's true." I was ready for another coffee and waved at the waitress. "I know it's unbelievable to people who haven't experienced it. I get that," I said and shrugged. "And that makes it worse because when you try to explain it, you feel even more humiliated and stupid for not seeing it and staying so long."

Mel reached over the table and grabbed my hand.

"Hey! I don't think you are stupid. I think you're really brave for sharing," she said and ordered two more cappuccinos.

"You do?" I asked and looked at her to truly weigh up her response.

"I do," she confirmed and didn't break eye contact. "And I can see why you would be worried about Beth, but I don't know what we can do to help her. She's too far in."

I went on to talk about love bombing and how narcissists choose their victims. All the red flags were there, but Beth was oblivious. She was so wrapped up in finally finding someone who loved and adored her that she was like a butterfly in a venus fly trap.

"So what happens now?" Mel asked.

I shook my head. "I can't control the fact that my ex is in town and I've done what I can to help Beth. I just need to get on with it and front it out," I said. "Maybe he'll get tired of her soon, or her family will see what's happening and step in. I don't think he's here for the long run. I think he'll get what he can and then discard her, unfortunately."

"Do you really think he's here to intimidate you, though? Could it not just be a coincidence?" Mel asked, and I sighed.

"It's definitely not a coincidence, Mel."

"Ok, but just let me play devil's advocate here for a minute. I know he's your ex and obviously a complete bastard, but why would he deliberately choose someone you know? Is it to make you jealous or something? What would he have to gain by coming here? Maybe he just met her online on one of those dating apps, and it turns out she lives near you and her kid goes to the same school. Stuff like this must happen all of the time, surely?"

"They did meet online, Mel. You're right about that."

"So maybe it's just one of those small world occurrences that he's turned up here, and maybe it's got nothing to do with you? I'm just saying that because I can see how it's affecting you, and I hate seeing you so anxious and worked up." She squeezed my hand again. "How do you know they met online?"

"Because they met on my Facebook page, I saw it play out."

"What do you mean? Facebook is a minefield for you. Between this and that weird stalker, maybe you should close your account."

"Jay started to leave comments on my page, and Beth and him got chatting. He made sure the conversation was public so I could see it, and he ended by saying he'd private message her." I sighed. "I can't really close my page. I need it for work. Being public is part of the deal, and the stalker guy looks like he's moved on anyway."

Mel nodded, then asked more about Jay. "Why would he do that, though? Why was he commenting on stuff on your page anyway?"

"Because he wanted to intimidate me and let me know he was watching. He wanted to remind me that he is in control and make me anxious just like before." I knew it was hard for people who had never been through this to understand, so I tried to be patient.

"Did you tell Damien?" Mel asked, "Please say you blocked him so he can't comment on anything else."

"I didn't do either," I confessed, "I thought it would blow over and there was no point upsetting Damien. After all, it's just a few comments on a Facebook page."

"But it isn't though, is it? Does Damien know how abusive Jay was to you?"

"Not exactly, because I've only just started to piece it together myself. He knows about some of the other stuff that happened but not the manipulation and isolation. I don't know how to explain the gaslighting or where to start. I was just hoping that if I stay in therapy, I could overcome it and stop feeling so anxious."

"You need to tell him, Steph, he loves you and he'll want to help."

"But help me with what though?" I could feel tears welling

up. "There's nothing to help me with. It all makes me sound like a jealous basket case, just like Jay said. I can't expect anyone to understand what I'm going through, not even Damien, and maybe not you either."

"Steph, it's upsetting you and that's enough. Like I said, you've probably got some post-traumatic stress or something? You need to stop being so hard on yourself."

If only you knew, Mel, if only you knew.

"I just hope he gives up on Beth soon and moves on again. Maybe we can help her pick up the pieces afterwards," I said and checked the time. The entire day stretched before me and I needed to write, but the mess I was in was all-consuming and wouldn't let me breathe, never mind think. I only needed to get through to 8pm and then I'd have my life back. This was the last push, the last lie and the last chance.

I could do this – I had to.

After coffee, my drive home was filled with thoughts of what lay ahead. Would I hand him the envelope of money in the car park? What if there was CCTV? Would he want to meet me inside?

Panic started to present all kinds of scenarios. What if it was a trap? What if he dragged me into the car and took me somewhere? I wouldn't put anything past him. If he was willing to take things this far, what else was he capable of?

It was sickening to think that the man I loved and shared a bed with for years was someone I never knew at all. Remorse knotted in my stomach, and I felt nauseous. I should tell someone where I'm going. Lizzie. After a quick call, she insisted on coming with me, and although I objected, I was relieved that I wouldn't be going alone.

I was exhausted already and it was only mid-morning, but I only had to get through a few more hours and one last big lie. Lizzie was my cover story. I could say she'd asked me to go out for some food and a catch-up. Easy breezy, a text to Damien would cover it. So easy that it took what felt like forever to compose and send because there is nothing easy or breezy about lying.

LIZZIE WANTS ME TO GO FOR FOOD AND A CATCH UP LATER, OK WITH YOU? X

OF COURSE LOVE I'LL PICK MYSELF UP A TAKEAWAY SO YOU CAN HAVE THE WHOLE NIGHT OFF X

The weight of guilt lay heavy on my heart.

CHAPTER 28

I was a horrible person, secretly unpicking our lives at the seams and then trying to stitch them back together. I loved Mia and Damien as much as I hated myself. Both feelings were as crushing as they were constant. Even when this was over, I knew it would haunt me forever. But what choice did I have? Maybe it was the penance I deserved and one that would stop me from doing anything as devastating in the future.

Time for a shower and change before the big meet-up. I needed to look as if I was going out for food with Lizzie, but not like I'd made any kind of effort for Jay.

What on earth did that look like?

I was clueless about fashion anyway, and my entire wardrobe screamed middle-aged mummy. The Four Seasons was quite posh, and if we ended up in reception, I'd stick out like a sore thumb if I rocked up in my version of smart casual, which was more like crocs and black leggings. The last thing I wanted to do was attract any attention. I just needed to give him the envelope and go, then a thought – should I put the money into something else? Giving someone a brown envelope looked a bit obvious, didn't it?

Would he want to count it?

I opted for a gift bag, unintended irony. A navy and red option with a ribbon handle that declared 'Happy Birthday' in cursive script. I nipped the two sides together and paperclipped them in the middle. Now it was time to find the one pair of smart jeans that might still fit me and think about doing something with my hair.

Pouring myself into the indigo denim and breathing in, I could see and feel that I'd definitely chubbed up. I'd been eating my feelings, but I promised myself that when I got out the other side of this shit show, I'd join Weight Watchers again and be a whole new woman, and an honest one at that.

I dabbed on a little make-up, left my hair tied up, and looked in the mirror again, instantly feeling sorry for myself. If I'd been asked to describe what I could see, I'd say I was desperately trying to be someone I wasn't. The concealer I'd used to hide the bags under my eyes was never going to be enough to hide the torment of the past few months, and although I'd pulled my top over my waistband, there was no hiding those extra pounds either. Shaking my head, I wanted to cry. I was so lonely and scared and hated who I'd become.

The doorbell made me jump. I peeped through the slats of the wooden blinds. Whoever was there had started knocking frantically, banging as hard as my heart was against my ribcage. Dusk had settled, and it had started to rain. My view was obscured, but then a car drove past and the headlights swept across Damien's outline. I exhaled and quickly made my way down the stairs.

"I'm sorry, I must have left the key in the door," I said as he dripped onto the doormat.

"Bloody hell, that rain is biblical!" he exclaimed and looked me up and down. "Wow, you look gorgeous!" He put the carrier bag down and the smell of fish and chips wafted upwards as he leaned in to kiss me. "I don't want to put a spanner in the works, Steph, but the weather is pretty bad. Can you not reschedule with Lizzie? The guy on the local traffic report said there was loads of surface water and I can vouch for the crappy driving conditions."

I can't. I need this over and done with.

"I'll text her and see, but don't worry, we aren't going far."

"Where did you decide to go?"

"The Four Seasons." In a liar's world, I was learning that keeping things close to the truth helps you remember the story later.

"For food?" Damien asked, taking off his wet coat and hanging it on the end of the bannister. "That's a bit posh. I thought you'd be going to that Italian that does three courses for a tenner."

"I think Lizzie wants to scope it out for some corporate thing, two birds with one stone and all that. Anyway, if she puts it on the company account, it doesn't matter how posh or expensive it is." I fussed with his coat so I didn't have to make eye contact, wishing he'd stop asking me about it.

"Fair enough," he said, making his way to the kitchen. "Don't mind if I eat, do you? I'm starving. Do you want some chips?"

"No, I'm fine, thanks. Mia might, though." I turned and made my way back upstairs, sat on the bed and as the rain poured down the windowpane, my tears fell silently into my hands. I covered my face and once again asked myself who on earth I'd become.

Chin up, Steph. It'll all be over in a couple of hours or so. And my marriage will be saved.

I walked downstairs and into the living room to see Damien sitting on the couch with his dinner on a tray and Mia next to him, choosing chips to dip in ketchup. *The Simpsons* was on the television and neither of them looked up when I said I was off. Mia mumbled a goodbye, and Damien told me to drive safely. With that, I headed for the door. Time for another date with destiny, and hopefully the last one.

CHAPTER 29

The Four Seasons was a hotel, golf resort and spa with a long, tree-lined drive. We arrived early, and I parked in a dark corner. It was quiet. The weather had done me a favour and kept most people at home.

"What happens now?" asked Lizzie as I turned off the engine and silence surrounded us.

"I honestly don't know," I replied. "I guess I either text him or just wait." I turned to look at her in the darkness and reminded her to stay hidden. Jay was expecting me to be alone, and he certainly wouldn't be expecting me to turn up with my lawyer, even if she was my friend.

"Have you told anyone else?" Lizzie asked, scanning the darkness for signs of his arrival.

"Not a soul. I can't risk it."

"That's smart. I hate him nearly as much as you do, Steph, and I really hope this is the end and you can finally get rid of the scumbag."

A taxi drove slowly into the car park and pulled into a space. My phone lit up.

I'M HERE

"What now?" I fumbled to unlock the screen and dropped it in the footwell. "Fuck's sake!" I bent over and searched with my fingertips until I felt the edge of the case.

"Steph, calm down," said Lizzie, but I could tell she was just as scared. "Take some deep breaths. This will be over in a couple of minutes. You've got this."

I held the phone in my hand, shaking with fear and

adrenalin. Time had slowed down and everything seemed so present and fragile.

HOW ARE WE DOING THIS?

Message marked as read. Three little dots.

HOTEL OR CAR, YOUR CALL

"What should I say?" I said, trying to slow my breathing. The windows were starting to steam up.

"Go to the car. I can see you from here, and if there is any funny business, I can run over," Lizzie said. "And I'll record it on my phone just in case."

"Just in case what? What do you think is going to happen?"

"Steph, you're panicking."

"Of course I'm panicking!"

"Text him back and just say 'car'. You can do this." Lizzie cracked her window open a little and fresh air filled my lungs. I was all in now. I just had to get it over with.

CAR - I'LL COME TO YOU

OK

The taxi door opened and I saw him light a cigarette. I stepped out into the dark, cold night and started to put one foot in front of the other. Jay swung around and looked in my direction. The wind carried the smell of smoke and his aftershave towards me. Familiarity taunted as I got closer.

"So nice to see you, Stephanie," he said, his voice dripping with sarcasm and charm.

"Here it is, you'll find it's all there as agreed." I passed him the bag and felt his fingers brush mine.

"I'm sure it is," he said and smiled, goading me.

Keep your eyes on the prize.

I turned on my heel and walked back to the car, hearing him drive off and not daring to turn around.

As I collapsed into the driver's seat, my whole body shook. His taillights were disappearing into the night, fading like a nightmare as you start waking up.

"Steph, you can't drive yet," Lizzie said, passing me a bottle of water.

I took it from her and sipped, spilling some onto my coat.

"Why don't we go into the hotel and get something to eat? You look like death warmed up, and it's too early to go back home," Lizzie suggested. "I'll drive up to the reception. They do valet parking from there."

"I can't face anyone though. I feel terrible." My head was pounding, but I had to admit I was hungry. I'd hardly eaten all day because of the cartwheels in my stomach. Food sounded good. Maybe I'd be able to eat now it was done, and keeping a lie as close to the truth as possible was a good strategy. Not that I needed strategies anymore, ever.

Because tonight is the last lie, it has to be.

"You won't have to face anyone. Who are we going to see here? It's midweek, it's been pissing down and it's too posh for your school mum brigade, no offence." Lizzie nudged me, "And anyway, I'm starving."

"Ok, I guess we could." I agreed and we swapped seats.

Lizzie circled the car park, driving past the spa and into the courtyard. She pulled into the valet parking space and we both made our way through a revolving glass door. I hoped tonight would be my first unbroken night's sleep in months. Who knows, if Damien was still awake maybe we'd have sex. I hadn't felt like it for weeks. Doing something that intimate when you are lying to someone feels so wrong. What I was doing was bad enough without bringing betrayal into our bed.

I'd made excuses about being tired and not feeling myself, both a version of the truth but with a foundation he would hopefully never want to excavate. Now there was a feeling of completion, and a need to be close to him.

I made my way to the bathroom while Lizzie asked for a table. Dabbing on some lip gloss, I told myself it was over. Things were going to get better now. Relief would find a way in, and although guilt and shame would be lifelong companions, I'd find a way to live with them once time had gifted me some distance from the present.

I'd done a very bad thing, but for a very good reason.

In the future, this would be a faded memory that I'd never have to revisit. I was on the up, and yes, I was hungry.

Even though I was exhausted, there was a little spring in my step I hadn't felt for ages and I was walking a little taller. Scanning the room for Lizzie, I heard her voice and followed it into the restaurant. She was talking to Ryan from the bank and his wife, Jenny.

Cue heart sink.

"Steph!" Jenny threw her arms around me. "It's been too long, how are you?"

Before I had time to answer, she went on to tell me Ryan said he'd seen me the other day and that although he couldn't talk about bank business, he could tell me something secret that was being planned for Damien. Excited and happy, she paused and waited for me to confirm.

How could I burst the bubble?

I'd make Ryan look like a liar and incriminate myself at the same time. There was only one liar here, and the spotlight was on me again. Lizzie filled the silence with a one-liner about being intrigued while I caught my breath.

"Yes, well, it has to be kept really secret, so please don't say a thing. I'm going to buy Damien a camper van," I said through a fake smile. Lizzie's jaw dropped, instantly joining up the dots.

She would be thinking right now about how we could buy more time to raise enough to *actually* buy a camper van – one that I didn't want and couldn't afford.

Even if I could raise the money, it would have to be a bank loan now, and Ryan literally was the bank. Unless I went somewhere else, but then Damien might see letters and statements from a different lender and wonder what was going on - I didn't know what was going on apart from I was standing listening to Jenny talking about going away together and touring the west coast of Scotland in our camper vans with our kids next summer. Things were galloping out of control and I couldn't stop them.

Whatever happened to no more lies?

But this wasn't a new lie. It was an old lie gathering pace.

Ryan chipped in a bit about campsites and beaches, and I nodded and kept smiling throughout, interjecting a vague statement here and there about them keeping us right, camper van virgins and all that. Jenny's phone pinged and she said they'd have to make tracks. The babysitter was taking her driving theory test early the following day so they couldn't be late.

After more hugging, Ryan rounded off with, "I thought I saw you in the car park earlier. I'd left my wallet in the glove box, and I saw you standing talking to a taxi driver. I came back and said to Jen, 'I hope that's not the sketchy bugger she's buying the camper van from!' But you gave him a gift bag so I'm guessing it was a friend's birthday or something."

He turned to Lizzie and laughed, "I'm not a stalker or anything!"

Lizzie smiled in acknowledgement and said it was someone she knew and that she was on the phone to a client when they pulled in to collect the bag, so I'd taken it instead. Thankfully, Jenny's phone started to ring.

"We're just leaving now, literally walking out now, love, ten minutes, I promise."

"Looks like we're off. It's been lovely to see you, ladies!" Jenny linked Ryan's arm, and as they made their way to the door, he turned and said one last thing. "Steph, let me know if I can help you with the camper van. You know I'm a petrolhead and don't need an excuse to go shopping for one – and I know you know this, but make sure it's all above board, no brown envelopes changing hands in car parks! Get it all documented and cover your back."

"Will do," I replied as the waiter appeared and walked us to our table without a single word being uttered between Lizzie and I until we sat down and he'd gone for the wine list.

"Fuck's. Actual. Sake," I whispered.

"I was just thinking that," Lizzie replied.

CHAPTER 30

Although it wasn't late when I got home, Damien was sleeping. I made a cup of tea and wondered how on earth I could cook up a camper van or twenty thousand pounds to buy one.

Either will do, thank you, Universe.

Yes, I knew about the Law of Attraction, and yes, I'd used it before, but this time I doubted myself. I'd spiralled into such a place of fear and regret there was no way I'd get into a happy feeling place and draw this in. Without feeling it, I couldn't create it. The gap between where I was and where I needed to be was too big. I needed to close it somehow, but the more I thought about getting unstuck, the more stuck I felt.

I needed to get back to basics - Be Open to Possibility, just like the very first lesson I'd had to live through. The kitchen clock said almost eleven, and my tea was cold. Standing up to pour it down the sink, I thought about that very first reading I'd had with Psychic Sue. Sidenote: if you'd told me back then that I'd be seeing a psychic and having my cards read, I'd have laughed in your face, but I certainly wasn't laughing during the days and weeks that followed.

I'd gone to a house party to make up the numbers. You could say I was a last resort. When my turn came to go upstairs and meet Sue, I was full of ego and Sauvignon Blanc, ready to discredit her or, at the very least, have a good laugh at her expense. I had no business being there and she felt it right away. She was kind but firm and I played along for a while until she hit an emotional nerve that proved nothing was being faked.

She was scarily accurate, and it shocked me to the core. Reading me like an open book, telling me things about my life that no one could ever have known, and more than that, telling me how I *felt;* feelings I'd locked away deep inside and banished into the shadows. They had settled somewhere I didn't want to uncover, lying dormant and undisturbed like the thick, wet layer of silt at the bottom of a river bed.

Sue saw through me and into the pain I was carrying. Turning cards and speaking softly, she dredged everything up in a blink, muddying my mind and heart with the past, present and future. She confronted me with ugly truths I'd been trying to hide from for years, making me face myself for the first time ever.

Humiliation had washed over me and I'd started to panic. I couldn't listen to any more of what she had to say, so I stood up to leave. To save face, I told her she was wrong and full of rubbish, but even as I stormed out, she told me that my life was about to unravel, and she'd be seeing me again very soon. How right she was on both counts.

Maybe Sue could help me this time too? She'd guided me through so much in the past, not just that first round of lessons. I'd sought her guidance many times since. I could count on her to be honest, and surely a bit of cosmic signposting would be a bonus right now?

If only Ryan hadn't known about the twenty thousand.

If only I hadn't mentioned the camper van.

If only I hadn't gone back to Jay's apartment in the first place.

If only, if only, if only.

CHAPTER 31

I don't know when I finally surrendered to sleep, but once I did, it was better than it had been in a long time. Today was the first day I didn't have to worry about Jay. I just had to tie up some camper van-sized loose ends and I was home free.

"Morning." Damien kissed the top of my head and put a coffee on the bedside drawers. "Did you have a good catch-up with Lizzie?"

"Yeah, it was really good to see her. She sends her love." I stretched and opened my eyes. It was still dark out, but cars were driving up and down the road so I knew it would be around six. Damien was dressed for work.

"I've got to run. I've got a couple of meetings this morning, but I'm hoping to be back home early as a trade-off." He stood up and smoothed down his shirt. "I'm having lunch with Ryan and his colleague, and I might bunk off after that."

Shit.

"Oh, I saw Ryan and Jenny last night at The Four Seasons. Just briefly, they were leaving as we were getting there."

I wish I'd waited five more minutes in the car park. That's literally all it would have taken for me to avoid those Universal sliding doors.

"I'm starting to feel left out here. I must be the only one who hasn't been!" Damien joked and straightened his tie in the mirror. "Right, I'm off, love. Have a good day."

I'd jumped out of the frying pan and straight into the fire, and the time I thought I'd have to put things right was evaporating fast. I sent Ryan a text, reminding him not to ruin the surprise. He sent back a laughing emoji and one of a camper van. If that was meant to make me feel better, however, it did exactly the opposite.

CHAPTER 32

Sue had a cancellation mid-morning. Perhaps The Universe was listening after all. I decided to take this as a sign she could definitely help, hoping that by thinking this, I'd start to feel it too and create the opportunity for this exact outcome.

I can do this.

She opened the door and the smell of incense wafted towards me. I could hear the soothing sound of tinkling bells in the hallway as the breeze made them gently chime.

As she hugged me tightly, I fought back tears, knowing she would sense them. I followed her into her therapy room and she made us coffee. When the small talk slowed down, she leaned in and asked how I was doing. Cue the floodgates. I started to splutter pieces of the story, some coherent and some not. She passed me a box of tissues and patted my hand.

"It's ok, love. Let's see what you need to know." Her energy was comforting and reassuring, and as she passed me the well-worn deck of tarot cards and asked me to shuffle, it felt like time had stood still. This room was like a cocoon, offering sanctuary and safety away from the outside world. It had saved me before and I prayed it would again.

She dealt six cards face-down on the table between us. I held my breath as she closed her eyes to connect and then turned the first one.

"Seven of Swords – this is about theft, deception and lies. It's an indication that someone is being sneaky and trying not to be caught out. Even if they are not caught, there is a huge cost to them and they may end up wondering if it's worth it. If I'm honest, it feels like there will be something of a hollow victory here." Sue looked at me for confirmation and I nodded.

"But it also comes with the feeling that it's not just one person involved. It feels like the deception is working in two different ways here." She paused and closed her eyes. "One is deliberate, and one is not. There is both a victim and a perpetrator here. One person is lying for personal gain and looking to take what they can get, and the other is lying to protect themselves and limit the damage."

"That's so on point," I whispered. "Jay is blackmailing me over a terrible mistake I made years ago, and I'm so scared it's all going to come out."

"Oh, Steph, that's horrendous! Actual blackmail? He's trying to get you to pay up?" Sue looked at me and I looked back, crying and nodding.

"It is, but I know I did this to myself. I went back to his place ages ago when I was drunk, and we had a bit of a fumble. I hate myself, I really do, but I swear I didn't have sex with him. I passed out not long after I got there, and he staged the bedroom like some Fifty Shades movie scene and took loads of photos of me."

Sue looked aghast and asked the obvious question about going to the police, and I told her I was terrified that Damien would leave me if he found out.

"But you're the victim here, Steph. Damien loves you and he'd support you in this." She tried to reassure me, but I couldn't see how this could go any other way.

"It gets worse than that, Sue. I gave him twenty grand yesterday from our nest egg, and I lied to our friend Ryan at the bank and said it was to buy Damien a surprise camper van, and now I'm in even deeper. Ryan is lovely, but he can't keep a secret. He's really excited about going away on family trips together in a non-existent van that I'm going to have to magic up to save my marriage. I've seriously messed up this time."

"I know you aren't going to hear this right now, Steph, but Damien loves you and he will forgive you for this. You really need to come clean and tell him, then go to the police."

"I can't. I just can't risk it." I knew she was trying to help, but I'd been over this scenario so many times now. It was impossible.

"Let's keep going then and see what else comes up," she said calmly, but the conversation about the police and Damien was not finished, and I knew she'd circle back once the cards were read.

"Justice." Sue read the word out loud at the bottom of the card. "Fairness, being held to account for your actions and a levelling up of the truth. This card shows there needs to be a reset. Something has happened that was unfair and unjust. The balance needs to be redressed. It can also mean legal matters, karma being repaid, and judgements being made. It's a card of consequence and cause and effect, reminding us that The Universe levels things up, and in human terms, this can mean punishments, losses and having to face up to what you've created."

I took a sharp intake of breath as she continued.

"However, I'm getting it through loud and clear that you will misinterpret this because you are locked in fear. You're going to think this is about you and it's not, not in the way you think it is anyway."

"What else could it possibly mean, Sue? I'm screwed and I'm going to get what I deserve." I knew this wasn't Sue's fault, and I tried to stay calm, but panic made me raise my voice.

"I'm glad you asked," Sue spoke with love and kindness. "This is about Jay, not you. You are going to experience a different version of this, and I'll come to that in a minute, but for now, focus on him. He's going to get what he gave out and you have no control over that at all, Steph. The Universe is going to square this up and it's out of your hands. Remember that you attract what you give out. He's taken from you and deliberately intimidated and frightened you. That's the energy he's in alignment with and he will get a helping of that back in return. It's already in motion and you have nothing to do with that, ok?"

I nodded half-heartedly. I wanted to believe what she was saying, but surely that would mean the whole story would have to come to light and with that, my karma would rain down on me, too.

"You are going to be able to observe justice being done, and when the time comes, you will get to choose whether you exercise compassion or go into ego and gloat about his downfall. Remember, what you give out, you'll get back, as always." Sue paused and took a breath. "Now, let's look at what this means to you because the two of you have co-created this situation to learn and evolve as souls, even if your human self doesn't agree or understand."

"Correct, I don't agree or understand at all right now."

"That's because you are in the fear of what's playing out. In spiritual terms, you're going through a growth spurt if you choose to surrender, that is. You're being protected here, Steph, even though it doesn't feel that way. This is going to come out and that's the best possible thing that could happen for you right now. You're exhausted and, quite honestly, heading for a breakdown if it doesn't. You can't hold back the tide on this, and I'm asking you to trust that what happens is meant to. The justice card is all about truth, and sometimes the truth is messy, but look at what lying has done."

"That's why I deserve a punishment, too, though."

"No, you don't because your intention was good. Yes, you behaved in a way that did not serve you, but you did that through fear, and you were being intimidated and manipulated. You did what you could to try and protect Damien from even more hurt, and in doing that, you multiplied your own hurt many times. You have carried this pain for you both and tried to hold back the tide all on your own. The energy that you put out was, of course, fear, but more so about love and protection. Jay, on the other hand, wanted to harm and take what was not his. It's very different."

I stared at the card and let the words sink in. Even though I was unwilling to accept them right now, I hoped I would in time.

"But what if it comes out? What will happen, Sue?"

"It's going to come out, love, and there's nothing you can do apart from tell Damien the truth and know he loves you. You need to have faith in yourself, the man you married and The Universe. You need to surrender and let it happen, and you'll not have to wait long."

"How soon?"

"Within the next two or three weeks, I'd say."

"Keep going, please," I said and Sue turned the next card.

"The Tower. I was probably expecting this one. It's a card about massive change, but it can be in a really good way. People talk about having your tower moment, which means a time of an old situation or paradigm crashing down around you. It can often be unexpected and mark life events you have no option but to surrender to. You have to allow the old life to fall apart for a new one to be built from what's left."

"Sounds terrifying."

"Yes, it can sound scary, but remember, you can choose what you make this mean, Steph. Tower moments are known for shattering illusions and deceptions and breaking down what is not working or serving you; they are opportunities to grow, evolve, and build resilience. These chapters in our lives are often the defining moments that help us discover who we are. They can redefine everything and be really positive experiences. Think of it as things falling apart so they can be built back together in a stronger and better way."

"It's the falling apart bit I'm scared of. Does this mean it's all going to come out?" I asked again.

"It's definitely feeling that way, but this is good because you have time to process the idea. It's not going to come as too much of a shock because you'll be expecting it."

"But by expecting it, am I not creating it? Is the Law of Attraction not going to send me it even more if I think about it? By the way, I haven't thought about anything else since this all started, so it's no wonder it's coming. Maybe I created this in the first place by going back with Jay and then went on to create the aftermath by going over and over all possible consequences. I'm an idiot as well as a liar." I hung my head and sighed. This was going from bad to worse.

"There is so much more to the Law of Attraction and our journey as souls in this human reality. Yes, we can and do draw experiences to us because we are energetically aligned and matched to them. But some people believe that everything happening in our lives is predetermined anyway and is always going to happen for our souls to learn and grow and our consciousness to expand. You came here incarnated as a human, as did all of us, to evolve and experience life in physical human form and become more enlightened on the journey before your time here is finished. It is in the lessons of life that we get the opportunity to do this, and there are great gifts to be had if you can find them."

"I can't find anything good in this," I mumbled and was starting to wonder why I'd bothered coming at all.

"Not yet, you can't, but that's when you must dig deep and trust. Remember what you went through all those years ago? None of that was easy, but those lessons changed you and shaped who you've become. You needed them in so many ways, and you wouldn't be who you are now without that journey."

"But I hate who I am now. I'm a liar and a cheat and a thief." I couldn't look at her. I was so ashamed.

"That's not who you are; it's what you *did*. There is an

obvious distinction here: your behaviour is not who you are, and that goes for all of us. It was driven by your emotions, which at the time were all over the place, and you did the best you could, which is all any of us can ever do in truth. You're a bit further down the path now and seeing things differently. When you know better, you can do better, and right now, you know better. You can see how handling these past lessons in a different way might have sent things on a different path, but here we are in the eternal present moment, and it is what it is. There is no point beating your former self up for her decisions. She did what she could in the moment, and right now, you are doing what you can, too."

"I don't know if I'll ever be able to forgive myself for this, especially if it all goes shits up," I said.

"In time you will because this is going to end up being a positive situation that you were always meant to go through and rise up from." Sue seemed certain that destiny had thrown this in my direction deliberately. She reached for the next card and turned it.

"The Lovers," she smiled. "Perfect!" The card depicted a man and a woman standing naked beneath the outstretched wings of an angel with trees and a mountain behind them and the sun beaming down. By Sue's reaction and, of course, the name of the card, this felt more positive.

"I hoped we'd see this card," she said and went on to tell me that it meant an opportunity for a deeply connected and soul honouring union with someone else, a soul mate or twin flame kind of love where the two of you felt like you'd found your missing piece, your other half and the one you had been looking for during your lifetime. It was both wonderful and heartbreaking. I knew this was true, that Damien was the love of my lifetime, and I'd been so blessed and fortunate to find him – yet I was risking losing him.

Sue seemed to think that the card was a positive sign of the bond between us deepening, and that this could be a result of everything coming to light. Me finally facing the truth about how scared and manipulated I'd been and that Damien loving me through it and help me to heal. She said we'd be closer than ever and I needed to get out of the fear that was holding me prisoner and, as soon as the opportunity arrived, I should tell him the whole story. She took a breath and corrected herself.

"Actually, you won't have to tell him. As soon as it's time, this will all be laid out before him as plain as day. He will have his own lessons to go through with regard to how he experiences and handles the situation, and there is great opportunity for him to grow as well. He will have the choice, as we all do, to go into the human drama, fear, judgement and ego or stay centred in his heart, taking a higher-self perspective and aligning with love. It's like you've all come together in this one pivotal moment of time to create an event that is so multi-faceted with so many different potential outcomes that you've given each other the best chance to learn as much as you can."

She looked at me for confirmation I'd heard what she'd said, and although I could give that with a nod, I couldn't say I agreed or even fully understood.

"I know you're going to need some processing time after this and it won't make sense straight away, but on the other side of this you're going to look back and it will all fall into place. You'll know why in some ways it was always going to play out, it was just the detail that your human-self chose that steered it in different ways."

"I'll have to borrow your belief on that one right now." I don't know what I needed or wanted by coming here, but this all felt very esoteric and not exactly the nuts and bolts plan I had to get busy hatching. No mention so far of a camper van showing up or a twenty-grand win on a scratch card.

Sue turned the next card and said it was the Ten of Pentacles.

"This is a brilliant card. It's all about money and financial security, but in the long term, and what you have worked to create. It's showing me no harm will come to your finances and you are in fact in a great position to accrue a whole lot more. The foundations are regarding money and family, you have prosperity in all areas of your life, and you're being asked to believe this and trust that it's with you for your entire lifetime. It feels to me that not only are you going to get your money back, but it will be multiplied. Where it's coming from, I can't say, but it's set up ready for you to allow in. You really need to do what you can to get out of money fear."

"That's easier said than done right now!" I said and she agreed.

"Yes it's not easy at the moment because your human self is stuck."

"So how on earth do I get out of it? I've seen the Law of Attraction work in the past, Sue. I know that it's a real possibility to change things, but you're dead right, I'm so scared that all I keep thinking of is the worst-case scenario here and I know that's not helpful."

"This is one of the challenges we face when we come to earth with a personality and an ego that we have to live with. When we get stuck in a loop of thinking and feeling the associated emotions, we get stuck in a loop of frequency. The more we think about something, the more we are in that energy. If we want to create change, we have to get out of that vibration – see?"

"I'm following you so far," I said and took a gulp of the cold coffee in front of me.

"There is another way to look at this that might help you." Sue paused and looked at me.

"Is there?" I asked. "If you can offer me anything right now, I'll consider it, Sue. I'm desperate, and yes, I realise this is part of the problem."

Sue nodded and told me that what she was about to explain

might feel difficult to get my heart and head around at the moment, and then went on to talk about there being a greater plan at work and how we all fit into it. She spoke of an innate intelligence that is a part of everything and that perhaps the situation I was going through was a part of it.

I shook my head at the very thought. Why would The Universe want me to experience this? It was all just some big mistake that had led to a catalogue of disasters based on my poor judgement, lying and fear. I'd done this to myself and there was no way I was going to give it some magical spin that let me off the hook. I needed to own it and get through it. That's why I'd come here not for some pixies and unicorns pep talk.

"Consider this," she said. "What if this has all come up so you can live your truth and finally heal from the abuse of your past? What if Damien finding out brings you even closer together and cements the relationship in ways you could never imagine? What if 'future you' needs you to go through this for a reason you don't yet understand?"

"I honestly can't think of one," I said and sighed.

"But can you go back to lesson one and be open to the possibility?" asked Sue.

"The possibility that it's happening for a reason?" I asked and laughed out loud. "I really can't see how."

"It's called 'The Law of Divine Order', and it states that there is a Divine Intelligence that oversees everything and seeks to ensure that all is happening as it should in the greater plan of our evolution. If you can lean into that, you can start to believe this is playing out as it needs to for everyone involved and will continue to do so."

"It sounds like you're saying Damien needs to experience his wife betraying and humiliating him, and I just don't believe that at all." I shook my head.

"Maybe Damien needs to learn about unconditional love in its truest sense, accepting your human flaws and loving you through them." Sue's statement sounded like a question I answered without invitation.

"But he's already done that."

"Maybe he's more conscious now and needs to go through another lesson to gain an even deeper understanding, and perhaps you need to trust that he loves you no matter what to finally get rid of your fear. There could be future situations and chapters in your lives that aren't written yet, but depend on this." She spoke directly but always with love.

"And if I can change how I think about it, I'll start sending out a different energy and draw in a different outcome?" I asked.

"Yes, that's exactly right. When you can release the emotional charge around something because you have changed what you made it mean, you no longer carry that negative emotion and vibration. So you get to release some resistance and raise your vibration at the same time." Sue seemed happy I was finally understanding.

"I just don't think I can," I said honestly, not wanting to deflate her.

"You said you don't *think* you can, but the truth is you don't *know* yet. Any kind of inner work is hard, and usually, it's something we come around to years after an event when we've had some time and distance and it doesn't feel as raw. That doesn't mean you can't do it, just that it might be harder. The phrase 'time heals' has some merit, but it's not the full story. Think about what I've said, Steph. I have a feeling this is going to be relevant." She waited for me to acknowledge her, so I shrugged in a non-committal way and let her continue.

"Let's see what the last two cards say," said Sue and turned card number five. "The Ace of Pentacles, a good sign! It's a card that speaks of new beginnings, opportunities, and the manifestation of your wishes. It can mean a windfall or an unexpected sum of money coming your way. It's about prosperity and abundance but in a holistic sense – so, in other words, it's a card that says you can have it all. It's not guaranteed, but The Universe is most definitely on board with your desires, and you are being Divinely Guided to take action in a way that will serve you best to get to your desired destination. Coming here is a great start towards that; it's showing you want to make progress and get as clued up as you can about the next steps you have to take. It's back to basics, Steph. You're going to have to look for the signs and synchronicities and do what you can to align with the overall feelings of what you want rather than what you don't. That's going to mean doing all that you can to heal the past, even the very recent past. The closer you can get to feeling more neutral about it, the better." She nodded as if in agreement with herself and The Universe.

"I'm not being pessimistic here, but even neutral feels like a long shot."

"I hear you; I do," said Sue. "But remember, the past has already happened. It's the effect it's having on you in the present that is relevant and will either serve you or not. You can't change what happened, only how you feel about it, and in essence, that is what will make a difference. Remember it could all be a part of a bigger plan, even if you can't see it right now."

I looked at the Ace of Pentacles, desperately wanting to be free from the angst and to surrender my ticket for the emotional rollercoaster. Was Sue giving me some life-changing wisdom here? My ego was in so much resistance that buying into the concept that this was in some way meant to happen would feel like I had to let Jay get away with it and, even worse, be some crazy shade of gratitude. Hanging on to resentment and a feeling of *fuck you* felt justified and ridiculously noble. I didn't actually want to let go of that yet, even though I believed it was in my best interests.

Incongruence – come on in and pull up a seat.

"There are parts of me that want to stay mad at him, and I want him to get some kind of punishment for what's happened. I feel like a bad person for saying it out loud, but it's the truth," I admitted.

"Of course you feel that way, you're human. And you haven't started to dig in and do the work yet, love, so don't beat yourself up." Sue turned the last card and started beaming. "The Empress. This card is about your feminine power and abundance, a connection with nature and nurturance. It has a strong connection to Mother Earth and encourages you to connect more with her, spend time in her beauty and give gratitude for her bounty. It's a card that can also lean towards a more literal sense of the word Mother and can indicate a pregnancy."

I looked up from my empty cup and laughed. "You know that can't happen, though, right? Damien's treatment and my age, seriously, Sue, that would be a miracle."

"I'm just telling you what the cards say," she said through her smile. "Have you been feeling any different?"

"Of course I've been feeling different. I've been worried to death and knackered because I'm being blackmailed and living some kind of weird double life where I'm apparently a liar and a thief."

"I know that, but I mean other kinds of different. Like pregnant different?"

"No, I don't think so. That would never cross my mind. The doctors told us there was a minuscule chance of us ever having another child, so we wrote it off and got on with life. It's not something I'd give any thought or consideration to now."

"Oh well, maybe it's just saying you need to connect with nature more and get more grounded." She said and smiled coyly before gathering up the cards and asking me to promise that I'd consider things could, in some way, be unfolding in my favour.

I said I'd try, but deep down, I thought it was going to be

both impossible and unfair. I knew this was about releasing me and had nothing to do with him. She wished me well and hugged me tight.

"Let me know how you get on, love," she said and I knew she meant the bigger picture stuff but specifically any pregnancy news, of which there is none and will be none and that's that.

STEPHANIE'S JOURNAL – LESSON 30
THE LAW OF DIVINE ORDER

*I trust that life is bigger than I can see. I trust that there is a
Divine Order beyond my control. And I trust that no matter
what happens I will be all right. ~ Oprah Winfrey*

This Universal Law states that everything and everyone exists
in perfect time and order, as directed by an Infinite Intelligence,
Source or Creator. It invites you to consider the existence of an
ever-present energy that helps sustain life in all ways in The
Universe.

Divine Order is present in beautiful and challenging
situations, in the pain and the pleasure and everything in
between. It's there in the mess and the messages, the joy and
the heartbreak. It gives us the best opportunities to become the
greatest versions of ourselves, and often in ways that we can't
possibly recognise when they are playing out. These moments
forge who we are becoming, and how we experience, process,
and integrate them reveals layers of self that we otherwise
would never have been able to access. By trusting in a Divine
Order, we are accepting that in every moment we are
experiencing what we need.

This does not mean we don't have free will as humans, but
throughout all our lessons, the following of our heart and
intuition, our growth and evolution and life experiences, The
Law of Divine Order could be working for our soul's Highest
Good.

The devastating divorce that taught you about resilience, the
financial loss that taught you to value people in your life more,
or the diagnosis that made you live for the moment and find
true joy and gratitude could all be examples of Divine Order
helping you behind the scenes in ways that you may not
immediately recognise. It's about trusting that you are in the

right place at the right time, even when it doesn't feel that way.

This is probably the hardest Universal Law for humans to accept and work with when we are facing difficulty and adversity, but after the storm, it can be both healing and helpful to reflect on what you have gained even in the darkest days and how The Law of Divine Order may have been serving you throughout.

CHAPTER 33

I stopped at the supermarket on the way home and bough the essentials, including a blueberry muffin, which was essential as I'd had no breakfast. Toothpaste and toilet rolls went into the basket, and then the pregnancy tests caught my eye. A double pack for less than a fiver, and I only needed one to dissolve the little niggle Sue had created. I could send her a picture of the negative test and go back to dragging myself through my current camper van dilemma. Peace of mind for five pounds was worth it.

Once home, I put the kettle on and settled down to write for a couple of hours before the school run, thinking that perhaps there was some merit in what Sue said about releasing myself from the past. Jay had taken way more than enough from me, and to let him have the present moment as well felt like the final insult. But to get my power back from him and the past, I had to find a way to release it, and fast. If this was the block between me manifesting what I wanted and needed, there was no question I had to find a way.

I started to write, and before I knew it, the reminder alarm was bleeping on my phone to tell me to get ready to leave. Stretching and looking at the word count, I knew the time was coming when I'd have to come clean to the agency about the subject matter. Tentatively, I drafted an email and attached the in-progress draft, explaining that I'd gone off the agreed topic but it hadn't been deliberate.

Before I put on my jacket, I nipped to the toilet and remembered the pregnancy tests. Better get that put to bed right now. I had bigger fish to fry, which included thinking of some kind of emotional enema that would flush any thoughts and feelings about Jay down the psychological u-bend as fast as I could.

I did the necessary and laid the test on the cistern as I washed my hands and breathed in to fasten my jeans. I should have gone for an apple instead of the muffin. Right – time to go. Mel would be waiting for me and it looked like it might rain. I wondered if the umbrella was still in the boot of the car as I picked the test up to throw it away, and there it was. The result.

I hadn't even read the instructions, so I had to dash back into the kitchen and get the box out of the bin. The tiniest writing on the reverse side, along with a picture, told me the news. Why didn't they make it easy for people? I blinked and blinked again. The picture showed two clear lines and underneath it was the word Pregnant. I went back to the bathroom and looked at the test – two lines.

Was this a false positive or something? Even the contraceptive pill was only ninety-seven percent effective; medical things were not completely bullet proof.

The alarm sounded on my phone again, telling me I had to leave, and I shoved the test in my pocket. If I didn't go now, I'd get stuck in the traffic and miss my parking space. I needed a reality check, surely? I was worried about a parking space when I had a positive pregnancy test in my pocket. A false positive, of course, because otherwise that would be, what exactly?

A miracle.

I'd written off any thoughts of having another child and so had Damien. We had both cried over it. Of course we wanted Mia to have a brother or sister and we wanted another baby for us too, but fate had intervened, and we'd accepted that what we had was more than enough and always would be. If I was honest with myself, there had been grief, but in the aftermath of Damien's treatment and him surviving the fight of his life, I just got on with it. Life showed me what mattered, and I was immensely grateful to still have him. Wishing for any more at that time felt somehow greedy.

The radio played in the background, the traffic hummed and the rain started to fall. I'd allowed myself to visit the land of What-If; feelings and desires I'd buried deep were surfacing. As I pulled up to the kerb and saw Mel waving, I burst into tears.

After a few minutes, I managed to tell her that I had a false positive on a pregnancy test and it had brought up a whole load of stuff related to Damien being ill and not being able to have another child. She listened and hugged me and held me at arm's length.

"You silly moo, Steph," she said through tears of her own. "You can't get a false positive."

"What do you mean? Of course you can." I shook my head in denial and disbelief.

"No, you can't. You're pregnant." Mel laughed. "You're actually pregnant."

"But I can't be!" I said and cried some more.

What the actual...?

"Have you got the test?" Mel asked and I produced it from my back pocket. She squinted at it for a couple of seconds and congratulated me. She asked me when my last period was and I couldn't tell her, and then I started to think about being overly tired and emotional. I'd definitely gained a little weight, but I hadn't been able to eat much at all due to feeling anxious and – yeah, sickly.

Oh my actual god.

"But they told us that after Damien's treatment, it would be very unlikely we would have another child. They even gave us leaflets about it and said they could refer us for counselling." I could hear myself speaking but felt like I wasn't present. If this was true, then how many weeks could I be? And what would Damien say? Mia was going to be a big sister. It was all feeling very overwhelming.

"You need to get an appointment with the midwife," piped up Mel.

"I need to tell Damien first!" I said and managed a weak smile. My hands naturally moved towards my stomach and I looked down at them. Within the next couple of months, I'd have a bump. A miracle baby was growing inside of me, and as I tentatively allowed the idea to settle in, happiness started to fill me up. The Universe was blessing us again, and nothing else mattered.

CHAPTER 34

Damien came through the door just as it was getting dark and kissed me on the cheek.

"How was your day, love?" he asked, as he always did. "And what are we eating? I'm starving!"

"It's been a strange day, to say the least." I took his hand, led him into the kitchen, and poured him a glass of wine. "We've got something to celebrate!"

"Have we now?" he looked at me quizzically. "News about the book?"

"No, better than that. Try again," I said, and he took a sip.

"Where's yours?" he asked, and I smiled. The penny hadn't dropped.

"I'm not drinking, but I'll raise a glass of this." I'd poured some sparkling water and added a dash of elderflower cordial, pretend prosecco.

"You aren't on another bloody detox thing, are you, Steph? Last time it wiped you out and you've been knackered and all fainty and distracted as it is. Just have some wine, for god's sake. I'm not going to have the whole bottle on my own; it's a weeknight." He sipped again.

"No, it's not a detox and it's not the book. Damien it's bigger and better than that and something you would probably never guess, so I'll tell you." I reached into my back pocket and put the positive pregnancy test on the table between us.

He caught his breath and sat perfectly still.

When he spoke, his voice was thick with emotion and I knew this was one of the rare occasions when my husband would cry.

"Are you sure?" he asked me, lifting his gaze from the table top and looking deep into my eyes.

He was going through what I had a couple of hours ago, afraid to step into hope and excitement because it couldn't possibly be true, or could it?

"I'm sure." I took his hands in mine and together we wept the happiest of tears, in our own private bubble of joy. A heart wish that had been taken from us both was now being granted, and life felt like it was smiling on us again, finally.

CHAPTER 35

That night in bed I felt closer to Damien than I had for months. As he started to drift towards sleep, I spooned into him and kissed the back of his neck, whispering goodnight. We'd agreed that I'd contact the midwife first thing and ask for a scan as soon as possible. I was guessing that I might be around ten weeks, but I couldn't be sure. There was an unspoken undercurrent between us. We were both waiting to hear that everything was alright and the baby looked healthy.

Turning over to set the alarm for the morning, I reached for my phone, hoping that I was nearing twelve weeks. When I was expecting Mia, I can remember suddenly feeling human again as the tiredness and nausea lifted at three months.

The message that was waiting for me choked all of my happy away in a blink.

I NEED ANOTHER MEET-UP. I NEED MORE.

No, no, no - this couldn't be happening.

I'd earned my new start and there was no way I could get any more money for Jay. I hadn't even worked out how I was going to get myself out of the mess I was in over the first twenty thousand, never mind risking taking any more. I didn't open the message, so it remained unread at his end.

Sitting on the edge of the bed in the dark with my heart pounding, trying to control my breathing so Damien didn't wake up, and another message lit up the screen, a picture this time. Were there pictures I hadn't seen yet? Could they be worse than the ones he'd already shown me? Was he saving the best for last?

Beads of sweat were gathering on my brow and I reached for the glass of water at my bedside. My hand was shaking, and I put the glass straight back down without daring to bring it to my lips. There was no way I'd be able to sleep now. I desperately wanted to open the picture he'd sent but knew it could crucify me. I didn't want him to know I was still awake by marking the messages as read, in case he sent more or perhaps felt like he was in control of me by waking me up late at night and scaring me. Both of which were true, of course.

What if I opened it and looked? Then I'd decide what to do. I wasn't going to sleep anyway, maybe it wasn't even that bad, perhaps I was overthinking this and maybe it wasn't a picture of me looking like a sex slave or a hooker after all.

Dream on, Steph.

I clicked, and at first there was relief. There was no bare skin, no compromising positions, and no sign of me at all. I breathed out slowly and closed my eyes. Then I looked harder, it was difficult to see the detail, the picture was dark and grainy. I tapped and zoomed in, then gasped and dropped the phone altogether. Damien stirred as I stood up and walked to the window, carefully peering out of the blinds at the taxi parked diagonally opposite my front door, the same front door in the picture I'd just opened and the same front door I'd hoped and prayed he would never find.

I heard the taxi's engine start and could see the headlights passing slowly as I stood statue-still. Yet again he had me cornered.

CHAPTER 36

"Steph, you look really tired, love. Do you want me to do the school run?" Damien said as I passed him a coffee at seven the next morning. "Didn't you sleep well? You could come back to bed and I'll take Mia."

I hadn't slept at all. I was exhausted but wired with anxiety.

"Do you mind?" I asked through a cloud of nausea and guilt. Damien was being a supportive husband and helping me because I was pregnant with his baby and he was a good person. Yet, I needed help because I'd been up all night trying to hatch a plan to cover up several layers of lies and betrayal that would break him.

Whatever happened to fair exchange?

"Not at all, love. You have to rest and look after yourself and baby." He sat up and stretched then made his way to the shower. "Anyway, you've got to call the surgery this morning and they might have an early appointment."

A message from Sue lit up my phone, simply a question mark. I replied with 'Yes!' and a heart emoji, and she sent back a row of happy faces in return. She'd said that things were going to be revealed within the next few weeks and I had no control over it all coming out, and even though I'd heard her and agreed in the moment, right now, I still felt like I'd do anything to stop that from happening. Maybe this would be one of those rare occasions she gets it wrong.

There was nothing more from Jay. Perhaps he was working a night shift last night and was still in bed. Maybe I had no option but to tell Damien the truth. Surely he wouldn't leave me now I was pregnant?

Who was I becoming?

Was I really willing to use our unborn baby as leverage to make Damien put up with my devastating behaviour? No, I could never do that, but I was desperate - really desperate now. I wondered if the police would have to uphold confidentiality in my favour if I went to them. I had no idea how any of this worked, and by calling them up and asking, I was spilling the beans anyway. They weren't going to believe the 'asking for a friend' thing, and they could trace phone numbers. Maybe they would end up knocking on the door regardless.

I couldn't think clearly and needed to be objective now more than ever. I'd text Lizzie for her advice. She might even know the answer to the police question. She replied straight away and said that I shouldn't engage any more; he'd had a big pay-off, and if I gave him more, this would give him the green light to keep coming back for more and I'd never be rid of him.

In the cold light of day, it felt like the right action to take, but of course, it wasn't the dead of night and he wasn't sitting outside my house in his taxi. Things feel very different in a moment like that.

Lizzie suggested blocking his number so that any texts he sent came back to him as undelivered. That way, he'd get the message there were no further negotiations. Fine in theory, but deep down I couldn't. Who was to say that he wouldn't approach me in the school yard or come to the house? Of course I *wanted* to block him, but not just from my phone. I wanted to block him from my whole life.

Damien popped his head around the bedroom door and said goodbye, told me to rest up, and said that he loved me. I said it back and swallowed my tears.

My phone pinged and I opened it to see Lizzie's response. But it wasn't from Lizzie.

The message was simply a question mark from Jay.

I didn't open the message, instead I ran to the bathroom and retched.

A warm shower and a piece of toast later and I was starting to feel slightly more human. Lizzie was right, if I gave Jay more money now, this would be the way of things and I'd be forever paying out, forever trapped. Emotionally, though, it felt like the slowest-ever ascension on the world's most scary rollercoaster, and I wasn't buckled in. The white-knuckle ride of my life might be to ignore him, I was hanging on and feeling every single mechanical click as he turned the screws tighter and tighter, waiting to get to the top and then fall off the edge. I just needed to take one day at a time and not respond, even one hour at a time if I had to. The ride would come to an end at some point. He'd get the hint and leave me alone.

I'd hardly thought about being pregnant. I remembered the joy and excitement of expecting Mia and although I felt that now, it was so overshadowed by Jay. That's not what this baby deserved, it was a miracle and would be loved and adored and I wanted to feel that happy anticipation and the bond between Damien and I growing along with my bump. Jay's toxicity was seeping into everything and contaminating every part of my life, stealing even the happiest moments.

My phone pinged and I jumped. Jeez! Incoming message from Ryan. This was probably about an imminent get-together that I was dreading because I'd have to eke out the lie of not having found a camper van yet, and well-meaning Ryan would be all over it so he could stop me from getting ripped off.

Far too late for that.

I opened the message to a garbled and cryptic couple of lines that didn't make sense about hoping I was ok and wanting to check in this morning. Jenny was their social secretary. This felt weird. I texted back 'ok', and within moments, the phone rang. He was overly pleasant and clearly building up to something. I didn't like this...

"So, erm, I couldn't really say this in a text, Steph, and I'm really uncomfortable saying it at all, to be honest," he said as he finally cut to the chase.

"Oh?" I asked, as my heart rate started increasing.

"Damien has been into the bank this morning in a hell of a state. Luckily I was in the branch and he asked for me, but Steph, it's not great."

"What's happened, Ryan?" My mouth was dry and I cleared my throat.

"He noticed that twenty thousand had been withdrawn from your joint savings account, and he was really confused that you hadn't told him about it. He was a bit panicked really, anxious and wound up. I told him that it's a joint account and the bank can't stop either of you from taking money out or paying it in, unless you have it set up for two signatures, but you two didn't want that."

"What did he say?" I asked, feeling fear creeping up my neck.

"He said that you would have told him if you were taking anything out of there, that you'd agreed not to touch it and it was your nest egg for the future. Steph, it was so awkward. I love you two to bits, you know that, but I could get fired for breaching confidentiality."

"But you didn't, though, so it's ok." I couldn't bear to think that my mess would have such a devastating ripple effect on someone else. "I'll take any responsibility for this that you need me to, Ryan. Please don't worry about that. You're right that it's our money and either of us can take whatever we want. The personal obligation we have to tell each other is out of your control."

"Yes, yes, you're right." He sighed, and I could hear him pacing around his office, the office I'd sat in whilst lying to his face. "But there's more, and I'm so sorry."

"What do you mean, more?" I asked, closing my eyes and saying a silent prayer.

"He was so worried, and I seriously thought he might start

to cry, he kept asking me if I was sure that you took the money. I had to fess up and say that not only was it you, it was me who authorised it. There was no point in lying; it's all logged on the system. If he asked to see the detailed records of the transactions, it's easy to prove what happened."

I could hear his voice but not the words. Damien had looked like he was going to cry. I knew it had nothing to do with the amount of money that had been withdrawn but everything to do with me lying. Maybe this was the beginning of The Tower moment that Sue saw in my cards. It sure felt like things were about to come crashing down around me and I'd have no way of limiting the fallout.

"So I had to tell him about the camper van, Steph, and I'm so sorry," Ryan said. "I know I've ruined the surprise and I've betrayed your trust as a client and even worse as a friend, but I felt like I had no choice. I kept saying that he needed to ask you what the money was for and I tried to get him to call you, but he was just so upset and confused. I had to give him something, and it just came out. I'm so, so sorry. I know I've messed up."

"It's ok, Ryan. It's my fault for lying," I said, choking on my words.

"Surprising someone isn't lying, it's a nice thing to do, and I'm sorry if I just ruined it for you I feel terrible. I can hear how upset you are."

"Don't feel bad, honestly. It's my fault for being all cloak and dagger about it. I didn't think it through properly. Of course Damien would see the transactions in that account. I thought I'd get away with it."

"You're making it sound like you stole it, Steph! There's no getting away with it; that was and is your own money, and you took it to do something lovely with." Ryan was trying to make things feel lighter, and in a way, he had. In essence, not that much had changed. I still needed to produce the money and put it back with a story of being unable to find exactly what I was looking for, or I had to produce the goods. That was always the case and the clock had always been ticking. The only difference now was that Damien knew.

"What did he say?" I asked, wiping tears from my face onto my sleeve.

"Once he calmed down he was made up, and if I'm honest, I think he felt pretty bad about it, so I wouldn't be expecting him to ask any questions. I told him you wanted to have a big reveal and make it a surprise, so I doubt he'll mention anything. In fact, by the time he left, he was quite happy and we'd talked a bit about the spec he'd really like, and he asked me to drop some hints in your direction. He said he'd send me some screenshots of ones he likes so I could steer you towards them if possible."

"Oh ok," I said, trying to sound upbeat, although I wanted to wrap this up asap so I could either puke or cry properly.

"So hopefully, all's well that ends well and he won't let on that he knows and neither will you, and this conversation didn't happen, right?"

"Right."

"I just thought I should let you know because honesty is the best policy and all that."

"Yes, definitely," I superficially agreed.

"Great, and if you want any help, you know where I am. Catch you later, Steph." He hung up and I sat with my head in my hands feeling absolutely shell-shocked. I knew time was running out, but I hadn't anticipated this. My phone lit up with a series of picture messages from Ryan, and I wanted the world to swallow me up. There might be no way out of this now apart from telling Damien the truth – the truth that I should have told him on that fateful day when I walked the walk of shame up our garden path.

My lies were drowning me more and more; my options had all but dried up, and any hope was evaporating with them.

That night, Damien came home with roses and hugged me tight. "I love you," he said and I burst into tears, for the second time that day.

"I'm sorry, it's my hormones," I said and busied myself looking for a vase.

He didn't mention the money and neither did I. The elephant in the room sat with us until bedtime and then followed us upstairs. I guessed it was going to be around for a while, at least long enough for me to either navigate through this or the shit to hit the fan.

CHAPTER 37

The following day in the schoolyard, Mel was asking me about scans and dates and baby names when Beth arrived with Rosie. They were talking loudly about how happy she was and that she hoped it would be next summer. I was sure they were both acting out the scene solely for my benefit as Beth presented her left hand to Rosie with a flourish, and Rosie theatrically held it out to catch the light. The diamond glistened, and the carat and the cut were mentioned, and, of course, the cost. Mel looked at me sympathetically, but she didn't know the half of it.

"You've got way more than her, Steph," she said, and I agreed in part, but then also thought about the fact that she was wearing five grand of my money on her left hand. A tiny little love bomb that might end up marking the beginning of her marriage and the end of mine.

"I don't want more than her. I just want them to piss off and stop rubbing my nose in it. I'm not jealous of her. It's not about the ring or the relationship, it's about him hanging around and being all in my face. It's suffocating and infuriating. I know he's a bastard and he's set me up to look like a psycho if I mention anything."

"Beth can't see it yet, though, it's not really her fault." Mel tried to be the voice of reason but I was having none of it.

"I tried to warn her, and she wouldn't listen, so that's on her. No one tried to warn me, and if they had, I'd have run a mile," I said confidently.

"Really?" Mel asked. "Come on now, Steph, it's shit but from what you've told me about him and the way he operates, it's not really her fault. She could be more sensitive to your feelings, though, and she certainly doesn't need to show off like that. It's kind of ugly."

"It's because she needs validation and significance. Her last relationship broke her and she's being tricked into thinking this is different. Narcissists go after people exactly like her and make them feel amazing to lure them in and trap them. She's showing off because she's got no self-worth to speak of."

"Ouch, that's judgy," Mel said.

"It's also the truth," I replied. "I know this because I was one of those people."

"Anyway, you've got more exciting things to focus on, like the scan. Are you going to wait until after that to tell Mia she's going to be a big sister?" Like a good friend, Mel was trying to deflect and change the subject.

"Yes, I think so. I hope she's made up and happy about it. We've always told her she would be an only child."

"I bet she'll be delighted. It's such an exciting time for you all. Is Damien happy?" Mel asked.

"Yes, after the initial shock. He's really happy, we both are." I could still hear Beth and Rosie giving it large about Mr and Mrs in the background. For Jay to spend my money on that ring and then ask me for more was a complete outrage.

The bell rang and the kids lined up. Mia was too busy talking to return my wave and I watched her walk into the building, wondering if this baby would look like her.

I felt my phone vibrate and sucked in a sharp breath of cold air. It was a picture message from Ryan and then three moving dots as he typed underneath.

YOU CAN TELL ME TO BUGGER OFF BUT I SAW THIS AND I KNOW IT'S EXACTLY THE ONE THAT DAMO WANTS AND ITS ONLY £21,000 – I MESSAGED THE SELLER AND THEY SAID THEY WOULD TAKE £20,000 FOR A QUICK SALE BECAUSE THEY ARE EMIGRATING, IT'S EVEN THE RIGHT COLOUR..... SO I PUT A DEPOSIT ON IT. IF YOU DON'T WANT IT I'LL ONLY LOSE FIFTY

QUID SO I THOUGHT I'D CHANCE IT, I CAN GO TONIGHT TO SEE IT WITH YOU IF YOU WANT ME TO? SMILEY FACE AND CAMPER VAN EMOJI.

I had no idea how to respond. I typed back that I was on the school run and I'd text later. How was I going to get out of this? I couldn't exactly say no I wasn't going. That would look really sketchy, but if I said yes and went along, that would be worse. I was literally in a no-win situation and needed to think fast. Maybe I could tell him I was pregnant and not feeling well. But then he would probably be lovely and understanding and say that he would go and have a look on my behalf, and I'd still be in the shit. Either way, he was going to see the van, with or without me, and it was going to be perfect.

After a couple of texts, we agreed to meet in Ryan's lunch break, and he sent me the address. I'd head home and do some research on Google, so I knew what to nit-pick about.

Another single question mark arrived from Jay.

I wanted to throw my phone out of the window. Was I doing the right thing by ignoring him?

Driving up our street used to fill me with such joy and happiness; the tree-lined road was beautiful and a nod to each season in turn. But now I found myself scanning left and right for a parked cab with my ex in the driving seat. I lived in a world of hypervigilance and checking. To say this had gone way too far was the understatement of the century. I briefly considered going to the police again and then reined the thought back in. I'd got this far, and if I ignored him, surely he would get the message and fuck all the way off, wouldn't he?

I double-locked the front door behind me and made my way upstairs. I typed 'VW Transporter Van' into the search bar and a million hits came up. After a few minutes and referencing Ryan's messages, I started searching the interior specifications. People had pull-out beds, televisions, cooking areas and more.

It seemed like nothing ignited a man's creativity like the inside of a van. Scrolling through different examples, I saw that people had even uploaded their bespoke plans to download and use; this was a whole new world. I was actually finding myself warming up to becoming a van owner when an email dropped in and brought me back to the now.

It was from my writing agent and the subject line was 'New Book Concept'. I hardly dared to open it; my life depended on it now. If they liked it and I finished it in double quick time, perhaps it would be on sale within the next six months, and the ebook could be even sooner. If I could tread water about the camper van until then, there might be a chance that I'd have money to squirrel away, money that I could produce later. I could tell Damien it would be better to wait because we wouldn't get any use out of it with a newborn, and it would depreciate while it was parked up. Much better to wait, surely? And what was the point in moving the money back into our savings account? The interest rate was terrible and it didn't matter where it was. It was all our money, after all?

What happened to no more lies?

Bad news would certainly impact any tower moment. I took a breath, clenched, and clicked. The email simply read, 'Steph, it's brilliant, keep going'.

I smiled from ear to ear and shook my head in disbelief. I was onto something here and a good job as well because there was no way I could stop writing now, regardless. I hoped this meant I was releasing resistance to opening future possibilities too.

Camper vans, money – stuff like that.

I knew that if I could think and feel differently, I would have a chance at being able to align with different outcomes, but the fear was so real and sometimes its grip was so relentless it choked me. I couldn't meditate or get into my happy place on the regular, *I was camped out right next to Shit Creek and it could burst its banks any day now and take me with it.*

The good news from my agent made me feel amazing briefly. Happiness faded to panic when I thought about the book being a bestseller. If I experienced more success, it would be like a lighthouse guiding him to me again, and although I was surrounded by an ocean of fear, I couldn't let it stop me from finishing the first draft.

I went back to the thought of changing how I felt about him. I was consciously aware that this would be a massive win for me, so why couldn't I do it? I sat with this question for a while, and the first thing I noticed was that I didn't even *want* to try. I was resistant to even considering feeling different, even though I knew it would help me and have no bearing on him. Interesting and infuriating at the same time.

I want to hate him.

I wanted to stay in this energy; it felt justified and was mine to keep hold of. There was ownership here, and a strong one, too. A misplaced righteousness and a feeling of entitlement, like I'd earned the right to experience this and I was going to hang on tight.

Where was this self-sabotage coming from?

A childhood memory flashed through my awareness. I was probably around twelve years old. Mum and I curled up on the couch one Christmas Eve, watching a movie while Dad was out at his work's party. We'd made hot chocolate and put on our new pyjamas, and just as the opening scene began, a key turned in the front door.

Dad came into the room saying that Barry from accounts had too many drinks and called him lazy. Everyone had burst out laughing and joined in, poking fun at him and making him feel like the butt of the joke. He'd laughed it off as best he could and then slinked off unnoticed and made his way home. No one would remember it in the days and weeks that followed, apart from Dad.

That was it for work gatherings. We missed out on summer barbeques and day trips to the coast that the company funded every year. There was no talking him out of it, even though Mum tried. He clung tight to what Barry had said, how it had wounded and humiliated him and the fact that he would never get the chance to do it again.

When Dad retired, the company put on a surprise after-work gathering. Mum and I were sworn to secrecy, both feeling compromised and disloyal, as well as worried about how he might react. Mum wanted to tell him it was happening but thought that he might not turn up, and Barry had organised a whip round and bought a gold watch to celebrate his long service.

I remembered getting dressed up and a taxi picking us up, then being sneaked into the board room with a load of excited employees and a buffet table laden with sandwiches and quiche.

"Shhh, he's coming!" someone whispered and silence fell in the darkness. Party poppers were at the ready and someone was ready with Cliff Richard singing 'Congratulations' on a cassette. Mum and I had sweaty palms and remained as clenched as we did quiet. We stole a sideways glance and it was clear we were both thinking the same thing.

The lights went on, the music started and the poppers popped.

Dad looked around and we could tell he was overwhelmed. He even started to cry as colleagues patted him on the back and shook his hand. The CEO picked up a glass and toasted his good health and retirement as Dad grinned from ear to ear. He seemed genuinely happy, and when Barry approached him to shake his hand, Dad opened his arms and hugged the bloke instead. We were too far away to hear what was being said over the music, but later we learned that Dad had said it was time to really put his feet up and *really be lazy* and Barry had looked confused. Dad reminded him light-heartedly about the quip that he'd made years ago, finally getting it off his chest.

We didn't hear Barry's reply, but I do clearly remember watching from a distance and seeing him step back and rub his forehead, then shrug. He stepped forward again and held Dad's shoulders in his hands and spoke directly to him. Then Dad hung his head and Barry patted him on the back two or maybe three times before he walked away, shaking his head. Dad sighed and shook his head too. Then, he was engulfed by more well-wishers, and a glass was thrust in his hand.

"What do you think Barry said?" I'd asked Mum.

"I don't know, love, but my sense is that there was something in there about your dad hanging on to bad feelings for far too long and us all missing out as a result." Mum was handed a drink and so was I, and we joined Dad in toasting his milestone moment. Barry was only ever mentioned once after that day by Dad and it was in the context of him being a good bloke, and simply that.

I sat with the memory a little longer and let myself feel into it. Right now, Jay was my Barry. Yes, what he had done was way more harmful, of course, but the essence was there. Someone had done something to me and I had reacted in an appropriate way at the time, but I was hanging on to it and maintaining it in different ways. It was normal to feel fear, anger, guilt and self-reproach in the moment and the aftermath too. Being human lends itself perfectly to that, and we have access to a full range of emotions. I was, however, hanging on to aspects that were contaminating my present. Maybe I wouldn't be able to release it all, but I could at least try to look at it objectively and see if there was anything I could do to help myself.

And just like that, a wave of resistance hit me. Why should I? He's a poisonous human being and he deserves my hatred and anger. He's trying to pull me down and take everything from me. Not a single part of me wants to feel any different about him.

And there it was, the key - my own reluctance to change.

Ever since I'd woken up in Jay's apartment, I'd been burdened with the crippling weight of not feeling good enough. I'd left the small amount of self-worth I still owned in his taxi before I entered the building.

I closed my eyes and took a breath, allowing the feelings to come into the present. My throat tightened and the tears started to flow, but tears of what exactly? Anger, blame, and, wait a minute – was that pity? I tried not to fight it; I'd messed up, but there was absolutely no way I'd intended to.

I was intoxicated, got carried away and had forgotten myself in a pocket of time that was held forever in my memory. I had a choice to attach a meaning to it, and so far, the meaning I'd given it was that I was a complete letdown and totally unworthy of Damien and his love for me. But was that the truth? And which truth mattered? Right now, the only truth that held any weight was my own, and I could change my truth as fast as I could change the meaning I was holding on to.

I wasn't unworthy. I made a mistake.

I'd been triggered and goaded, and I was drunk, but I was not a bad person, and I had not done any of this deliberately. In addition to this, my running back to Jay and feeling like I desperately wanted a connection with him was a result of the abuse I'd lived through. Thanks to Robin, I understood now that I'd lived in a weird and manipulated reality that had isolated me and made me behave in ways that were adapted to my toxic environment, an environment that was carefully stage-managed by Jay to keep me under control and make me feel small.

Throughout our whole relationship, I'd craved the love and connection he showered me with initially. He'd love bombed me into feeling like I was living a fairy tale – when he started to withhold the thing I wanted most, I worked hard to get it back, albeit briefly, and just enough to condition me to think that maybe one day it would last.

That night, when I went back to his apartment, I was vulnerable. The old wounds had not fully healed, and how could they? I hadn't known the extent of the calculated and strategic emotional abuse I'd been through, and when he turned on the charm and said everything I'd wanted to hear, my defences crumbled. As we kissed, a rush of emotion and lust ignited the touch paper, and there was no going back. Like an addict who'd taken a drop, I couldn't stop. I was on a sex and serotonin high that I couldn't fight, and he knew it.

I could see now that I'd been conditioned to respond to any kind of attention from him in this way. He used control and manipulation to make me feel worthless and then he'd throw me a scrap of affection which he knew I needed. I'd work hard for more, scratching around for shreds of self-worth in every interaction. People-pleasing, degrading myself in the bedroom by doing things I didn't want to, cooking the best food ever and not seeing my friends and family. While I was in this mode, things were usually good. I was rewarded with more affection and attention and so the cycle played out until he switched to phase two and the drama started, of course.

I could see why and how I'd ended up at Jay's apartment that night and how it had played out. I'd also believed that Damien might have been cheating on me, creating the perfect emotional storm. The combination of circumstances all came together in one moment and overwhelmed me, triggered me and dredged up a heap of past pain and programming. I was to blame for what happened. But in truth, was there ever going to be a different outcome?

I sat with the sadness. This was a completely different feeling from the guilt, shame and self-reproach I had been carrying. Still uncomfortable but easier to bear. I needed to let go of the energetic charge around this and the horrible feelings that had been eating me up all this time. I might even be able to let go of their frequency and shift my point of attraction – lesson one was Be Open to Possibility, after all, and in this exact moment, I felt like I could.

I stretched and felt a flutter in my stomach that caught me by surprise. I'd forgotten the fizzy feeling in early pregnancy when you first start to detect movement, so subtle, like a butterfly gently moving its wings. My hand rested on my soon-to-be bump and I smiled. Things felt lighter and more hopeful, until I remembered I had to meet Ryan.

STEPHANIE'S JOURNAL – LESSON 31
YOU ARE NOT YOUR MISTAKES

You make mistakes, mistakes don't make you.
~ Maxwell Maltz

We are all prone to behave, at times, in ways that we regret, and we refer to this as making mistakes – newsflash, humans are fallible and we *all* make mistakes. It's an unavoidable fact of life.

Mistakes, however, should be considered along with context. The way we behave is driven by how we feel at that time. If we are tired, scared, stressed, jealous or wounded we will behave differently to the way we would if we were calm, centred, loved, happy and relaxed.

We are all in essence doing a version of our best in that exact moment. Although our behaviour is of course our responsibility, mistakes do not define who we are as a person.

Mistakes are made in the moment, within context. If you feel like you made a mistake, step back and look at the bigger picture.

Based on everything that was going on and how you were feeling at that time, could you have really done anything differently? Maybe the mistake was inevitable? Or perhaps the odds were stacked against you, you acted unconsciously, or you were scared. There will be reasons for the mistake, and once you have defined them you can perhaps be kinder to yourself and see this as being human. It's unproductive to allow this moment in time or period in your life to define you, see it instead as an opportunity to learn.

You are *who* you are, not what you did.

Please learn, forgive yourself, make amends and move on.

CHAPTER 38

I drove to the address Ryan had sent me, with no idea how I was going to pull this off. He was already in dialogue with the seller, and I felt like I was watching an episode of someone else's life. I walked over to them, mentally kicking myself for showing up at all and wondering why I hadn't sent a text saying I couldn't make it. I'd set myself up for the most embarrassing and ridiculous face-to-face scenario with this really nice man who needed to sell his van, and I had no money to buy it.

"Steph, this is Jack. He's *American!*" Ryan said enthusiastically and Jack stretched his hand out to shake mine.

"Nice to meet you," I mumbled through a fake smile, hoping he wouldn't hate me for what was about to happen.

"You too," said Jack, smiling back. His was genuine. He radiated a kindness and peace that made me kick myself even more as he went into an explanation of needing to sell the van because he was travelling back to the United States to start a new chapter of his life with a woman he believed to be the love of his life.

"It's one of those small world stories, to be honest," he said whilst leaning against the bonnet. "If I hadn't moved out here, our paths would have ended up crossing at some point over there, I'm sure, but the timing wasn't right on either side."

"Oh?" I asked, not just to buy time but to find out more.

"Seven years ago I came here to start over after a nasty breakup. I lived with my brother and his family for about a year while I got myself together - never with the intention of staying, but life just rumbles by and I was kind of coming around to it when my brother and I got word that a great aunt had passed away. We flew back home and after he returned to be with his family, I stayed on for another week, and that's when I met her. Not for the first time either. Once we got talking, we realised we'd been like ships in the night for years. Turns out that Gail and I had been moving in and out of the same circles but never truly connected because, of course, we were both married."

"And she wasn't married then?" I asked as Ryan circled the van.

"No, she'd been through a messy divorce the year before, so we were both footloose and fancy-free." Jack smiled. Even though he was of retirement age, there was a twinkle in his eye that you'd see in a young buck. "And the rest is history."

"Was it love at first sight?" I asked, thinking back to destiny connecting Damien and I at Prospect House and that feeling of knowing when someone is the one.

"I'd say so, and I think that we were probably always meant to be together; it was just a timing thing. We weren't ready for each other until we were ready for each other if you catch my drift. We had stuff that we needed to learn about life and ourselves so we could have something amazing. I guess I'm saying I'm a great believer that you need to find yourself first." Jack smiled at me again and I smiled back.

"Steph, it's perfect," Ryan shouted from inside the van and the moment was gone. "It's exactly the spec that Damien would want and the paperwork is all in order." He climbed out and stood back, admiring the black, shiny paint job and silver wheels. "You've done a great job here, Jack. She's a beauty."

"Thanks, it's been a labour of love for sure and we've only been able to take one real trip in her, but I have to say she drives like a dream."

"Where did you go?" Ryan asked, "I'm always looking for new places to adventure."

"You've got a van?" Jack asked.

"Yeah, but not as classy as this. My mate will be winning at life if the Mrs goes for it." He laughed and nodded in my direction.

"Van life, man, it's the way forward. So much freedom on the road. Gail was here in the spring and we toured Scotland for two weeks. It was breathtaking."

"Don't say you did the NC500?" said Ryan. "I'm so jealous!"

"Well, as a matter of fact, we did and you have every right to be jealous. It was the trip of a lifetime." Jack laughed as Ryan asked him for the highlights.

"Where do I start?" asked Jack. "There was so much to see and the scenery is spectacular."

"Did you do Applecross Pass and Balach Na Bar?" asked Ryan, his eyes wide and his enthusiasm evident. He may as well have been speaking a foreign language as far as I was concerned.

"That we did." Jack was enjoying reminiscing and went on to tell us about Callum the stag in the car park at Torridon once you had braved the famous Applecross Pass. He's so used to tourists that he wanders around, letting folks stroke him and feed him titbits. He described the rugged beauty of the beach at Sango Sands and licked his lips at the memory of the best hot chocolate in the world at Cocoa Mountain. Patting the side of the van affectionately and smiling, he told us that she came with a ton of happy memories.

"And low mileage and a full-service history," piped up Ryan. "Steph, she's everything Damo would want, seriously."

All eyes were on me. I could feel myself starting to blush, and I felt flustered and didn't know what on earth to say, so I said I'd think about it.

Ryan looked at me in anticipation, clearing his throat. "Can we have a word, Steph?" he asked and made his way up the street a little, with me following and panicking but trying to hide it as best I could.

"Look, I'm not telling you what to do here, but I am telling you that this is a steal, and it's exactly what Damo wants. You won't find anything better; don't let it get away. He just put it up for sale a couple of days ago and if you aren't quick, it's gonna go."

"I have to think about it, Ryan. I'm not sure." The lie forced me to look at the pavement instead of him.

"What are you not sure about? If you want me to go through the spec or anything I can?" He was getting frustrated and I totally understood. I'd be the same in his shoes.

"I'm just not sure about a camper van now if I'm honest." I dared to steal a glance and his expression was one of confusion.

"What?"

"I know you probably think I'm crazy, but the truth is I found out a few days ago that I'm pregnant, and I don't know if this will work now. I should have told you before we came, but I wanted to see if there might be enough room for, well four." Half a lie might be better than a whole one.

"That's amazing!" he said and threw his arms around me. "I thought the doctors said you couldn't have another one?"

"They said it was really, really unlikely." I smiled weakly and patted my belly. "Yet here we are."

"And everything's ok?" he asked.

"I've got the first scan booked for next week, so we'll know more then and go public after that, but please don't tell anyone beforehand. I mean, I know you'll tell Jen, but please ask her to keep it a secret for now. And don't tell Damien that you know, or he'll know we've been talking."

Welcome to my web of lies, Ryan. For what it's worth, I'm sorry.

I breathed out a sigh of something nearing relief. I'd managed to wriggle out of this one graciously and by telling the truth, kind of. Honesty was the best policy, after all. If only I'd stuck to it sooner, I wouldn't be standing here now stringing Jack along and lying to our friend.

"But Steph, this is perfect timing! We bought our van when the two girls were younger and it worked brilliantly!" Ryan was grinning from ear to ear. "It's the best thing you could do, seriously. Think about being able to just pack up and go, no booking references, no departure lounge, no flight delays with a newborn baby in your arms who won't settle. It's the most family-friendly thing you could do. I'm made up for you! This is going to be great."

Here's me thinking I'd managed to put the fire of enthusiasm out when in fact, I'd just stoked it.

"I'm not sure. I need time to think; it's all a bit overwhelming, the baby and everything." I started trying to untangle myself. I would be roasted alive on that fire if I didn't find a way to shut this down.

"No, honestly, Steph, it's great!" and so he kept going, Mr Camper Van of the year. I knew he was well-meaning, and under different circumstances, he would be completely right. He absolutely would be helping me and doing me a massive favour, doing *us* a massive favour. And I could see that it would be a brilliant option for us as a family. Of course I'd love to go all in and say yes, but I'd managed to fuck this up royally, and Beth was wearing a quarter of the payment on her left hand, with the rest earmarked for the wedding of the century along with whatever else he could squeeze out of me.

"Ryan, it's not great because *I'm* not sure," I mumbled at the kerb.

If he heard me, he didn't acknowledge it, and he threw an arm around my shoulders as we walked back to Jack.

"Well, you two, what's it going to be?" Jack asked and I could feel my eyes welling up.

"I can't take it, Jack. I'm sorry," I said and they both turned to look at me. "The thing is I just found out a few days ago that I'm pregnant, and it's a complete surprise." I fanned my face with my hands and then wiped the tears with my coat sleeve.

"Sorry, hormones."

"Hey, hey, it's fine." His voice was calm and he walked over to hug me. "Life has a habit of throwing us a curve ball here and there, I should know."

"I'm really sorry I've wasted your time." I sniffed and searched in my pocket for a tissue.

"No, no, you haven't at all. I've enjoyed our trip down memory lane. You've done me a favour." He smiled and I really wanted to tell him the truth, and if Ryan hadn't been there, I might. He just had the kind of presence that made you feel safe. Gail was a lucky lady.

Ryan reluctantly shook Jack's hand, and we made our way back to our own cars. He asked me once more in a serious tone if I was sure before we hit the road. He was deflated and confused, probably even angry, and I could understand all of it.

As I drove away feeling all kinds of terrible, I could see Jack waving in the rear-view mirror. I wondered how much time I had left before Ryan joined the dots up and sussed things out. I thought again about telling Damien the truth. As each day passed, I was getting in deeper and deeper and dragging others with me. Time felt like it was running out – I needed a miracle and fast. And then, right on cue, another flutter. I had my miracle. I just needed to believe I was worthy of one more.

CHAPTER 39

Scan day arrived. I was meeting Damien at the hospital mid-morning and definitely had nervicitement, as Beth's mum Mo called it once. The excitement of seeing the baby on the monitor and everything feeling so real at last, but feeling nervous until you find out everything looks fine. Measurements would be taken for an estimated due date, and we'd get our teeny black and white scan photo to show friends and family.

I wondered how Mo was for a moment; she'd been very present when the kids were at nursery and helped Beth to pull around after her breakup. I liked her. She brought life experience and wisdom as well as fun and good humour when it was needed. I'd turned to her for advice before and she'd been lovely, a safe space and someone you could rely on. I hoped she was ok and wondered again why I hadn't seen her. Then it clicked. I hadn't seen her lately because Jay's plan was working. He'd be turning the screws behind the scenes and strategically and covertly isolating Beth from anyone who would question his motives or challenge his intentions. Maybe Mo would listen to me and we could save Beth after all?

I found a parking space and made my way to reception.

"Fancy seeing you here!" I looked up to see a friendly face and, for a moment, couldn't place her. She sat down beside me and started chatting, thankfully mentioning something about not leaving Tuppy too long, and the penny dropped.

Gemma was there for a counselling appointment. She went on to tell me she'd been referred because of domestic violence and followed up with confirmation that he'd never actually hit her, of course. I'd said exactly that to Mel, not to minimise what had happened, but to give context. Most people don't realise that emotional abuse is domestic violence, and I didn't either.

As Gemma talked, I could see that her story was in many ways so like mine. She had no idea it was going on either, and it had messed with her head and her heart in ways that maybe only other victims would ever fully understand.

"I had no idea. I'm so sorry you've been through that." I wanted to tell her about me, but Damien would arrive any minute.

"Ah, thank you, part of life's rich tapestry, you could say. I'll be ok in time, and he will sadly continue doing what he's always done to other women and end up ruining other lives on the way." Gemma sighed. "But you can't do anything to expose them or help the next victim because by the time you get to them, they think you're a psycho. Things could be worse, though. The moment I realised what was happening to me, I Googled covert narcissism and you wouldn't believe some of the stories. I'm in a couple of Facebook support groups now and it's mind-blowing." She shook her head. "Seriously, it's like some kind of psychological thriller."

"Oh?" I asked, curious and making a mental note to find said groups.

"One woman posted that her husband had told her he was in the military and he'd gone out regularly in a uniform, but they later found out it was from eBay." Gemma nodded. "He was living this weird double life and even shot himself in the leg to make her think he'd been in active combat and been injured."

"He actually shot himself?" I asked.

"Yes with an air rifle or a spud gun, nail gun or something, not an actual gun. He didn't have a real gun because, guess what? He wasn't in the army!" Gemma laughed and so did I.

"My god, that's crazy," I said and thought that my blackmail story would be something people would find just as unbelievable.

"He even promoted himself too! He came home one day,

preening and peacocking around the place, then asked his wife to sew some badges onto his 'uniform' because he'd had a big promotion." Gemma was on a roll. "And when the shit hit the fan and he was exposed and she chucked him out, they found a delivery envelope and receipts from Etsy for the badges." She laughed and shook her head.

"Unbelievable," I said and I meant it.

"Of course, the failed relationships before her had nothing to do with him and everything to do with the horrible women he'd fallen victim to. That's why he had nothing when he met her; he'd been ripped off – poor him and all that. Truth be told, he'd lived like a low-life leech for years and moved from woman to woman, bleeding them dry, then slagging them off to the victim."

"The smear campaign," I said, and Gemma's eyes lit up.

"Yes! Do you know about this stuff?" she asked. "So many people just don't get it."

"I know a bit," I said, not wanting to give too much away.

"Seriously, these people are hand grenades in their victims' lives. Maybe more of a life landmine because you can't see them until it's too late."

"I wonder if they just keep getting away with it?" I said, thinking about Jay and the landmine he'd hidden in my life that I was currently tip-toeing around.

"I don't think he did with the next victim," said Gemma. "His ex-wife posted an update last week to say a woman had been in touch with her, realising there were massive holes in his story. He'd raged about her not trusting him and then staged a pity party, threatening to harm himself." Gemma rolled her eyes. "Who would even say that to manipulate others? It's sick."

"Did she listen to the ex-wife and call it off?" I asked, thinking about Beth.

"Yes, and now she's way more clued up on what to look for.

He was back on the dating sites straight away with an updated profile, of course, that was full of lies and talking about trust and loyalty being important in a relationship. He knows how to lure people in, the ones who have been cheated on and hurt, because they are vulnerable and easy to manipulate."

"That's so calculated," I said and waved at Damien as he approached the reception desk.

"Oh, they know what they are doing, believe me," Gemma said just as her name was called and she stood up. "Anyway, nice to see you. I didn't even ask why you're here? I hope you're ok."

"Oh, for a scan, I'm pregnant," I smiled as Damien walked towards us and Gemma congratulated me. Damien took her seat and patted my knee. I could feel his nervicitement on top of my own, but we didn't have long to wait before my name was called.

CHAPTER 40

We were ushered into the small room by a young-looking woman in a green uniform. She took my coat and asked me to climb onto the bed as the radiographer arrived. The room was painted regulatory magnolia with hard-wearing grey-speckled flooring and dimmed lights, and the bed had a long sheet of paper across it that slipped a little beneath me. The middle-aged radiographer was kind and professional, with a lovely smile, and she asked me to roll down my jeans to expose my thickening abdomen. The gel was cold and the room was silent, apart from a ticking clock and a soft but ever-present whirring of ducted heating.

She pushed her glasses up her nose and peered into the snowy screen facing her but away from us. I tried to read her reaction but couldn't.

"Everything looks fine," she finally said and smiled, turning the screen round for us both to see.

Damien and I breathed a joint sigh of relief. There was the outline of our baby, a tiny little fist waving in slow motion, tiny legs and feet and a little pot belly. I stared at the screen in a daze. Yes, I'd known that I felt different, and yes, I'd done a pregnancy test, but this was the exact moment when it all became real.

I felt Damien squeeze my hand and I turned my head to look at him, tears rolling down his face.

"It's a miracle," he whispered as my heart blew wide open with love for him.

"They are indeed little miracles, and like I said, everything looks fine," the radiographer repeated and I breathed a deep sigh of relief. Now I could have more excitement and less nerves. She went on to take some measurements and said that I looked to be around ten or eleven weeks and that my next scan would be at twenty weeks, which would be here before we knew it.

"Because of your age, we need to monitor you a bit more closely, so although we will scan baby at week twenty, you will need to see a consultant as well as the midwife. It's nothing to worry about. You seem fit and healthy, and so does baby. It's just that some hospitals prefer to have that extra layer of expertise just in case it's needed at any stage." She asked if we had any questions.

"What kind of risks do you mean?" asked Damien and I squeezed his hand back.

"Well, it's things like blood pressure that we need to monitor for mum and just generally keeping a closer eye, and for baby, there is an increased risk of miscarriage, but please don't worry, everything looks really good." Her tone was reassuring, but from past experience, I knew that you didn't stop worrying about the baby being healthy until you held it in your arms and could see for yourself. As soon as that worry faded, it made room for anything and everything else a new parent frets about.

"We can make the consultant appointment at this end. You'll get a letter in the post and it's likely to be sooner rather than later. Not because anything is wrong with your scan, because there isn't. It's simply because if anything does come up, the sooner we know about it, the sooner it can be resolved. Any more questions?" She looked at us both and I shook my head.

"Well, you're free to go, and the ladies' loo is three doors down on the left," she laughed. "Everyone is desperate to go after they've had me pressing on their bladder for ten minutes."

STEPHANIE'S JOURNAL – LESSON 32
TREAD CAREFULLY IN THE LIVES OF OTHERS

Walk gently in the lives of others. All wounds are not visible.
~ Uknown

We are all fighting invisible battles in the best way we know how. We often have no idea what other people are going through or how it's affecting them. What we say and do, and how we show up in the lives of others, can make a difference that ripples through their day in different ways, and we may never know the effect we have had, be it good or bad.

You are responsible for how you show up. You get to choose your attitude, tone of voice, language, humour, kindness, level of tolerance and everything else. Self-awareness is part of being conscious and owning the energy you bring. This is not to say that you are expected to navigate around the world being a pushover or spreading toxic positivity, neither of which are healthy or realistic. You can still experience your own life lessons and the full range of human emotions and remain conscious.

Be kind and patient, compassionate and tolerant where you can. The world is a hard enough place to navigate, and we can all lighten the load for ourselves and each other. Look to pass on goodness when possible. You could start a ripple effect of positive emotions with a compliment, lift someone up with a smile or raise someone's self-worth by praising a job well done. A nasty comment or being mean-spirited with someone when their resilience is low could have far-reaching consequences you are unaware of.

Seek to contribute, not contaminate.

CHAPTER 41

"Here we go again, another big adventure," Damien said and hugged me close. "Do you want to go for a quick coffee before I go back to work? We could stop at that place just down the road?"

"Yes, I'll see you there," I said and buckled up, ready to follow him.

The drive was short but long enough for me to imagine for a few moments that things might turn out alright. If we'd been given this miracle baby against all odds, perhaps I could somehow beat the rest of them. The agency liked my work, and every day I was getting closer to finishing the first draft. In a couple of weeks, my energy will be back, and I'll be able to write more. If I could maintain a few thousand words a day, I'd be submitting in just three or four weeks. Depending on a possible second draft and edits, the publishers could consider releasing it in the spring. As soon as I had earned out on my advance, I'd be making money again, and I could pay the twenty thousand back. Damien would never know.

Reality check, he did know.

I was even lying to myself now as well. I could blame pregnancy hormones, but I should also make a mental note that I might be *actually mental*. Should I even be left in charge of a baby? Damien knew and he hadn't said anything. Now, why was that? Because Ryan made him promise not to, and he doesn't know that I know. All so complicated, all so self-created and all so avoidable.

Yes I am mental – confirmed.

As I pulled into the car park, my phone lit up.

Another question mark from Jay, this time followed by:

I CAN'T WAIT MUCH LONGER STEPH.

Ignoring it, I slipped the phone into my handbag. He wasn't getting any more from me and the sooner he got the memo, the better. I had to have the courage to stay the course.

Damien had found us a window seat and had already ordered. He held my hands and looked at me with so much love I wanted to confess right there and then. For the first time ever, I felt I could risk it and be safe. Surely he would understand and he'd forgive me. I took a breath and cleared my throat.

"Steph, I need to tell you something." It sounded serious.

"Oh?" I said and waited. I pulled my hands away from Damien's and put them on my lap to hide the tremble that was starting. I looked at the wood grain on the table and started to count the stripes between the edge that faced me and a knot near the centre. Was this the moment that things started to unravel? Had Jay followed through and sent the pictures? The tower moment was coming. I started to quickly rehearse an explanation, but there was nothing new, nothing of substance and nothing that sounded like it would make a difference.

"Or rather, you need to tell me something, I believe?" the question hung in the air between us.

I breathed in deeply and out slowly. Before me sat the man of my dreams, holding my heart in his hands. I was about to crush him by finally telling him the truth.

"Look, I'll make this easy for you," he said and I stole a quick glance. Was he smiling?

"I'm really sorry, but I accidentally found out about your idea to get us a camper van, so I want you to know that I know, and I'm really stoked and excited about it."

"You are?" I said and tried to sound happy, but at the same time, I realised I was absolutely screwed.

"It was my own fault really, and you mustn't blame Ryan, but I put him in a position where he had to tell me what was going on. I saw that you'd withdrawn twenty thousand from our joint savings account and I panicked. I'm sorry if I doubted you."

Oh my god. Damien was actually apologising to *me*. Any shred of dignity I had left was going, going gone.

How could I sit there and let him do this?

"And Ryan says you found one that would be perfect. He's shown me pictures of it and I think it's the best idea ever, Steph, I really do. I wanted to tell you as soon as I knew, but I didn't want to throw you before the scan. We were both so nervous about it. I know you haven't been yourself for a couple of months and now we know why – it's our little miracle, Steph, and I'm so made up."

"Me too," I mumbled.

"What's wrong, love?" Damien leaned in closer. "I know it's all a bit overwhelming and I'm sorry I ruined your surprise. You're such a sweetheart for wanting to do this for me. I really love you for it, so don't feel embarrassed or anything. It's all good."

"I'm ok. I just feel a bit sick," I said and stood up.

The walk to the ladies felt like a mile, and I was relieved to be the only occupant. I hadn't been lying about feeling sick, but it was with anxiety, not hormones. I dry-heaved a couple of times into the bowl, spat into a tissue and flushed. None of this was Ryan's fault, but I could cheerfully choke him right now.

Making my way back to the table, I told Damien I needed to head home and lie down. Lie down and think about how I could engage in any kind of damage limitation before my life crumbled.

"You do look really washed out. I think you need to go back and rest up. Do you want to leave your car here for now and I'll bring you back for it later?" The love and kindness that had been our solid foundation for years now felt like it was made of glass. One wrong move and it would shatter. I'd fall into the abyss where I deserved to be.

"That's a good idea, I think," I said and picked up my bag.

"Your phone was pinging. I had a quick look in case it was school, but it was just a load of question marks. You know some weird people." Damien shrugged and reached into his pocket to find change for a tip.

Too close, way too close.

"That van you went to see with Ryan," said Damien, opening the door. "Don't feel bad about it. Ryan knew it was perfect for us, so he went back and put a deposit down on it. We had a chat and please don't be mad, but we thought that baby brain might be getting in the way of you making decisions, so we went ahead and held it."

I didn't say anything, mainly because I felt like I was about to pass out.

"Steph, you're not mad at me, are you?"

"No, I'm not, but can we do this later? I feel really wobbly," I said and linked Damien's arm.

I looked out of the window the whole way home, hardly speaking a word. This had to be the beginning of the end, the happiest day and the saddest day, both at the same time. All I needed to do was pick my moment and tell him everything, then try to hold it together as he packed and left.

I wanted to cry, but there were no tears left.

"I can work from home today. I'll call the office when I get back," he said and patted my knee.

"Ok, thank you," I replied weakly and thought that The Universe was at least lining this up for me. "I think I'll go straight to bed for an hour. I'll put Mel on standby for the school run if you like."

"That would be good. I'd rather not leave you."

I'd rather you didn't leave me too, but I think it's inevitable.

Nothing ever goes away until it has taught us what we need to know. ~ Pema Chodron

We come to Earth to grow, expand our consciousness and evolve through our own unique Soul Curriculum. This contains the lessons we need to experience about ourselves, other people, life, and the human condition generally. Sometimes the lesson is obvious, and sometimes not. If we don't learn it, it can repeat until we do. This repetition may be needed several times, much to our Human Self's frustration, and can show up in different scenarios over time until we finally get it.

Perhaps we attract the same type of relationships, or maybe we are always in the same financial circumstances. The theme may have variations, but the essence is the same.

In order to learn a lesson and gain the growth and wisdom it offers, you need to bring it into your conscious awareness. That means looking at what keeps coming up for you and reviewing it from a present-moment, conscious standpoint. Without being judgemental of yourself, you must still own the fact that this is constantly being drawn in, so there must be an energetic match to this pattern.

Maybe there is a historical worthiness wound that triggers a pattern of people-pleasing? Perhaps relationships feel out of exchange because you are an overgiver.

Does an experience of living in financial lack as a child affect your money mindset now?

Once you have found the core of the lesson and identified what keeps it active within your vibration, you can empower yourself to heal and change. Once learned and integrated, you won't need to draw in the repeating experiences associated with that lesson.

CHAPTER 42

I sat on the edge of the bed and stared into space. I had to come clean and devastate the man I loved, the man who loved me , our daughter and our unborn baby. I held our whole fragile world in the palm of my hand and I was just about to drop it. I had no idea what to say or where to start. How do you begin the conversations that you know are such pivotal moments in life and relationships? The Universe had set up the time and space to do it and the clock was ticking. Damien would ask me for the twenty thousand later today or tomorrow so that he and Ryan could pick up the van, and I'd have to confess. I could wait until the very last minute, or I could do it soon. Both felt horrendous.

I sent Lizzie a message. She'd know what to say.

ARE YOU THERE I NEED ADVICE?

GIVE ME 2 MINS X

I'M BACK. ARE YOU OK?

NOT REALLY. FIRST OF ALL GOOD NEWS I'M PREGNANT.
OMG THAT'S AMAZING!

I THOUGHT YOU SAID YOU COULD HAVE NO MORE?

YES IT'S AMAZING, SCAN TODAY AND ALL GOOD.

IS DAMO MADE UP?
YES WE BOTH ARE.

SEND SCAN PIC!
WHAT'S THE DILEMMA?

I THINK I NEED TO TELL DAMIEN THE TRUTH.

OH?

YEAH, RYAN ACCIDENTALLY TOLD HIM ABOUT THE 20K CAMPER VAN THING. AND THEN HE ONLY WENT AND FOUND ONE THAT IS PERFECT AND THEY ARE EXPECTING ME TO PRODUCE THE FUNDS.

FUCK.

YEAH.

WHEN?

DUNNO BUT SOON, LIKE MAYBE TODAY OR TOMORROW. RYAN PUT A DEPOSIT ON IT.

FUCKS SAKE.

SO WHAT DO I DO? WHEN HE ASKS ME FOR THE CASH I'M GOING TO HAVE TO SAY I DON'T HAVE IT.

YOU'RE EITHER GOING TO HAVE TO TELL A LIE ABOUT WHERE IT'S GONE OR COME CLEAN ALTOGETHER.

I KNOW BUT HE'LL BE ABSOLUTELY BROKEN AND THEN HE'LL LEAVE.
WHERE COULD YOU SAY THE MONEY HAD GONE? CAN YOU SAY YOU LOANED IT TO ME?

HE'D NEVER BUY THAT, HE KNOWS YOU EARN A FORTUNE. AND THEN IT'S JUST ANOTHER LIE TO MAINTAIN.

BUT IT WOULD BUY US A BIT OF BREATHING SPACE SO YOU COULD EARN THE MONEY BACK? OR I COULD GIVE YOU SOME CASH. I HAVEN'T GOT THE WHOLE TWENTY BUT I HAVE ABOUT HALF IN MY BUFFER ACCOUNT. IT'S A START? YOU COULD PAY ME BACK OVER TIME.

THANK YOU FOR OFFERING BUT THAT WOULD STILL LEAVE ME SHORT, I DON'T THINK I'VE GOT ANY OPTION BUT TO TELL HIM EVERYTHING.

THE WHOLE THING?

I THINK IT'S THE ONLY WAY.

EVEN THE PART WHERE YOU MET UP WITH YOUR EX AT A HOTEL AND GAVE HIM A BAG OF CASH?

I THINK I HAVE TO.

IF YOUR GUT IS TELLING YOU THAT YOU HAVE TO TELL HIM THEN IT'S THE RIGHT THING TO DO. IF IT GOES BAD YOU CAN COME AND STAY WITH ME AND OF COURSE BRING MIA, DAY OR NIGHT.

THANK YOU.

HAS HE STOPPED TEXTING YOU?
NO, AND DAMIEN SAW A MESSAGE FROM HIM TODAY. HE DIDN'T REALISE WHO IT WAS BUT IT'S GETTING WAY TOO CLOSE.

OMG THAT IS CLOSE.

IT WAS JUST A LOAD OF QUESTION MARKS BECAUSE I'M IGNORING HIM.

THANK GOD IT WASN'T ONE OF THOSE PICTURES.

I KNOW – THIS IS WHY I NEED TO TELL HIM. IT'S GOING TO COME OUT ANYWAY AND I'VE AVOIDED IT FOR LONG ENOUGH.

KEEP ME POSTED AND KNOW THAT I'M HERE FOR YOU. HE LOVES YOU SO MUCH, I HOPE THINGS END UP OK.

ME TOO X

I closed my eyes. The sickness had subsided and made way for sadness, a feeling I'd become very familiar with and carried for what seemed like forever. Fluttering in my belly and a brief moment of happiness, but then the thought that I've done this to you, my baby, and you aren't even here yet. Who knows where your daddy will be when you are born into the world? I can't guarantee he'll be here.

I felt scruffy. There was residual gel from the scan on my tummy and I needed to feel clean. After a shower, I pulled on some comfy leggings and an oversized t-shirt, bobbled up my wet hair and, full of dread, padded down the stairs.

The radio was on in the kitchen, and I took a breath. One step at a time, you can do this. Damien wasn't there. On the countertop was a handwritten note. Brief and impersonal, not his usual style, no kiss at the end and no 'I love you'. It said he had to go out and that he'd be in touch. Be in touch? What did he mean by that? I was probably overthinking things. I was tired, full of hormones and the most anxious I'd probably ever been. He might have been called to a meeting or a property in a hurry and gone to do some firefighting. No need to panic … yet.

I went back upstairs, dried my hair, put on a little make-up to stop me from looking like the walking dead and opened my laptop. I'd received another email from the agency telling me they thought this work was very timely, and it would hopefully help so many people and, of course, sell many copies.

If there was any kind of gift in the relationship I'd endured with Jay - and cheerfully endured at times, in a deluded and messed up way - it was that I had so much to write about now. Although it was ironic that my perfect and beautiful life was now hanging in the balance. At least I could continue working, and the best thing was, it didn't feel like work. It felt like therapy, an outlet. I'd anonymise and generalise so the readers could identify themselves within the words, but the essence would be me telling my story, what I'd learned and how I'd rebuilt it. The final chapter might even be about what was to come, how to rebuild after a tower moment. Hopefully, there will be a happy ending.

I heard Damien's key turn in the front door and his footsteps echo in the hallway. It was now or never. I made my way downstairs slowly, each step taking me closer to ground zero. I had about an hour before Mel dropped Mia off, and with fear gripping me tightly, I readied myself to start talking. He was in the kitchen pulling his phone charger out of the wall and winding up the wire to put it in his backpack.

"Damien," I started talking, wondering what was going on. He hadn't mentioned a trip or overnighter, and the last thing I knew was that he was so concerned he couldn't leave me. And yet he had, for at least a couple of hours, so where had he been and what was going on?

He looked at me and I could see he'd been crying.

"What's happened?" I asked and walked towards him.

He extended his arm to keep me out of his personal space

and simply said, "No, Steph, don't."

"But what's happened?" I asked again. "Damien, what's wrong? What's going on?"

"I'm going away for a while because I need to think. I need space and I need to weigh things up, Steph. I can't be here right now with you." He was fighting the urge to cry again, although I couldn't.

The tower was crumbling, and I had no idea how or why. I reached for him again and he stepped backwards, bumping into the kitchen table.

"Don't touch me, Steph," he said. "I have to go and I'm going to ask you to let me."

"I don't know what's going on here!" I shouted.

Damien turned around and matched my tone. "Oh, but you do. You fucking do!"

Oh my god, he knows.

"Do I? Then tell me!" I was desperate to know what he'd found out so I could fill in the blanks with the truth, finally, the truth that I should never, ever have steered away from. "Damien!"

He left the room and made his way upstairs. I could hear him in the bathroom gathering up his razor and toothbrush. The bedroom was next, and I heard drawers open and close, and the wardrobe door creak open, then slam shut. He appeared at the top of the stairs with enough clothes packed for at least a week and enough emotion to sink the *Titanic*.

"Just let me go," he said through gritted teeth. "I don't want to say things I'll regret. I need to go and I need to go *now.*"

"Please, please tell me what's wrong!" I begged him as he made his way towards me and the front door.

"What's wrong?" He yelled at me, and my hands flew to my mouth. "What's fucking wrong? You really want to know, do you?"

He'd seen the pictures; I should have told him earlier today before this all exploded. Jay obviously had been willing to follow through with his threats, and he'd sent them, and now Damien had no context, timeline, or explanation. All he had were images of his wife looking like a hooker in some other man's bed.

"I can explain, I really can. I've been meaning to tell you everything, but I've been trying to pick my moment and find a way to explain it in a way you might understand and not hate me. But I didn't know where to start…" I was rambling, and he stood in front of me, waiting for my sorry explanation.

"Everything? That sounds like a whole lot of explaining you need to start doing, Steph, but I'm afraid you're going to have to save it for another day because I need to go. I can't bear to look at you right now, never mind listen to your half-arsed excuses and lies. I know more than enough already."

"But Damien, I love you, and I'm so, so sorry for whatever you think I've done," I spoke through hysterical sobs and he closed his eyes tight in fury.

"Steph, I can't do this right now. I love you too and that's why I need to go. You've broken me, perhaps forever. I don't know yet. Never in a million years did I think you would betray me like this, and especially with him. But the worst part of it all," he said with his hand on the doorknob, "was that you let me think this was *our* miracle baby. What kind of sick fuckery is that?" he walked through the door, and as it slammed shut, I fell to my knees, screaming silently before howling like an animal caught in a trap.

STEPHANIE'S JOURNAL – 34
TOWER MOMENTS

*Never be afraid to start over. It's a chance to rebuild your life
the way you wanted it all along. ~ Unknown*

Tower moments in our lives make reference to the Tower card
in the tarot. The illustration shows a tower being hit by
lightning and starting to fall. Although at first sight, it can
appear worrying, the message that comes with it is twofold and
positive. Initially, there could be unexpected change and a
shake-up in your life, typically disassembling what is no longer
working or serving you on some level. Your human self may be
unaware of the need for this and you could go into fear and
resistance. This is a time to surrender as much as you can and
accept. Much of what plays out during a tower moment can be
out of our control.

Once the old paradigm or situation has collapsed, it's time
to rebuild in a much healthier way. A tower moment in your life
is a forced change that is ultimately going to lead to something
good. Do your best to have faith that this is the case and hold
the intention for your Highest Good. Use the bricks that
tumbled down to create something new which serves you much
better.

CHAPTER 43

"Steph, slow down," Lizzie said. "I can't make out what you're saying."

I could hardly breathe, never mind speak. I was crying and shouting like someone possessed. Lizzie hung up and a text came through straight away saying she was on her way. I paced up and down and called Damien over and over until she arrived.

Each call went to voicemail, and each time, I left a message pleading for him to come home.

"What the hell happened?" Lizzie asked, scooping me up tightly.

"He knows and he's gone," I managed to say. "But I don't know what he knows or how he found out. He just came home and said that I had fucking broken him and then he left."

"Oh, Steph, that's awful!" Lizzie said, rocking me from side to side. "I thought you'd told him and it had all gone bad. I presume you tried to tell him?"

"I did, I did, of course I did! I was too late. I should have told him earlier. I should have told him a lot fucking earlier, like back at the start of this absolute shit cart of a situation that I can't mend now. My marriage is broken and I've broken me and the man who loves me. I'm poisonous, Lizzie, I'm garbage."

"No, no, no, Steph, you're absolutely not. You made a mistake and that's all. Now don't we need to go and pick Mia up from school around now?"

"No, it's ok I've got a friend doing that," I snivelled.

"Good. Do you think it might be a good idea for her to have a sleepover at that friend's house tonight? Just while we pull you round a bit and make a plan?"

"I couldn't put on her like that, really I couldn't."

"Have you ever done her a favour?" asked Lizzie.

"Yes, plenty of times, we help each other out a lot," I said.

"So it shouldn't be a problem then, should it?" said Lizzie and asked me for my phone. "Let's text her and sound her out, shall we?"

"What are you going to say, though?"

"I'll say that you don't feel great and that we are going to go through to the hospital to get you checked over. Does this friend know you're pregnant?"

"Yes, but Mia doesn't know yet. We were going to tell her in a few days. I wanted to buy her one of those t-shirts that says 'I am the big sister' and wrap it up as a surprise."

"And you still can. We can still get that sorted, so don't worry."

"I'll text her. I'm ok," I said and started with:

HI MEL.

I told her the scan results were fine and I had a picture to show her, but I was exhausted and asked if Mia could go for tea at their house straight from school. That would give me enough breathing space for now without having to think about toothbrushes and pyjamas.

Another lie: when will this nightmare end?

"I'll put the kettle on," said Lizzie, leading me into the kitchen.

"How could he have found out?" I said, shaking my head.

"Because that snake Jay has sent him the pictures, I'll bet. Damien's mobile number is plastered all over the company website. He's not hard to find." Lizzie made coffee that I knew I wouldn't drink, but I'd huddle up with it anyway.

"That's what I thought too, and he'll have no idea when it was or the truth of what happened. Jay knew exactly what he was doing when he staged those photographs. It looks terrible, I look terrible."

"Hopefully, Damien will calm down and at least let you explain. Maybe there is some damage limitation that we can do once he knows the truth."

"The truth that I went back to my ex-husband's apartment with the intention of getting laid before I passed out drunk? That's hardly damage limitation."

"I mean the truth of you being blackmailed, Steph, the truth that you had very few options in this, and you've been at the mercy of someone hellbent on taking you down and stealing your money. The truth is that you made one mistake, you didn't sleep with Jay and you're the victim of a crime and a hideous, manipulative, harmful one at that. You've been terrified and terrorized for months, and you've been scared to tell anyone. That's the truth of what's happened here and that's what Damien needs to hear, and the police."

"I can't go to the police, Lizzie, you know that."

"Yes you can, and you have to now. You didn't want to go because you were scared Damien would find out, and he'd see the pictures. But newsflash, he's probably seen them by now. You've got nothing to lose, and you might even get your money back if you report him."

"I need to think this through. Damien thinks I'm having an affair with Jay."

"What?"

"He thinks that the baby is Jay's."

"Oh my god, Steph! Call the police, this all needs to come out now, you have no choice! The only way you can try to save your marriage is by telling Damien everything, and you know that because it's exactly what you were going to do a few hours ago anyway." Lizzie handed me my phone.

"I will, I promise. I just need to regroup a bit first." I put the phone down despite her objections. I was exhausted, reeling and literally couldn't take any more. Nothing from Damien, he'd gone to ground and who knows when I'd hear from him. For all I knew, there might be a divorce petition on the doormat within the next few days.

"Steph, he could be facing a serious punishment for this, and he deserves everything he gets. I'll send you some info to motivate you about how long people get for this kind of crime and to show you how serious it is."

My phone pinged with message notifications as Lizzie found the newspaper stories she wanted to share and I promised I'd look later when my head stopped spinning.

"I need to lie down. I'm exhausted," I said and stood up.

"That's understandable. I've got some work I can do while you rest." Lizzie reached for her oversized handbag and pulled out a diary and pen. "Go on, Steph, I'll bring you a cuppa in an hour."

I made my way upstairs, sat on the bed and clicked to see what Lizzie had sent. It had already been opened and was marked as read.

"Lizzie, send me a message on messenger, would you please?" I shouted.

"Saying what?"

"Anything."

I closed the app and my phone pinged, I didn't open the message envelope. When I went to it, the message was marked as read.

Lizzie sent me a string of messages, and the same thing happened each time. Maybe on top of everything else, this horrendous day had to offer me, it was now serving up a side order of hacker. I'd have to go through the whole password reset thing and alert Facebook, and for the life of me, I couldn't remember any of my login details. I'd have to wade through that later when I felt a little more human, a little less sick and a lot less devastated – as if that was going to happen any day soon.

Surely if I'd been hacked, they would be posting loads of stuff on my page, though? I knew people who had gone through this and they'd woken up one morning with a whole load of porn or activist posts plastered all over their pages. Maybe Jay had hacked into my account somehow and that was his plan? Was he going to share the pictures on there?

I can't face this right now.

Lizzie was right; I had no option but to go to the police. As well as my marriage, it looked like I could lose my income and my reputation at the same time. Was this at the expense of ignoring his messages? Heads of government didn't negotiate with terrorists. But I'd already done just that, and twenty thousand pounds later he knew without a doubt that when the screws were turned, I would pay up. One more turn and I'd crack, one way or another, and Jay knew it. That's why he'd hacked into my Facebook account. He was getting ready to ask me again and tell me there was about to be a social media takeover.

Right on cue, my phone alerted me to a message from him.

WHEN AM I SEEING YOU AGAIN I NEED MORE

If I give him more this will never stop.

YOU'RE NOT GETTING ANY MORE THIS HAS ENDED

SO YOU WANT ME TO GO PUBLIC ABOUT US?

THERE IS NO US AND I KNOW YOU HACKED MY FACEBOOK

PHOTOS TELL A DIFFERENT STORY - I DIDN'T HACK YOU BUT IT'S A GREAT IDEA

IT'S OVER JAY FUCK OFF AND LEAVE ME ALONE

NO CHANCE OF THAT I'M AFRAID I'M INVESTED

IF YOU POST ANYTHING ON MY PAGE I'LL GET THE POLICE INVOLVED

YOU KNOW WHAT I WANT STEPH AND ITS MORE OF THE SAME

I was feeding his ego and making things worse, like a fly caught in a web that starts to struggle and alerts the spider to move in for the kill. I needed to stop engaging. I shut down my laptop and wished it was that easy in real life to shut him down. Messages kept coming through on my phone, one after another. I didn't open any of them until the final straw.

I KNOW YOU ARE SEEING THESE MESSAGES SO STOP PRETENDING YOU AREN'T

What did he mean?
Something was nagging at me, a memory of something I'd seen on TV perhaps, one of those six-part dramas you can download as a box set. I could remember the woman sitting upstairs and typing something on her laptop on Zoom and her husband reading the conversation downstairs in the kitchen on the family laptop because she hadn't logged out.
What if?
Dread and realisation washed over me. All messages were marked as read. Of course Jay thought I'd seen them, but it wasn't him that had hacked into my account - it was me who hadn't logged out. I ran to the side of the bed where Damien kept the iPad he sometimes used to watch movies when he couldn't sleep. The headphones were curled up on the carpet, but the charger was gone and so was the iPad, the iPad I

sometimes used to update my Facebook page when I couldn't be bothered to boot up my laptop. The penny dropped as my heart sank even more.

Damien hadn't seen the pictures, he'd read the messages. I scrolled back through them in a panic and tried to read them through Damien's eyes. Yes, this could be misconstrued as me having an affair, and if I were in Damien's shoes, I'd have probably thought exactly that.

Jay had been deliberately vague. Nothing he said was incriminating or a direct nod to me being blackmailed. None of the messages sounded flirtatious, but they were clipped and direct and could have simply been his style. References to meeting up at The Four Seasons and taking an envelope of money with me, it was easy to see how this would look like I was having an affair and planning to start a new life with my ex, and the worst of it – that Jay and I were having a baby.

Damien, please let me explain.

Maybe if he wouldn't pick up my calls, I could get through to him on a Facebook message. I could message myself and see if he picked it up? Anything was worth a try, so I quickly typed a nuts and bolts overview of what had happened and said there had never been an affair and that I was being blackmailed by Jay.

The message was opened and I gasped, imagining him reading it in my mind's eye. I begged him for forgiveness and asked him to come home. If I could only have a chance, I could make him see. Finally, a message came back.

HE SAID YOU'D SAY THAT. I'M SIGNING OFF NOW.

I stared at the screen dumbfounded.

He'd had contact with Jay?

I went back through the message thread and sure enough there was an exchange between the two of them.

THIS IS DAMIEN STEPH'S HUSBAND AND I'M GOING TO BE BRIEF AND DIRECT. WHAT THE FUCK IS GOING ON HERE AND HOW LONG HAS IT BEEN GOING ON FOR? YOU WILL UNDERSTAND I HAVE DECISIONS TO MAKE BASED ON WHAT YOU SAY NEXT. I WOULD APPRECIATE YOU BEING HONEST.

WE'VE BEEN HAVING AN AFFAIR ON AND OFF FOR A WHILE NOW SHE'S STAYED AT MY PLACE ONCE BUT WE HAVE MET AT A HOTEL

DID SHE EVER GIVE YOU ANY MONEY?

LET'S JUST SAY WE HAD PLANS

Damien hadn't responded, that will be have been the moment his whole world caved in. Jay had managed to do exactly what he set out to do; take my money and ruin my life. I curled into a ball on my bed and screamed into my pillow. The walls started to close in on me and I wondered how I was going to keep going. Lying in misery and darkness for who knows how long, I opened my eyes as Lizzie put a cup of tea on the nightstand and pulled a blanket over me.

"How are you feeling?" she asked and I explained the whole messaging mess. "Oh, Steph, you have to go to the police now. This is bigger than just you and it's the only chance you have of getting Damien to see the truth."

"It's too late. I think the damage is done. Jay is a master manipulator. He's already got Damien believing him," I whispered. "It's what they do. They break lives apart for their own gain and then they move on."

I gasped, and my hands flew to my abdomen.

"Steph?"

"I'm ok, it's probably trapped wind. I haven't been able to eat properly." It happened again but this time it took my breath away. I stood up, and Lizzie steadied me. With one hand on the wall, I walked the few steps to the bathroom.

"Don't lock the door," said Lizzie, and I knew that she was perching on the bed to be close by just in case I felt faint.

Before this moment, I thought things couldn't get any worse. Yes, I'd risen from hardship before, but this time, it was different. Back then it had only been me. The stakes were a million times higher now I had two children to consider, two other little lives to protect and two other hearts to stop breaking as well as my own as we walked through the wilderness of being a broken family.

And there it was, a bright red smudge.

"Lizzie!" I cried out, and within seconds, she was there.

"Stay there. I'll get a pad and we'll go straight to hospital."

CHAPTER 44

The drive to the emergency room seemed longer than usual. We'd hit rush hour.

"Maybe I should have called an ambulance," said Lizzie, trying to change lanes and navigate the heavy traffic.

"It's ok. It wouldn't have been any quicker," I spoke between long, slow breaths, trying to stay as calm as possible but failing big style.

I'd called and texted Damien to no avail. I could feel the pad was doing its job, and I'd had two more cramps that made me double up. I closed my eyes and prayed with everything I had that I wouldn't lose this baby or this baby's father.

Lizzie pulled into the drop-off zone right in front of the doors and left me in the car while she went inside. A porter soon appeared with a wheelchair and helped me out of the passenger seat. I was taken straight to emergency, where I was thankfully given a private triage room with an en-suite.

"We're going to get you scanned, Stephanie, to see what's going on. Your blood pressure is sky high, so please do your best to relax. I know it sounds impossible when you're stressed and worried, but can you try, please?" She smiled and patted my hand as a memory of the radiographer came back to me telling us that miscarriage was far more common when you are an older parent.

"Can I get you a cup of tea or anything?" she asked and I declined politely. The truth was I felt like I was going to vomit, and then another cramp hit. I whimpered and started to cry. The tears flowed because it hurt and I was exhausted, but they were mainly for our baby and the horror of losing this pregnancy, as well as everything else.

The lovely nurse rubbed my back and told me they had paged a consultant to see me and booked the scan, which they'd do on a mobile unit that would arrive within the hour.

"Am I going to lose this baby?" I asked weakly.

"I can't say what's going to happen, I'm afraid," she was trying to remain neutral, but I couldn't detect any hope in her voice. "Is there anyone you want me to call for you?"

That certainly didn't sound optimistic.

"No, it's ok, thanks." I turned my face towards the stark white wall and whispered a prayer, not only because deep down I still believed in a higher power but also because that's all I had left.

The scan was nerve-wracking, and the time gap between the beginning and hearing that the baby was still here and doing well for now seemed like forever. My blood pressure was starting to lower a little, but there were no guarantees.

The afternoon soon faded into evening, and Lizzie tried to tempt me with something to eat. I grazed a little, but ate nothing of substance. I'd sent Damien what felt like a million messages, but as yet, there was no response. Although the medical care was excellent, this was a wait-and-see scenario. All of the language used was empathic but considered, careful not to sprinkle the seeds of false hope or equally of doom and gloom but to provide a safe space for whatever happened next. I was being kept in overnight for observation, and depending on how events unfolded, it could be longer. Lizzie yawned and I told her to go home. She objected, of course, but in truth, we both knew there was nothing she could do. In all honesty, there was nothing anyone could do, no matter how medically trained they were. Nature and destiny were in charge now, and my only option was to surrender.

"I wish I knew where Damien was," I said as Lizzie pulled on her coat. "I just want to know that he's ok."

"You need to focus on you being ok, Steph," she said, and I

knew she was right.

"I know, but a big part of me being ok is knowing that he is. He's holed up somewhere believing that I've cheated on him with my ex, planned to leave him and that I'm carrying another man's child. That's devastating, Lizzie, it really is."

"When you put it as bluntly as that, yes, it is," she sighed and pulled on her jacket. "I hear you, Steph, but you must remember you are the victim here. Nothing has really changed from the moment you went back to Jay's apartment and came home to Damien. You've done nothing wrong."

"Nothing *else* wrong."

"If you want to see it that way then yes, nothing else wrong. But you didn't do much wrong in the first place. We both know Jay is a narcissist and from what you've told me about your sessions with Robin, you can see that even more clearly. It's no wonder it played out like this when you look at how beaten down you were and how desperate you were for love and affection from him. You need to remember he's an abuser, just like Robin says, and that you had one human moment because you were drunk and upset. Nothing much happened. I know you kissed him, and that's a big deal, but this wasn't a regular lapse of morality, Steph; it was a set-up."

"Do you really think that?" I asked.

"Yes of course I do. You fell back into an old trap that he'd set for you. You were vulnerable to him specifically because of all the triggers and past conditioning. You would never have done this with some random taxi driver. It was always a combination of your past and his intention for the present to collide and get what he could again. You are not a cheater. You'd never deliberately hurt Damien. You were lured into this so Jay could extort money from you and control you just like he did in the past. It's a shame there was that brief encounter between you because that makes it really sting, but this is way bigger, and you have to go to the police as soon as you've pulled around."

"I wish you could tell him all of that," I said. "I don't think I've got any chance of him listening to me."

"Steph, I'd tell him all day long because it's the truth and because you two are meant for each other. I'll even give him some of the sordid details of how Jay manipulated me and nearly ruined this friendship for good. When you look back, can you see how it was totally out of character for me to do something like that to a friend?" She sighed and shook her head. "I still feel terrible about it."

"You don't need to. I knew then how manipulated and fucked up he'd made you feel and it wasn't your fault at all."

"And I know how manipulated and fucked up he's made *you* feel and it's not your fault at all."

After confirming that I'd call if I needed anything, Lizzie kissed my forehead and squeezed my hand.

I dozed for a while after she left; it was shallow and full of nightmarish metaphors about loss and regret. Sleep and processing had merged together and I couldn't tell the difference anymore. The nurses came in regularly to check on me and it wasn't until around midnight that the background noises started to become familiar enough that I drifted off properly, only to wake at around 2am with another stabbing pain.

I buzzed for help and the night staff came quickly. There was no time to call Lizzie.

CHAPTER 45

The next day, I was weak but managed to shower, glad of the grab rails around the wet room. If only I could wash away the pain down the plug hole too, but it would cling to me for years to come. The hospital towel felt scratchy on my skin, fitting, as I didn't deserve any comfort. My bed had been changed overnight, and when I returned to it, two slices of toast and a cup of tea were waiting for me.

Fear had made room for emptiness, an emotional numbing that came with an enforced surrender. There was literally nothing I could do. The tower had fallen, and my life as I knew it had been demolished. I felt hollow.

A nurse came in to take away the toast I'd barely nibbled and check my blood pressure. She asked me kindly how I was doing, and I said I was tired and wanted to go home. The ward round was usually around 11am and she said it was up to the consultant to make that decision and in the meantime, I should get some rest.

About four hours to wait. When I got home, I'd have to tell Mum a version of the truth, a diluted version, and I'd have to watch her heart break along with my own. The nurse returned with a charger I'd asked to borrow. My battery died overnight, but now it lit up with messages and missed calls. Damien had tried to call me! I fumbled with the handset and voicemail.

"Steph, I'm so sorry. I just don't know what else to say." There was a whole load of sobbing and then a quick "I love you."

I frantically started to scroll through the texts, one from Mum late last night telling me to take care of myself, and from about midnight, there were several from Lizzie. She was going to meet Damien and explain everything to him, not to panic or worry, and things would be ok. This was the only way. Two hours later, she'd messaged again with the news that he'd listened and was absolutely devastated, and that devastation wasn't because he felt even more betrayed, it was because he couldn't bear to hear what I'd been through.

Thank you, thank you, thank you.

Lizzie had filled in all of the blanks, and most importantly, Damien knew I'd been set up and I hadn't had sex with Jay. Tears filled my eyes, this time with relief, not devastation. Maybe there was a version of a happy ending that I could still hang on to? Could Sue be right for a second time?

I opened Damien's first text message, saying he loved me more than ever and couldn't keep going if anything happened to us. I knew as soon as visiting hours began, he'd be with me, and we would start the process of piecing ourselves back together again. Holding the phone to my chest, I imagined his arms around me. This was all such a mess, but in that moment I felt like maybe it could be mended. Love is the strongest force in The Universe, and I could feel his surrounding me and filling me up. Drying my eyes with a tissue, I typed back that I loved him, waiting to see if the message had been read. Maybe he was in the shower or still asleep, it didn't really matter; I'd see him soon and that was the very, very best thing ever.

Messenger sent me a message envelope from Jay and my anxiety spiked. I told myself I didn't need to worry now, it had all come out just as predicted and he couldn't harm me anymore. I might even mention that I was going to the police. Why shouldn't he be looking over his shoulder and living on his nerves just like I'd had to? I opened the message to respond and saw that apparently I already had, or rather Damien had – as me.

There had been an arrangement to meet at The Four Seasons later in the day with another payment. No numbers had been mentioned, but it was made clear that it was the final instalment. Was Damien going to pay him off altogether? My head was spinning. I texted Damien again and there was still no response. Lizzie's phone went straight to voicemail.

What is going on?

There was nothing I could do but wait. Seconds felt like minutes, minutes felt like hours. Checking my phone, fretting, pacing. Waiting for the consultant, flicking channels on the television that I wasn't watching anyway.

My phone rang and I nearly jumped out of my skin. Mum. Taking a breath, I tried to sound more composed than I felt, updated her in brief and told her that I hoped I'd be home later today. She confirmed that Mel was doing the school pick-up and sends her love. I swallowed down guilt for being so vague, but I didn't want to go into upsetting detail on the phone, I'd rather have the chance to talk properly and privately. Face to face and in a safe setting, both her and Dad would need time and space to process this, and we would have to support each other.

After goodbyes, I checked again for word from Damien. Surely he'd be out of the shower now? Why wasn't he responding? This was all really sketchy and weird. Even if he was driving, he could use hands-free. I tried him again and it rang out. This was not great for my anxiety or blood pressure, both of which I had to keep in check if I wanted to get home and start to heal – myself and my marriage.

A nurse opened the door and asked if I was ok and that she had a surprise. She spoke in a stage whisper and said it would have to be quick, and I wasn't to tell anyone, or she'd been in trouble for breaking the rules, but ten minutes wouldn't harm, and my husband can be *very* persuasive.

That's why he hadn't answered the phone!

He wanted to surprise me and sweep me up in his arms, hold me tight and tell me he loved me. I looked and felt a complete mess, but it made no difference. Damien had seen me like this before and helped put me back together - there was nothing we couldn't do. I felt like a child on Christmas morning, excited and overwhelmed. The nurse left the room and I tucked my hair behind my ears, keeping my eyes on the small square window.

Sue had been right about The Tower; it had to come out, and all fall apart so it could be rebuilt stronger and better than ever and on foundations that were still intact.

Footsteps walked up to my door, and my phone rang. What was Damien playing at? I smiled and answered the call, knowing that any second now, I'd see his face. The call connected and it sounded like he was driving. He started to ask how I was as the door opened wide. Jay stood in front of me with a bouquet of flowers, smiling like the proverbial alleycat. The nurse scurried off in the background. As I dropped the phone onto the bed, my jaw dropped too.

"What the hell are you doing here?" I wondered if I should scream.

"Do I need a reason?" he said in a tone dripping with charm and implication. "I was passing and I thought I'd drop in to see how you were."

"To intimidate me, to make your presence felt so I keep paying up. That's why you're here."

"Now, now, Stephanie, don't get yourself all worked up." Jay smirked and I wanted to slap him into next week. "Think about your blood pressure."

"Fuck you, Jay. Why are you here and when are you leaving?"

"There are some things you can't say over a message, Steph, the context gets lost. So I thought I'd come and have an in-person chat with you to check we are on the same page."

"The only page I am on is the final page. It's over, Jay. You are getting nothing else from me." And then I remembered that Damien had promised a final meet-up. "After today, this is done."

"Well, if that's the way you feel, we'd better make sure it counts then."

There he stood, arrogant and oblivious to the fact that the game was up.

"How did you know I was here?"

"Because I don't miss a thing, Stephanie, that's why."

"Why can't you just fuck off and live your life with Beth or, even better, leave her alone and find someone else, someone that lives miles away so I never have to see you again?"

"Ah, the lovely Beth," he smirked. "Such a sweet girl, but not really my cup of tea."

"You're poison," I spat at him and noticed out of the corner of my eye that the call with Damien was still connected. "You've got my twenty thousand and that's way more than you deserve. Just tell me why you're here and then go."

"Twenty thousand is a drop in the ocean for you, Steph. Double it and I'll consider leaving you alone."

I laughed out loud and his expression remained neutral. "You want another twenty thousand? There is no way on earth you're getting that from me. I shouldn't have given you the first twenty and I'll forever regret that almost as much as ever having anything to do with you, you fucking snake."

"I think you'll reconsider." A sinister smile spread across his face. "You see, you haven't seen all the pictures yet." He reached into his pocket and brought out his phone, clicked an icon or two and held it up for me to see. My stomach flipped. My shame was clearly written all over my face because now it was his turn to laugh. "You'd passed out cold so I could do whatever I needed to, and you had no idea. Lifting your legs up and over to get the right position in that one was like a workout. You haven't lost any weight, have you, porky?"

"I hate you," I said. "And I want you to go."

"I'm done here anyway. I just wanted to come and tell you

what I was expecting when we meet up later. I don't like putting numbers in messages; it's all a bit tacky."

"You mean you don't want any evidence lying around that you're blackmailing me and threatening me in case the police get involved?"

"That's just an added bonus, really." He shrugged. "Anyway, I just wanted to be clear – double bubble, Steph."

"Fuck you, Jay."

"No thanks, Steph. I've had an upgrade in that department and I've realised that I like my women on the small to medium side rather than extra large. I bet Damien has to get pissed and turn the lights off with you. How ironic that the pictures will make him think we had a night of passion together when, in fact, I couldn't think of anything worse."

I cringed and wanted to cry, but didn't want to give him the satisfaction.

"Get out, get out now before I scream."

"If you ever offered to get down on your knees, though, that would be a different story. You're really good at that. I'd close my eyes and pretend you were someone else, someone attractive and sexy, and I wouldn't be able to hear you because you'd have your mouth full…"

Just then, the nurse opened the door and told Jay he would have to leave, and I couldn't have agreed more. He passed her the flowers and winked at me.

"See you later, love."

The nurse blushed as he winked at her too. As she left, I lurched to pick up my phone. Thankfully, Damien was still on the line.

"Damien, are you there?" I could hear he was still driving.

"Yes, yes, I'm here," he said after a moment or two.

"Did you hear all that?" I asked, torn between wishing he had and hadn't.

"Yes, I heard it all."

I couldn't read his tone apart from knowing that whatever emotions lay beneath the surface, he was working hard to control them right now.

"I'll be there as soon as I can, Steph. You need to tell the staff who he is and not to let him back in, ok?"

"Ok, I will."

"I mean it, do it as soon as we've finished talking. He's fucking dangerous and I don't want him anywhere near you or us. I love you and I'll be there soon."

With that, the call ended.

The nurse returned with the flowers and started saying what a lovely husband I had. I corrected her as politely as I could and she stopped arranging the stems.

"But he said he was!" she wiped the palms of her hands on her uniform and shook her head. "He was so convincing. I can't believe it. I'm so sorry."

"It's not your fault. He *is* so convincing and I could have said as soon as you walked in with him that I wanted him to go, but I didn't."

"Are you ok though? I mean the flowers, and he seemed so desperate to see you that I just presumed he was telling the truth." She was embarrassed and I didn't want to make it any worse.

"Look, what he told you was half right. He used to be my husband, but we're divorced and I'm happily married to a man who will be here any minute to take me home as soon as I'm discharged."

"Oh!" she said and nodded, pressing her lips together into a thin line. "I see." She explained that the ward round had started and the doctor wouldn't be long and asked if I'd like a tea or coffee. Her face was flushed, and I could see she wanted to be anywhere else but here. I wanted neither but asked for a coffee, giving her permission to busy herself elsewhere and me a chance to catch my breath.

"Please don't let that man back in," I said as she turned to leave, and she nodded, closing the door softly behind her.

CHAPTER 46

When Damien walked into the room it felt like time had stood still. I looked at him and burst into tears, and he held me so tenderly it felt otherworldly. After a few moments, he held me at arm's length and said he never, ever wanted me to keep anything from him again. I promised not to and said I was sorry over and over again, and he told me I didn't need to be sorry. I sat on the edge of the bed and he sat in the seat next to it, holding both of my hands in his and staring into my soul.

"I feel so bad that you went through this without me to help," he said, full of love and authenticity.

"I just couldn't tell you it was him. You said it would break you if it hadn't been someone faceless and anonymous, and I felt like I'd done more than enough damage." I shook my head in shame.

"But, Steph, I just said that out of pain and fear, and you took it so literally. I shouldn't have said it to you. I'm so sorry that it's brought us here." He pulled me close again.

"It was me who brought us here, not you. You have nothing to be sorry about. It was me who messed up." I had to own this, and I couldn't let Damien think it was anything to do with him.

"Steph, you messed up because you've been messed up by him. Lizzie explained it all and I've had time to do some research. I'm not saying it doesn't hurt because it does, but I can understand why it happened."

"You can? Really?" I asked in disbelief.

"Yes I can, and now I know what I know, I can see that this would never have happened with someone random. You're never going to have a one-nighter with a guy you just met. This was specific to this freak and his agenda. You'd been primed in the past to respond, just like when Pavlov rang the bell and the dogs knew it was feeding time. He manipulated you for years and when you got into that taxi, you were drunk and vulnerable, and he saw it as an opportunity." Damien rocked me in his arms. I closed my eyes tightly and said he was being far too nice.

"I'm not, Steph, I'm being honest. It makes it easier to understand and dare I say it, it hurts a bit less when I look at it this way too." He sighed and lifted my chin with his index finger. "Never mind me, how are you feeling? You've been through such a lot and I should have been with you."

"I'm fine now I know that we're going to be ok," I whispered and he kissed my forehead.

"We are going to be more than ok, Steph. You're the love of my life and I'm never letting you go." He looked away for a second as if to compose himself and then tentatively mentioned the pregnancy. "We can try again, you know, for a baby, I mean."

My words caught in my throat briefly until I composed myself. "No, it's ok," I said softly and squeezed his hands.

"But it's happened once, Steph. I know the odds are against us, but we might fall lucky again." His voice was full of hope and tears glistened in his eyes.

"I said it's ok." As I spoke, a smile started to light up my face and Damien looked confused. "It's ok because I'm still pregnant."

"Are you sure? Are they sure?" he asked and I confirmed I'd had a scan in the early hours and everything seemed to be ok. I was still pregnant and the baby looked healthy.

The door opened and the consultant knocked before he entered. Looking at my blood pressure readings and the scan picture, he asked how I was feeling. After a brief exchange, he said I could go home as long as I took it easy and had as little stress as possible. Damien held my hand the whole time, grinning from ear to ear, and confirmed that I wouldn't be lifting a finger once I was at home.

The house was warm and cosy when we got back. I made my way straight to bed and Damien followed me with a cup of tea and plumped up my pillows. For the first time in a long time, I felt cocoon-like dreams envelop me and hold me safe, finally without the fear of being found out. I woke about an hour later to see Damien's note on the nightstand saying he'd gone out and wouldn't be long. Closing my eyes again, I sank deeper into the pillow. A little while later, I heard the front door gently close and the familiar sound of him padding upstairs.

"I need to tell you something," said Damien, suddenly sounding serious. "Jay has been arrested, so the police are going to call for a statement. I said you'd just come out of hospital and you wouldn't be up to it for a few days."

"What do you mean arrested? How do you know?" I asked.

"I set him up. I pretended to be you and agreed to another payment in the car park at The Four Seasons. Lizzie and I had already told the police the full story, so they nicked him. He'll be questioned and probably charged with extortion, defamation of character and blackmail. He could get up to fourteen years depending on the judge on the day, how he pleads and any previous convictions."

"I don't know what to say," my hand flew to my mouth.

"You don't need to say anything, just know it's been taken care of. He's not getting away with it; this is his own doing and he's brought it all on himself. No normal person treats someone the way he has treated you. He's a head case and the world's a safer place with him locked up."

"What did the police say? Didn't they want proof?" I asked, still struggling to take it all in.

"I gave them proof. You know that old work phone I've got, the one I keep charged up in the glove box for emergency backup? I used it to record your conversation with him in the hospital. I'd already spoken to the police before that and they were going to start an investigation, but this accelerated things."

"Isn't it entrapment or something? You're not going to get into trouble over this, are you?"

"I don't know and I don't care. I'm sure if anything, I'd get a slap on the wrist or community service or something, but who gives a flying fuck? He's been caught and that's the end of it. Apparently the kind of abuse you went through is a crime, Steph. It really messes people up. One of the officers I spoke to this morning said this is domestic violence and it's treated really seriously, gaslighting and manipulation are strategic brain-washing. Offenders can go to prison if it's proven."

"And you don't even know it's happening until it's too late."

"Yes! And that's why he needs locking up, so he can't do it to anyone else. I pulled the car up right behind him so he couldn't drive off and the police did the rest. He obviously knew something was up because I saw him fiddling with his phone before they opened the driver's door. He's probably put some stupid status online or trying for damage limitation and texting a lawyer."

"I've had nothing tonight," I answered honestly.

"Well, let's hope it stays that way," Damien said. "I need a drink after that."

I heard ice cubes clink into a glass and the sound of pouring. Damien would be having a Jack Daniel's on the rocks, a treble at least, and I didn't blame him one bit.

"Steph, please stop punishing yourself," he said as his arm encircled my waist, and he pulled me close. "I'm so sorry I said what I did about you not knowing who you'd erm…"

"Been with?" I whispered, hanging my head.

"Yes, that."

"Don't be sorry. This is my fault, Damien. None of the blame lies with you. I don't know if I'll ever be able to forgive myself for making such a stupid mistake and then making things a million times worse by lying to you." I sniffed back tears and Damien leaned in to kiss me. I could taste the whiskey on his lips.

"Like I said, you took what I said literally, and that's what led to you lying," he said with conviction. "You had no choice, my love. I can see that. I know you were scared and didn't want to make it worse, so you thought it best not to tell me."

"Yes. Exactly!" I said and pulled him into me. "I'll always regret it."

"And I'm telling you now that you don't need to. In fact, I'm asking you from the bottom of my heart to forgive yourself because I forgive you."

STEPHANIE'S JOURNAL – LESSON 35
CHOOSE WHAT YOU MAKE THINGS MEAN

Nothing has any meaning except the meaning we give it.
~ Tony Robbins

Our lives are filled with information, and as humans, we attach various meanings to this. These meanings can come from our past experiences, old beliefs, observations, what we have been told, the media and many other sources. We can attach meanings in an automated and unconscious way, leading to generalisations and presumptions about people and situations. We then generate self-talk and feelings around this story and use it to modify our opinions and behaviour.

An example might be that your partner doesn't feel like being intimate with you because they are tired and stressed after a long week at work. If you have unfinished emotional business from your past, or if you carry beliefs that make you interpret this differently, you give this a whole different meaning. Suddenly, you're worried they don't find you attractive anymore, they are falling out of love, and this might be the beginning of the end. This self-talk makes you panic and feel needy. You adapt your behaviour to 'win them over' and become too intense, stressing you both out even more. You chose to make something mean something it didn't, and a cascade of emotions and events ensued from this moment. They were just tired, but you made it mean something different that wasn't true.

Remember, you get to choose what you make things mean. Staying conscious, stepping back and observing your own self talk can help you to identify the meaning you are giving to someone or something. Once you know what that meaning is, you can weigh up how true and relevant it might be, and challenge yourself to look for alterative meanings that might serve you more.

CHAPTER 47

The next day felt different. There was still a backdrop of anxiety, but it was diluted. I even allowed myself to consider that this wasn't my fault, and perhaps things would be alright after all. Damien was in full-on protection mode, and if the police hadn't been watching from the other side of the car park, I was pretty sure he would have taken his chance and punched Jay into next week.

I'd had a lie-in, the last one for a while, as Mia was coming home today and we'd be back in the school run groove in a blink. Mel and Mum had tag-teamed brilliantly. I was so grateful to them both and must remember to get two bunches of flowers with my next food shop, and the big sister t-shirt for Mia. The hospital had confirmed I was carrying a girl and I knew Mia would be thrilled. Life was slowly getting back on track, and it seemed that Sue had been right after all. I made a mental note to send her an update.

I'd called Mum from the hospital to tell her the baby was safe, and we'd both been emotional. I had so much more explaining to do, and I wasn't looking forward to it, but with Damien by my side, I could hopefully share a version of events that wouldn't be too distressing.

There was a knock on the door and I opened it wide, expecting Mum to throw her arms around me, but she was on the verge of tears, and Dad looked furious.

"Put the kettle on, love," she said, patting my arm but avoiding eye contact. "How are you today?"

"I'm fine, Mum, just tired. I'm so grateful for all your help with Mia. I don't know what I'd have done without you." Treading carefully, eggshells cracking underfoot, Dad huffed and puffed past me into the kitchen.

"Have I done something to upset you both? What's going on?" I asked, looking from one to the other, trying to read them.

"This," said Dad, pulling out a copy of a newspaper he'd been holding under his arm. The headline read 'Fifty Shades of Spiritual' and was accompanied by one of the pictures in Jay's possession. You couldn't tell it was me from the picture alone, and some of it was shaded out to reduce the porn factor, I presumed, but the story named me and told of a sordid love tryst with a taxi driver. It laboured the point that I was married with a child and had written books that claimed to be life-changing and spiritual, yet I was a cheating adulteress with no morals who loved nothing better than a bit of S&M at the weekend. The complete story was about discrediting and humiliating me, exactly what Jay had threatened to do.

Right now, I didn't care what the rest of the world thought. I only cared about my parents. Mum was in bits and Dad wasn't far behind.

"How could you do this, Stephanie?" he asked, his eyes closed. When he opened them, he turned the paper over so all we could see was something about football.

"I didn't, Dad, it's all made up," I whispered, horrified and looked at Mum. "I've been blackmailed, and the police are involved. That's why I ended up in hospital. My blood pressure was sky high."

"I told you it wouldn't be true," Mum said to Dad, and for probably the third time in my life, I saw my father start to cry.

"If it's not true, then where did these bloody pictures come from?" Dad spoke through gritted teeth and I could see his hands gripping the kitchen countertop and a vein in the side of his head starting to throb. He turned his back to me, unable to look in my direction, wiping his face with the sleeve of his jacket and sighing. "I just can't believe it, any of it. How could you, Stephanie?"

"It's Jay. He's been blackmailing me for months. This picture is one of many. I'll let you know that now in case others come out."

"Jesus Christ!" he said through gritted teeth, and Mum put her face into her hands. "How could you do this to Damien? And it's all over the front page, for god's sake."

"Give her a chance to explain." Mum sniffed and sobbed, smiling weakly in my direction.

"Go on then!" Dad turned around and I saw the extent of what this was doing to him. I started crying too, and tried to give them both an account that would make some shred of sense in this horrible world of pain, blame and confusion.

"I'm going to tell you something you might not believe." I began with a summary of the backstory of abuse, not knowing it was happening, and then I fast-forwarded to the night in the apartment with Jay. Lastly, I mentioned the twenty thousand pounds and the arrest. Silence filled the room.

I cleared my throat and asked if I could keep the paper to show the police, and they both nodded. Humiliation meant I couldn't look at them, and I was sure it wouldn't be any easier producing pictures of me lying on my back with my bush blurred out to a police officer. Named and shamed in print, on every forecourt, in every newsagent and supermarket that sold papers. Not to mention social media and the internet generally, I'd be a meme by lunchtime. No matter what happened next, the damage was done. Shit sticks, and that's a fact. I wondered if any school mums had seen it; I bet Rosie was giving out copies at the gate.

"Do you want us to stay until they get here?" asked Mum, and I said no, giving them instructions to head home and not open the door to anyone. I didn't want to scare them, but the press might try to get a scoop and ambush them. What I'd been through was terrible enough, but the knock-on effect on my family was crushing. I knew there and then that I'd never forgive myself for dragging my parents into this, never mind my husband and children.

After they left, I called Damien.

"I've seen it. I'm on my way home," he said.

The police arrived at the same time as he did and took our statements. As they asked questions, I heard the office phone ring upstairs and the apologetic voice on the answer phone of my agent cancelling our agreement and saying that the publishers were dropping all of my titles. I thought I'd reached ground zero, but there's obviously a basement.

Once the police left, I dared to look at my social media and saw exactly what I'd been expecting. My career was over and my income was gone. I'd never recover from this. Some of the comments made my stomach turn, and some made me furious, and all were totally unfounded.

Even if Jay went to prison, and even if my name was cleared, it would make no difference. He'd done what he set out to do, and he'd taken me down, lock, stock and barrel. There was little to no chance of ever coming back from this personally or professionally. I'd have to move house, change Mia's school, and find a job, and Damien might have to close his business. The devastation would be all-encompassing and permanent. I doubted I'd be able to leave the house ever again, so much for new beginnings.

This was the final round, and he'd won.

He'd actually won.

EPILOGUE

I sat in a high, wing-backed chair with a warm breeze gently moving the leaves of the trees that surrounded me. The stage had been set on an Italian stone patio, surrounded by greenery and peace. The chair opposite me was empty for now.

I took a deep breath and closed my eyes to calm my nerves and bring my energy and focus into the present moment. I'd not long been out of hair and make-up and was as prepared as I could be, knowing there might be some surprise questions and my reactions would be closely captured. That didn't faze me these days. I'd had enough scrutiny to last a lifetime and knew that no matter how you presented yourself or what you told some people, they would always want to judge you and pull you down.

Thankfully, they were in the minority now. Time heals, they say, and it's true: time, truth, and an excellent legal team.

People were doing lighting and sound checks, and I was miked up, ready to roll. Cameras were in position, and two tumblers of water sat on the glass table in front of me. It was showtime, and I was ready.

"Welcome to this week's show. We have a very special guest that many of you will have heard of, given her astronomical rise to fame through her best-selling book *Love Blind*. The book was born out of a real-life survival story, and it's one that many people have lived a version of and may even still be doing so. It shines a conscious light on the silent pandemic of narcissistic abuse in our society today and has sold millions of copies worldwide. It's hard to believe this is a book that was nearly never published, and even harder to believe it was her abuser who ironically helped this author to achieve such success through his attempts to ruin her. It is my absolute pleasure to speak with Stephanie Anderson today and find out what really happened all those years ago and why it's taken so long for her to give this, her very first interview since her life and career fell apart. Welcome, Stephanie. Please start at the beginning. I don't want to miss a thing."

"Thank you. I'm so honoured to be here. Thank you for creating a safe space to share my story and finally have my voice heard." I took a breath and paused. "It's taken me so long because I had to know my daughters wouldn't be harmed even more by me sharing this story. When it first broke, Mia was in primary school and I was pregnant with X. I protected them as much as I could, but Mia especially was called names and bullied once the other kids found out, usually in a really unconscious way because their parents had bought into the media scrum. Even when my name was cleared in court, the damage had been done, and, unsurprisingly, that story didn't warrant a front-page splash. We had no option but to buckle up and engage in as much damage limitation as possible, and the people in our inner circle were the ones we held close and leaned on."

"I see. Wow. And how old are your girls now, Stephanie?"

"Mia is twenty and Ella is fifteen. They are both resilient and confident young women. They've got great friends who know the story and can handle any questions eloquently and honestly. When your people approached me to do this interview, I knew it was time."

"So take me back to the day when your publishers dropped you. You must have felt like your whole world was collapsing in that moment. You'd just come out of hospital after a heavy bleed and almost lost the baby you were carrying. You'd saved your marriage by the skin of your teeth, you'd just found out that your husband Damien had set up your narcissistic ex and had him arrested. And you'd almost finished the first draft of

Love Blind, which was, at that point, completely pointless. Add to that the fact that your parents came to show you the newspaper headline that had naturally devastated *them,* and yet you've been quoted as saying that this was, in hindsight, one of the best days of your life."

"Yes, and so it was, although I had no idea at the time. Starting with the newspaper headline, that had started brewing years earlier, with one moment in time where I'd lost my sense of who I was and what I stood for. Rewind further and I can tell you that I was married to a narcissist and I had no idea. For years, I slowly slipped away and became a shell of myself and didn't see or feel a thing. It was insidious, calculated and strategic, and, of course, incredibly harmful."

"So just to fill in some blanks here, the man you were married to was what you would describe as a covert narcissist, and you're saying right now and of course in the book *Love Blind,* that you were manipulated by him and had no idea it was happening, is that right? Because for a lot of people, that's going to be hard to understand."

"That's exactly what I'm saying, yes. And I know it's hard to understand for those who haven't experienced it and even those who have lived through it or might be in it right now. Being in an emotionally abusive relationship is like being in a cult. But it's more dangerous because people around you know when you've been recruited into a cult. They have no idea you are in an abusive relationship because often, you don't know either."

"And was that what drove you to write *Love Blind?* To educate people?"

"Yes, I wrote it for the people in those situations to help them see it's not healthy. It's also for those who have been able to leave and rebuild their lives. And it's for the observers and family members, who are helplessly watching the person they love being hollowed out and isolated."

"Right. Right. I understand. So, getting back to that moment when the headline hit as being one of the best days of your life, can you tell us more about that?"

"Sure. Ok, so it didn't start that way. As you mentioned, my parents were devastated by the headline and picture. The papers then harassed them to sell their story or any photos of me. They were shunned by friends and neighbours, and life became incredibly hard for them. In the background, we were fighting a legal battle with the press and suing for libel, which, of course, we won, but the time lapse between the headline and the win felt like decades for us all.

It was only actually seven months, but it was seven months of hell. During that time, though, my social media blew up, and I mean *blew up*. I very quickly hit one million followers and doubled it within a few more weeks. Initially, it was a mixture of people wanting to troll me and some sympathisers. Some were just curious to see if I really was that kinky. Since I had no income and no one to represent or publish me, I also had nothing to lose. Total autonomy, and I played full out. I started to post excerpts of *Love Blind* on my Facebook and Instagram pages and hashtagged things like gaslighting, Stockholm Syndrome, breadcrumbing, love bombing and more and the engagement just kept growing."

"So through the newspaper headline and photograph you started getting social media famous?"

"I guess I did, in a way. And then, only a few weeks in, my agent called me and said that my original publisher wanted the new book after all and wanted to revise their offer and that there was another offer on the table from someone else."

"And that's when the bidding war broke out?"

"Yes, and it was all because I suddenly had credibility and tabloid front-page fame. I was talking in the book about emotional abuse and manipulation, and then I was lured into my ex-husband's lair, passed out drunk, tied up in a heap of compromising positions and photographed so he could extort money from me. As soon as the court case broke and it was obvious I'd been blackmailed and abused, book sales went crazy. The publishers could hardly keep up with demand, and I was suddenly getting so much recognition for helping to lift the veil on emotional abuse. None of this would have happened if Jay hadn't sold his story to the press."

"And was that something he did out of spite at the last minute when you wouldn't give him any more money?"

"Yes, he had a media contact, and the story was ready to break if I didn't pay up. He'd promised some pictures to go with it, and on the day he was arrested, he sent them from the car park as the police approached him. I think it was partly about the money and partly about a final chance to hurt me. But whatever his intention was, it completely backfired because it ended up with me here, talking to you in front of millions of people."

"And it ended up with him in prison serving fourteen years for blackmail and extortion. Can I ask if you believe in karma, Stephanie? Do you think your ex got what was coming to him?"

"I believe we get what we give out, whether you call it karma, payback or Law of Attraction, there is some kind of squaring up that happens in The Universe, and we get what we are meant to."

"And do you believe you got what you were meant to?"

"Yes, yes, I do. I believe that I am a better person because of what I've been through and although there are moments where it still stings, I have softened my feelings towards my ex. Manipulative people know no better. They aren't emotionally healthy, and they don't see the world the way healthy people do. They can't hold down healthy relationships, they don't take any responsibility, and they ruin every good opportunity that comes their way. It's sad."

"So if you had a final message, what would it be?"

"It would be that you are worthy of being loved and appreciated for who you are, and you shouldn't have to change a thing. Compromising is different to changing who you are. Compromising is healthy and a good thing to do if it's for the right reasons. But never, ever lose who you are and never, ever allow someone to make you feel less than, even for a split second, because you have the light of The Universe at your fingertips. You are made from stardust and you came here to shine. If you don't believe it right away, go back to lesson one and Be Open to Possibility."

"Stephanie Anderson, it's been an absolute pleasure to talk to you today, and I'd encourage anyone listening who is in resonance with your message to get their hands on a copy of *Love Blind*. It's much needed, and it's a book that can change the very fabric of our modern-day culture."

I smiled and tears of gratitude welled up as I composed myself and took a breath before speaking.

"Oprah, please believe me when I say the pleasure is truly all mine."

STEPHANIE'S JOURNAL – LESSON 36
THE HARDEST TIMES OFFER THE GREATEST GROWTH

Grow through what you go through. ~ Unknown

It is during the hardest times in our lives that we are forced to dig deep and find out who we really are. Although we would never choose difficult or traumatic circumstances, they often come with huge leaps forward in our personal and spiritual growth. They can forge a deeper connection with ourselves and others, revealing immense inner strength and resources we may have been unaware of. We can also experience a new purpose and meaning moving forward, an increased reverence ad gratitude for life and the people in it, raising our vibration more and helping to attract more goodness and joy.

Sometimes referred to as 'Post-Traumatic Growth', this phenomenon is almost impossible to experience whilst in the midst of the trauma. After the event has passed and we start to regroup, process and heal, we can look back from a more objective standpoint and recognise the ways we have grown. We can sometimes even look for opportunities to be grateful when the time is right, forging a wisdom and deeper meaning to life that we would otherwise not have been able to access.

SUMMARY OF THE TWELVE LESSONS

Ready to connect with Kate?

Visit her website: www.kate-spencer.com

If you have been affected by the themes in this book, please reach out to a friend, family member, or someone trusted for support. Therapy is available through licensed and trained therapists worldwide at www.betterhelp.com. You don't have to face the legacy of emotional abuse on your own.

ACKNOWLEDGEMENTS

A heartfelt thank you goes out to everyone who has followed Stephanie's transformation and begun their own through *Twelve Lessons*. I feel immensely privileged to have been the custodian of a story that has been so life-changing for many.

I owe a huge amount of gratitude to The Universe.

My life is blessed with family and close friends who offer unwavering love and support. I never take this lightly and understand it's what my foundations are made from.

The process of writing *Twelve Lessons* changed me. It forced me to reflect deeply on who I was and who I was becoming, and it made me walk into my own shadow and sit with myself. Some of it was confronting, and some of it brought up shame - old wounds that I needed to bring into the light of consciousness and heal.

Like all of you I am a work in progress, but I've done enough to claim my new beginning. As Stephanie's story comes to a close, and her happy ever after begins in earnest, so does mine.

I asked The Universe to bring me the perfect partner at the perfect time, and it delivered. He has helped me to finally feel worthy of living the life that I always wanted. You were worth waiting for, Johnny. It's a cliché, but I had no idea what true love was until you walked into my life and changed it forever.

Twelve Lessons feels complete now, and so do I.

Thank you for being part of Stephanie's journey, and of course mine too.

Love Kate x

Professional Acknowledgements

A BIG thank you to the following people.

I couldn't have done this without your endless patience, encouragement and fabulous skill set.

Michelle Emerson, content edit and typesetting
~ www.michelleemerson.co.uk

Mo Prowse, friend, business assistant & book lover
~ @mjprowse | Linktree

Leanne Kelly, cover design
~ www.facebook.com/Jakenna.creative.design

David Mark, writer & literary mentor
~ www.davidmarkwriter.co.uk

Claire Mitchell, marketing & business coach
~ www.thegirlsmeabusiness.com

LET'S GET SOCIAL

There are lots of ways we can stay connected!

Website: www.kate-spencer.com

Facebook - www.facebook.com/RealKateSpencer1/

Instagram - www.instagram.com/real_katespencer/

YouTube - @katespencer9524

Tik Tok – tiktok.com/@kate.spencerauthor

Podcast – Kate Spencer's Life With Soul Podcast

Join my newsletter for updates about Twelve Lessons Products and other books and projects:
katespencer.simplero.com/katespencerbooks

TWELVE LESSONS CLUB

If you love Stephanie's story, love *Twelve Lessons*, and love the idea of living your best life, then I've got something perfect for you...

The Twelve Lessons Club is a deeper dive into each lesson, with me right by your side. Just as these lessons changed my own life and Stephanie's, they can change yours too. I've created bitesized workshops for each lesson, journal questions and exercises to help you to apply what you're learning and experiencing in the real world.

Just like Stephanie in the original Twelve Lessons novel, you'll get one lesson each month to lean right into, experience and live through. Life-changing transform-ations can happen with each lesson learned and integrated as we shed layers of our former selves and allow our true selves to shine. Healing the wounds of the past, ditching the drama, releasing resistance, letting go of self-sabotage, loving ourselves and finally feeling worthy.

All of the above can ripple through your whole life and bring you more joy, happiness, connection, and love. These experiences can raise your vibration and help you to manifest more of what you want through Law of Attraction.

You'll get access to a members' area where your lessons will be loaded up monthly, along with bonus meditations, worksheets, checklists and affirmations. You'll also be invited to a private Facebook Community where we can share our experiences, our own life lessons and have fun! You'll be able to tag me, ask me questions, find out more about my life and hang out with people just like us.

By reading *Twelve Lessons*, people have changed their lives in amazing ways. Imagine what these lessons could do for you if you went even deeper?

I'm sending an intention to The Universe that the right people come ~ the people that I can support, connect with and help to create the life they really want, through the power of Twelve Lessons.

If that's YOU then why not start living lesson one right now and Be Open to Possibility?

The Twelve Lessons Club costs £12 per month and you can cancel or pause your subscription anytime, if it's calling to you – I'll see you there!

http://www.twelvelessonsclub.com/

Love Kate x

PRAISE FOR *TWELVE LESSONS*
– AMAZON REVIEWS

"I read this book on my kindle while on holiday this summer, I had had an awful year of two very close family bereavements, a very poorly daughter and the usual obstacles and realities of a working mum trying to juggle work, home and a new business. I had lost my mojo, my motivation and will had got up and walked away. My holiday was a time to rest and gain some clarity on where I wanted to be, my journey and close some chapters from the past. This book was an inspiration, the most inspiring read I have ever come across, it made me realise only I have the power and mindset to change my life and go out there and reach my goals. It's given me my motivation I so needed to build my business, also gave me the tools to look at and change my relationships too in a positive way. If you are juggling life, facing challenges and do not know where to turn then this is the book for you!"

"Fantastic! I've never read anything like this book before! It's a self-help book and novel all wrapped into one. (You can heal your life by Louise hay and Bridget Jones all wrapped into one!) If you like anything from Hay house publications, you will love this book. I am not a 'novel' reader normally but I happened across the author on Facebook and her page is wonderful (lady with a truly beautiful soul) so I thought I'd give this book a go :) I'm so glad I did!! This is one of the best books I've ever read, it has a wonderful story that will keep you hooked, and has a wealth of law of attraction information (all in everyday terms that I can completely relate to)."

"My gosh what an inspiration to think positively and keep putting out to the world what u want in life. I've read this book within 2 weeks I just couldn't put it down. I also feel that my outlook on life has changed and I feel more empowered and hopeful for what lies ahead. Anyone and everyone should read this book no matter what journey you find yourself on. I have never ever read a book from start to finish this was my 1st and I'm 31."

"I am a very busy mother of 5, but I still was compelled to read the book every moment I could over 48 hours. Kate you send your message very eloquently to the reader offering so many nuggets of gold along Steph's journey to a new energy of self-awareness, involving several serendipitous moments which can't help her resist the universe's plan for her journey here on Earth. My consciousness has always been searching for answers, and being an avid reader for the past 20+ of the 'self-help' section of the book stores, alas twelve lessons is up there at the top for me. Kate's you're a wee genius and I can't thank you enough, The visions and events which have evolved so very quickly for me is astounding, I only finished the book 3 days ago, which is only a testament your teachings Kate. it's like I've been in the darkness my whole life and you enabled me to strike the match that was in my hand the whole time. Thank you."

Go to your local Amazon store to read thousands more!

ALSO AVAILABLE

Twelve

Lessons

Journal

KATE SPENCER

A deeper dive into each of the 36 lessons from Stephanie's Journal, and the perfect companion guide to The *Twelve Lessons* Novel Series.

A personal and spiritual development manifesto to help you create and live your best life.

Be Open to Possibility and download the first three lessons as a gift from here: katespencer.simplero.com/threefreelessons

COMING SOON

Love Bomb

KATE SPENCER

A single moment in time can define everything that comes after.

The one-night stand that results in a pregnancy.
That drink before driving.
Saying "I do".
Reading texts on your husband's phone.
The first domino falls, and there is no going back.

I hadn't suspected a thing.
People usually say they had a feeling something was going on. Well, I didn't.
I saw a text on Adam's phone and opened it.
I read it, statue still.
This went back weeks, perhaps even a couple of months.
Beginning with pleasantries and turning filthy fast.

I scanned the messages.

Words jumped out that made me gasp and blush.

He'd never said those things to me.

She'd sent breathy voice notes back in an Eastern Block accent that made me feel sick.

There was no photograph of her on his camera roll and no new friend on Facebook.

But she was real, and she was *really* invested in meeting up with him.

And the saddest thing is, so was he.

Arrangements had been made for this weekend when he was supposed to play golf.

His key turned in the lock and I returned his phone.

He walked over and kissed me, picked up his phone and left for work.

Leaving me shell-shocked, bereft and wanting to scratch Natalia's eyes out.

Becky

It's not like I needed to meet someone.

I was settled in suburbia.

The divorce had been quick, and life was good, but recently I'd felt very single.

Not lonely exactly, but an absence.

Or maybe a longing? Someone to share my life with and my bed.

"I can't believe I'm doing this," I muttered. It was a balmy August night with a slight breeze. The stars had begun to pinprick the ink-black sky. We'd been outside since sunset, and the wine bottle was empty.

"Do I need a filter or anything?" I asked and turned my phone to show Sarah the selfie I'd chosen. I could always rely on my sister for an honest opinion.

"No, you need to look like yourself. If this bags you a date, you need to look like you do in real life. You're gorgeous, Becky."

"Ok!" I said with a confidence I wasn't feeling and clicked to complete the dating profile.

Anxiety and excitement bubbled in tandem.

I drained my glass and started to scroll.

Where are you Mr Right?

Joe

Maybe this time would be better.

It's not like I want anything special, but I'd best make a mental note not to say that because they all want to hear that they're special.

I wondered about reactivating my old profile. Would it show the creation date as today, or the date I had initially created it? I didn't want to look like some kind of desperate loser who had been on the scene for the last eighteen months.

I knew how I wanted to present, how I *needed* to.

Confidence without arrogance.

Emotional intelligence without weakness.

Success without bragging.

The old profile just needed a tweak here and there and perhaps a new photo. I added a couple of recent achievements and a picture of a car I'd seen at a motor show last month; everyone does it.

I clicked complete and confirmed that the start date was today - game on.

Draining the can of lager, I picked up the last slice of pizza.

Pepperoni with stuffed crust, a payday treat and the last takeaway for a while if I was back on the circuit. Cold pizza in one hand and my phone in the other. Not exactly living my best life – yet. But all of that could change with a swipe or a click.

I had a good feeling this time.

The odds were finally going to be in my favour. With optimism, I started to scroll. *Who's the lucky lady?*

Becky

We moved back indoors, and I opened another bottle of wine, the glug of a glass filling, and then a quick sip. Dry and fruity just like the label said.

I thought of Adam. Maybe he had been my person after all? I stopped myself. This was a rabbit hole I sometimes fell down when I'd had too much to drink.

It wasn't Adam I missed. It was having *someone*. It might have been better if we'd shredded each other, had that final Armageddon where I'd smashed up our wedding photos and ripped his suits to shreds right up in his face while ugly crying and spitting with fury. But the pain ran deeper than that; it had numbed me with disbelief and dragged me into an abyss where all I could feel was cold detachment. I couldn't face him after his weekend away. I didn't want to talk, or listen or imagine. I had to shut it out. I had no choice.

The locks were changed and I pinned a note to the door. I hoped he'd had a nice time with Natalia and my solicitor would be in touch.

He shouted through the letterbox for a while, and I'm sure I heard him cry.

When I didn't answer, he blew up my phone with all kinds of ridiculous excuses, which I ignored.

He recycled them all again through mutual friends and even my parents, but I wasn't buying any of it.

Too raw, too sore, too broken.

He probably thought I was being unreasonable, but the truth was that I was trying to stop myself from withering up and dying. A process that had crept up close and been whispering to me from the shadows.

I had to shut Adam out, or I wouldn't survive this.

The memories, the hopes and the dreams all got locked away in a vault I never wanted to open again. If they started to spill out, they might be so beautifully fragile and precious that they'd shatter me into a million fragments, and I'd never be able to piece myself back together.

Once he knew nothing would change my mind, he made it easy for me.

His change of heart was abrupt and left a tiny open loop that I could easily have picked back up. A dropped stitch in our marriage. But the trouble was I knew it was there, and I always would. Invisible to others, but to me, the whole pattern was ruined.

Three years had passed, but I still thought of him. We were like a novel with an ending that invites a sequel, perhaps. But actually, no, because there could never be a happy ending now, not once the trust was gone.

I closed my eyes and sighed. I missed our big old house. *The marital home* as it was referred to on the court order. I could have fought for it, but I needed a new start, a blank slate. Maybe that was selfish? I got to pack up and leave the echoes of the past, which Adam still lives with.

Together, we had loved that old house back to life. It was part of a disputed inheritance and had been standing empty for years.

We viewed it one bright autumn morning, with the sun shining through copper beech trees that lined the drive, and as we walked towards the front door I squeezed his hand and he squeezed mine back. Gravel and flame-coloured leaves crunched underfoot.

The front door was painted black but flaking; time had tarnished the heavy brass knocker. Yet, from the moment we stepped inside, we both knew.

Walking through the hallway just as many people had before, with old, dusty Victorian tiles underfoot and high ceilings edged with cornices and cobwebs above, it was exactly what we'd been looking for. As the estate agent talked about fireplaces and original sash windows, we stole sideways glances that confirmed this house was going to be ours.

Milton Keynes UK
Ingram Content Group UK Ltd.
UKHW020630070524
442340UK00006B/284